Philipa Lowe is in search of a house, ⟨...⟩
approve, particularly of the one she ⟨dearly⟩ wishes to see. In spite of
his reluctance, she goes ahead, and on her first sight of it she is full
of enthusiasm. True, it is too big for her, true that she could barely
afford it, but at once she falls in love with it.

Oliver's reluctance is soon explained, as this was the house
where a murder took place. Six years before, Clare Steadman was
committed to prison for the murder of her husband. This, to
Philipa, is not discouraging. She is intrigued. When she discovers
that Oliver himself was intimately involved, she is fascinated.

It is when Oliver declares that he believes Clare to have been
innocent that Philipa interests herself in the evidence – but then the
facts come to light, and seem undeniable.

For how could Clare, with the gunroom doors locked against
her, and the french windows jammed by her own efforts with a
shot-gun, have reached her husband, in order to make use of the
second barrel?

And at what was the third shot fired? At nothing?

A SHOT AT NOTHING

Roger Ormerod

Constable · London

First published in Great Britain 1993
by Constable & Company Ltd
3 The Lanchesters, 162 Fulham Palace Road
London W6 9ER
Copyright © 1993 by Roger Ormerod
The right of Roger Ormerod to be
identified as the author of this work
has been asserted by him in accordance
with the Copyright, Designs and Patents Act 1988
ISBN 0 09 472510 1
Set in Palatino 10pt and
printed in Great Britain by
Redwood Books
Trowbridge, Wiltshire

A CIP catalogue record for this book
is available from the British Library

1

Oliver and I were standing beside my car in the town of Asherton's only car-park, looking through what we had and rejecting the obvious non-starters. The estate agent had been over-generous with her hand-outs, as she hadn't seemed to understand the kind of property in which I was interested. She had even seemed confused.

'We're getting nowhere, Phillie,' said Oliver wearily. 'You're always looking for the impossible.'

'I don't see why it should be impossible. I can produce the money, so why can't anybody find me a house?'

'You're too particular.'

'I am *not*. And what's that you're throwing away? Let me see. You haven't even given me a chance to glance at it.'

'It's not for you, Phil.'

'I wish you'd let me make up my own mind.'

We were being short-tempered with each other, both of us limp with the continuing heat-wave, and because we had been scouring the county for a suitable property for nearly three weeks. And Oliver hadn't been at all encouraging. He didn't approve. Oh no.

'Let me see it.' I held out my hand.

Reluctantly, he unfolded the crushed ball he'd turned it into, made a poor job of smoothing the creases, and handed it over.

'I'm sure you'll hate it,' he said morosely.

Hate it! I was looking at a colour photograph of a sprawling and magnificent house, and eagerly reading the prospectus. Four beds, three baths, commodious kitchen with modern fittings. Four receps. Garage – four cars. Two stables ... it went on and on, and in a mixture of excitement and a despair that I would never be able to afford such a place, I turned it over to discover the asking price. It was just a little less than my capital would allow.

'It's wonderful,' I whispered.

'But it's not for you, Phil.'

'What the devil do you mean, Oliver?' But now I was happily ribbing him, willing to forget his strange attitude. 'It's just what I've been looking for.'

'It's too big for you.'

'We could convert it into a country hotel, Oliver. Wouldn't that be splendid? We'd make it pay its way, you the *maître d'hôtel*, me the manageress...'

'You're talking nonsense, Philipa. Let's look elsewhere – if you insist on going on with it.' And he turned away, having reverted to my full Christian name in a most chilling manner.

It was unlike him. We could argue, we could shout at each other ... then laugh together. Normally, he would have developed on my fantasy hotel theme. Never before had he been so curtly dismissive.

'Whatever you say, I want to see it,' I told him firmly. 'You'll know how to find the place, I'm sure. I assume we're still in your district?'

'Yes.' He kicked a tyre. He had worked that area, from constable to inspector.

'So you could guide us there?'

'If you insist.'

'I do insist. Let's go back and ask about the keys.'

'We could look without going in.'

'Peering through windows, like burglars casing the joint, if that's the phrase? No, thank you!'

'All right then ...' Oliver drew back his shoulders, expressing disapproval.

Turning, I headed diagonally across the road, not checking whether he followed, but he was there at my shoulder when I asked if I could have the keys.

The young woman was hesitant. No doubt it would normally have been necessary for her to accompany us, but she seemed to be alone in that small branch office. Then she almost thrust the keys at me, and with a strange smile I couldn't understand. She flicked an entirely different smile at Oliver.

'I'll be back,' I said to her.

She pouted her lower lip at me and nodded. 'I know.'

Once outside I simply said, 'There. You see.' Then, when we reached my car, I asked, 'What did she mean ... I know?'

'She'd seen she could trust you, Phil. With the keys.'

I shook my head. It hadn't been like that. Had the young woman been *too* anxious to let me have the keys? That her and Oliver's

6

attitudes conflicted was not surprising, she eager for a sale and Oliver strangely reluctant. Then why had I seen that tiny smile, almost conspiratorial, pass between them? I dismissed the thought. Oliver's reluctance alone would have encouraged me. He ought to have known that I respond adversely to discouragement.

Nevertheless, I asked him what he had against it.

'You'll see.' He didn't enlarge on that.

He was acting very strangely, but nevertheless he directed me faithfully, if coolly, until we found ourselves in a minor lane that was weaving itself gradually downwards.

'Is it down here?' I asked.

'Yes.'

'There's supposed to be a fine view across the valley. In its own grounds, it said.'

'I know.' He was silent, staring ahead and seeing, I reckoned, nothing of the road. 'Wasn't I there?'

I assumed he meant: there, beside me, chatting to the young lady behind the desk.

'Of course you were,' I agreed.

'There's no of course about it.'

While I was considering the obscurity of that observation we rounded a bend, and the view under discussion abruptly revealed itself. An open prospect across the valley, had been the description. That was completely inadequate – it was breathtaking. We had not run through a village, so I had begun to wonder whether 'in its own grounds' really meant 'isolated'. But clearly this was it: Collington House. A FOR SALE board peered discreetly at us over the hedge, and there was, after all, a village. It was clustered together, from our position, as no more than a few grey and red roofs just beyond a belt of trees, and lower down to the right.

I swung into the partial set-back in front of a five-barred gate, and parked the BMW. We got out to have a look, Oliver taking his time about it, but I had very little attention to spare for him. I leaned on the top bar of the gate, and was captivated by the view.

I had no idea what an acre of ground looked like, out in the open and placidly soaking up the sunlight. I had seen a mention in the prospectus of nearly five of them. It sloped upwards to my left, disappearing over the horizon, whilst in front of me and to the right it swept down in a saucer, with a glimpse of water, possibly a lake, and hedges marching away ... away ... to be lost beyond another rise. Flowing, heaving vastnesses of grass faced me.

7

'That'd take a bit of mowing,' Oliver said morosely, at my shoulder.

'And *this* is four-point-eight acres?'

'You misread it, my sweet. It's forty-eight acres.'

'You and your blasted crumpling.' But I could put no force into it – the prospect seemed to calm me. This wasn't a 'property'. It was an estate.

'There're horses over there,' he said, pointing, and indeed there were, three of them, two chestnuts and a grey. 'Somebody's obviously renting the grazing.'

Three horses, though, wouldn't be able to control that quantity of grass. But Oliver reassured me.

'You'd be able to rent it to cattle farmers, even sheep farmers. Sheep crop it shorter, I believe. Or you could breed cattle yourself. Aberdeen Angus, or something. The bullocks are a bit skittish, mind you, and don't know their own strength. You'd have enough ground to employ your own vet. Or what about a racing stable ...'

'You're being facetious,' I accused him. 'You're doing your best to put me off.'

'No, no.'

I turned and stared him in the eye. He tried a weak smile. 'It's what I've dreamed of, Oliver, and you know it.'

'It's not. It's what you've dreamed *up*, with all your low cunning. I can see right through you, Philipa Lowe. You're crafty.' He grinned at me, evilly I thought, and added, 'You haven't even seen the house yet. It's over there, to your left.'

I looked where he gestured, refusing to rise to his bait regarding my cunning plans, because he was quite correct on that point.

In effect, we had driven past it, the house being to our left as we stood facing the thorn hedge and higher up the rise, with a clump or plantation of trees beyond it. Presumably the front of the house and its drive faced away from us, yet I'd noticed no entrance along the road.

'The surrounding hedges would all be yours too,' Oliver pointed out. 'Probably a mile of them, and you'd have to keep them trimmed.'

'No, I wouldn't. I'm a conservationist. I'd let them grow as they wished, and attract all the wildlife.'

'The local hunt wouldn't approve.'

'To hell with the local hunt. They're not going to hunt over my territory.'

'Yours, Phillie? It's not yours, yet. You haven't even looked over the house.'

But there's nothing like opposition for strengthening the resolve, and I was getting my full share. 'I've already decided. Let's go and look at it – if we can find the way in, that is.'

He took my elbow companionably, I thought with some authority, and turned me back to the car. 'It's just round the next bend.'

'You know the district very well,' I observed.

'Well, yes. On motor patrol you get to know every byway. Come on, the house is worth looking at, anyway – even if the whole damned place *is* too big.'

I sensed a slight change in his attitude. He had tried his putting-off tactics, and realised they weren't working. Now he was verging on encouragement, which had to mean he had something in reserve. Abruptly my interest in Collington House put on a vigorous surge. I couldn't wait, now, to put my foot inside it. It was true that the price was high for me, and would poach a large amount of my invested capital, but that was what it was all about, after all, and Oliver appeared to have realised it. His present stance was not influenced by any problem involving size. I would have considered a much smaller and less attractive property, but Oliver's attitude would have been exactly the same.

When we came to it, the drive entrance was no more than a gap in the hedge. Perhaps decorative gates had once hung there, but if so their stone buttresses were now no more than desolate piles. I would have to allow for replacements.

At first the drive, gravelled and amazingly weed-free, ran downhill and apparently away from the house, but having given the impression it had no intention of reaching the house, it made a wide sweep to the left and continued in a mounting S, which clearly would take us beyond a sweep of glorious beeches and startlingly high spruces, eventually to the front of the house. The original owner had possibly possessed a whimsical streak, as the drive performed this manoeuvre simply in order to plunge us into a tunnel through the trees, and out again to a sudden and startling vision of the house frontage. Gravel still predominated, but it now swept around an island apparently consisting of one solid box hedge, seven or so feet high, but uniformly shaped in a precise circle twenty yards across.

'What's that?' I asked, parking in front of it.

'It's the Collington maze. Famous, that is. It's one of the few circular mazes ever constructed, but in fact it never reaches a centre. The original idea was that visitors had to find a way through it in order to get to the front door. It discouraged unwanted callers.'

'It certainly would. Was he crazy, this man who built it?'

'Oh yes. Completely. Mad Harry Collings, they called him. The family name. Collings. But it was a cheeky, happy madness, in no way violent. For instance, you can walk round the maze to the front door – drive round it if you like – or if you wanted to use the maze there's a straight path through. Well ... nearly straight. Only the ones who didn't know ever ventured into the side paths. Mad Harry used to say he welcomed straightforward callers, not the devious ones.'

'A philosopher.'

'Indeed.' Oliver seemed in a sunnier mood now. He sounded quite proprietorial, as though Mad Harry could have been his own invention.

'You know a lot about him.'

'He's a local legend. But why don't you stand back and look at the place, before we go inside.'

I stood back. Oliver joined me. Except for the porch and the main entrance, hiding behind the maze, the whole frontage was spread facing us. It was a wide and quite squat row of mullioned windows, above which was a balcony that seemed to run all round the roof, protected by stone balusters and a run of stone coping. The roof had a very shallow pitch, apart from three peaks of roofing, one at each end and one over the door, each of which had one window in the gable facing us. And there were seven tall, twisted chimneys.

'Seven chimneys,' I said.

'Yes. He loved chimneys. Only two fireplaces, though. Five are fakes. In effect, it's a bungalow. There're bedrooms beneath the three roof peaks, but not lately used, and lots of rooms downstairs, stuck around all over the place. Built long before bungalows became popular.'

I glanced at him. 'You know it well?'

'Oh yes.' He kicked at a large pebble.

'Let's go inside, then.'

It had been something of a surprise to me that the estate agent had handed over the keys without question. I had imagined that we would be accompanied, if only to see that we didn't lift any-thing, though I'd assumed it would be stripped of furniture and fittings. But she had clearly recognised Oliver as a former police officer in the district, prior to his altercation with a shot-gun. In any event, I could now dangle the keys from one finger as we walked round the maze, feeling headily like the owner, returning from watching my horse come in third at Ascot.

As Oliver had said, we could have driven round the maze, as there was a clear ten-foot-wide stretch of gravel in front of the portico. And here again the humorist had left his mark. The porch steps were at least thirty feet wide, a little crumbly now, and there were four fluted columns. But most of this width was occupied by a run of six windows in stained glass. The door itself was tucked in at the right-hand corner, hiding coyly behind one of the columns.

'Allow me,' said Oliver, taking the keys from my fingers.

I looked at him with surprise. He flicked an eyebrow at me.

'If I hadn't been with you, Evelyn wouldn't have trusted you with the keys,' he explained.

'You know her?' I was a little jealous of any other woman who had known Oliver.

'Oh yes,' he said casually. 'In an official capacity, of course.'

'Of course.'

'The point is,' he explained, 'that the place is like a fortress. The father of the present owner, Clare Steadman, had it laced with alarms, and connected to the nearest police station. This grey box, here, is the monitor.'

The grey box was fixed to the side wall of the porch, and had on its surface one peculiar cylindrical keyhole. On the ring was a tubular key with little spikes. He inserted this and turned it once. A small green light flicked at us as a small red one went out.

'It's still connected,' he said. 'I guessed it would be. Now the alarm's turned off, and we can open the door.' This he did. It opened with a quiet and stately grace. He gestured me inside.

I walked into the hallway. This was a square box-shape with a high ceiling and panelled walls of dark mahogany, up to chest height. From it led long halls, sideways in both directions. There was a beautiful hallstand against the facing wall, almost black now from years of dust polished into its carvings, companion to a tall, stately cupboard on the facing wall. There was another of those alarm boxes just inside the door, but this one had two buttons, green and red, marked 'off' and 'on'.

'But ... it's furnished!' I cried.

'Yes.'

'There was no mention – '

11

'In the brochure ... something about: and contents. You read it yourself, Phil.'

'But ... but ...' I was now completely confounded. One sight of the grounds, one glimpse of the house itself, had convinced me that it was worth well above the asking price. But ... furnished, too! And I'd seen nothing yet of the rest of it.

'This is ridiculous, Oliver. Why is it so cheap?'

'Cheap! It'd just about ruin you, Phil, and you know it. Even though the market's depressed.'

'Cheap for what it is,' I persisted. 'This is the seventh place we've seen, in my financial bracket, and not one of them has been anywhere near as grand as this. What's the snag? That's what I want to know.'

'Upkeep...'

'Nonsense.'

He shrugged, but his eyes were steadily on me. Then, presumably so that I shouldn't turn away from him, he put both hands on my shoulders and smiled sadly at me. His injured right arm was improving all the while, and there was considerable, though encouraging, strength in the fingers digging into my left shoulder.

'I know what you're up to, Phillie my love,' he said quietly. 'And it's not going to work.'

'If you're so clever...'

'I don't need to be clever. Oh Phillie, you know I love you. It's just that I don't see why we need to get married.'

Perhaps I'd been too adamant about it. Perhaps we were too much alike, and he persisted in his attitude only because I did in mine. We'd touched on it so often ... and now here it was again.

'Don't want to be tied to me, you mean. Free to troll around after other women. Free to walk out on me...'

'You know it's not that.'

'It's because I've got the money and you haven't.'

'Not *that*.' But his statement was contradicted by its emphasis.

'Oh yes. Oh yes.' I was on the attack now. We hadn't before laid it out in words which couldn't be withdrawn, that was the difference. It had simply hovered between us like an oppressive cloud, with thunder lurking in it. He saw no reason why we shouldn't live together without marriage. Everybody's doing it, he had informed me. I saw no reason for living together except with marriage. And all that was holding him back...

'All you're thinking about', I shouted (and in somebody else's house ... it was unpardonable), 'is this ridiculous idea that the man

12

has to be the provider. Stupid! Antiquated! Revoltingly sexist! You make me sick, Oliver. So I intend – '

'You intend to squander the bulk of your considerable fortune on a house, and then we'd have to exist on my police pension. *That* is what's so ridiculous.'

This idea had occurred to me while we'd been staying at the house of my friend, Heather Payne. But I couldn't remember having expressed it.

'And you', I snapped back, goaded to it, 'are forgetting that my considerable fortune, as you call it, comes from the artistic talent of my previous husband. A *man* has earned it. Isn't that good enough for you?'

But it was a mistake. I had said the wrong thing.

'It's because it comes from your previous husband, you silly woman you.'

'Oh.'

He smiled at my no doubt empty expression, then leaned forward and kissed me on the tip of my nose. I felt my lips quivering, and wasn't certain whether I was about to break out in tears or laughter.

'Let go my shoulders, you big oaf!' I shouted, and the tears were mine, the laughter his.

'We clearly wouldn't last long as a married couple,' he observed, his head on one side. 'Virago, that's the word for you.'

'It's beneath my dignity to tell you what you are, Oliver.' I sniffed.

'Let's go and see the rest of the house.'

But I caught at his sleeve. 'I'd make you a solemn promise,' I said, 'that if you married me you could have a divorce at any time, and I wouldn't oppose it.'

He frowned. 'Divorce is even more painful than marriage.' He cocked an eyebrow at me.

'You'd be able to claim maintenance from *me*. Doesn't that appeal to you?'

'Hah!' he said. 'Let's go and see – '

'You wouldn't need to feel yourself bound to me, nor chained, nor riveted . . .'

He laughed. 'Divorce is when the rivet falls out. Like a pair of scissors. Then the separated two halves are useless on their own. Except for stabbing, of course, and usually in the back.'

'I'd expect my scissors to have a firm rivet.'

'You're contradicting yourself, my sweet. You've just said – '

'Let's go and see the rest of the house. You're spoiling it for me, Oliver.'

'It's already spoilt.'

This time I allowed him the last word, because I didn't know what he meant. We went to see the rest. I heard him muttering to himself about my being hopelessly old-fashioned, but I didn't take him up on it.

The whole place was crazy, a mixture of Victorian fussiness and what would have been, at that time, a courageous thrust at originality. Of course, I fell in love with it, as I had with Oliver because of his craziness, which is what it must have been if he wanted to live with me when I was quite aware that I'd be difficult to live with. Maybe, married, a little less, I assured myself.

The house ought to have appealed to him, the criss-crossing of passages, and doors where you wouldn't expect to find them, these usually opening into corners of large rooms when the centres of the walls were bare and available. But he made no comment – and placidly continued to make no comment – as though he'd decided I was past hope and the decisions were all to be mine; as though he knew there was no likelihood that we would ever be living there. That was how it was, his aloofness probably intentional, but I had to take a generous attitude as to his silence, and assume he wanted me to make an uninfluenced decision. Yet he must have observed the fact that I could barely contain my delight. I loved the strangely proportioned rooms. Long and narrow or nearly square; high-ceilinged and low-ceilinged, they were all delightful. In some way that I couldn't tie down in my mind, the proportions seemed always to be right and the windows in exactly the correct places, even though not the obvious ones. And the furniture! Venerable and revered, now very dusty and without dust covers, it had previously been treated with care and affection.

'But why ... why,' I asked, 'shouldn't it be more expensive? Several times what's being asked. And how long has it been empty? Tell me that.'

I didn't intend him to take this as a question, not expecting he would have the answer. But he had.

'Just under six years.'

'So why hasn't it been sold?' I nodded. 'And why is the furniture still here?'

'Presumably because it was cheaper than storing it. And of course, she'd have to bear in mind the possibility that she would

14

return to it. But she might have found it difficult to imagine herself living here again.'

'She, she! Who?' I asked.

'Clare Steadman. I told you that, Phil. Mad Harry's granddaughter.'

'But why wouldn't she come back? And where is she now?'

At that time we were in a wide room, rather barely furnished, whose double french windows looked out over a paved terrace and a lawn at the rear. Oliver walked over to the windows and stood there, his back to me.

'I believe,' he said, 'unless they've moved her, that she's in Benfield women's prison, serving out a life sentence for murder.' He turned to face me. 'Heavens, Phil, if she were to get full remission she could well be out around now. I reckon you're wasting your time looking at it.'

It was as though this was what he'd been holding back in reserve, to throw it at me – though whether the fact of murder or of the imminent remission, I couldn't tell. Why he hadn't come out with this before I put down to his cussedness.

'Poor woman,' I said. 'And the house empty for so long.'

He was annoyed that I hadn't asked the obvious questions. 'Nobody cares to live in a house where murder has been committed.'

'It was here? The murder?'

'In this room,' he said, his voice empty of emotion.

I paused. The room was quiet and placid, with no murmurs left of violence. 'And who was it this Clare Steadman killed?'

'Her husband. One very dark and stormy September evening. She shot him ... Harris Steadman. Mind you, he was about due for some kind of violent end. It's just a pity that she was the one who did it.'

'A pity for her?' I asked, probing and suddenly alert, though I tried to sound casual.

'Yes. A pity for her. There were numerous people, male and female, he'd been goading to a pitch where they'd have happily removed him from the district – permanently. I suppose she was the closest, so she got the most goading.'

He was skating around it cautiously, but on thin ice.

'Like the backmarker in a herd of cows?' I asked, regretting the ineptitude the moment I said it.

He didn't reply to that, and was walking slowly round the room, idly opening the tall glass-fronted and now empty showcases that

15

lined the walls. I knew he was seeing them full, and peopling this room with movement and frantic action. I walked over to the french windows and stared out over the terrace and the lawn beyond it. Rhododendrons, a little past their flowering period now, enclosed the lawn. Beyond them was the stretch of territory comprising the grounds. Now I could see the distant sheen of water clearly, and it was indeed a lake. I had always dreamed of owning my own lake.

'This was Clare's house,' he said at last, having decided how best to present it to me. 'Her father's before that, his father's before him. Mad Harry Collings, that was. Clare's father had his own fixations, and transformed the place into an almost unassailable fortress. *He* was eccentric, too.'

'I'll bet she's not too stable, either,' I said. 'Runs in the family, does it?'

I turned. He was frowning at me.

'Stable enough,' he said flatly. Then he went on, 'If you'll only let me explain. Clare's father, as I said, turned the house into a fortress. You've seen the alarm lock at the front – that's connected to the nearest police station, and the whole system runs right through the house. After the final locking-up at night, open one window or one external door, and they – the police – know at once. No alarms blasting away in the house, though. The idea was that we could sneak in on them and lay a hand on their collars.'

'That sounds rather crafty. But wait a minute ... it'd mean you could be lying in your bed with a burglar *in* the house, and there's been nothing to warn you. I'd prefer the alarms. You could at least grab a poker.'

'Ah yes. You'd send 'em running, Phil. But what her father did do, to make things more secure, was have proper mortice locks put in every internal door in the place. Look ...' He turned to the door by which we had entered. It had a lock as well as a normal door handle. Oliver turned the key, and the lock made a reassuring clashing sound, then he rattled the door to demonstrate how firm it was, how, in fact, it didn't even rattle. 'The idea was that if a burglar did get in, he'd have to start work again even to get beyond the room he'd entered, and then more work to get inside the next one – and so on.'

'By which time the gallant police would have swooped in and cut off his retreat? I see. Very clever. But hold on. In that event ... Oliver! Are you telling me that you were the gallant police on that particular evening? The murder evening, I mean. I wondered how you seemed to know so much about it – the house and the murder.'

He pouted, then nodded his head ruefully. 'Too much, for my liking.'

But – after nearly six years – that didn't explain his reluctance even to come here, I thought.

I was beginning to understand Oliver rather comprehensively. He was about to tell me something he knew I wouldn't be pleased to hear, and was approaching it cautiously, edging round it as he tidied up the facts in his mind. I had to adopt a casual and almost disinterested attitude, so that he wouldn't detect that I was critically alert. Otherwise I'd have had to drag it from him, and our delicate relationship would have been in jeopardy.

'You did tell me you'd patrolled this district in a police car,' I offered tentatively.

'True. But that was a year or so before this all happened. I'd transferred to the CID by that time, and just happened to be the closest when the burglar alarm call came through. I'd been to see a farmer who'd had trouble with his neighbour about a fence. It was late ... ten thirty-ish ... when I picked up the call. The alarm system had been triggered at Collington House. I knew where it was ...'

'Of course.'

He hesitated, then got on with it. 'There was a thunderstorm, and that delayed me a bit. The rain was bucketing down. It must've been Harris Steadman himself who'd triggered the alarm when he threw open the french windows. These windows here. Or it could have been Clare, when she opened the front door and ran out. Which meant that Harris Steadman must have set the alarm when he got home, by punching the button in the hall. In any event, when I got here the front door was closed, but unlocked. Of course, I'd come about a possible break-in, so I had a quick look round outside, and then, as the front door wasn't locked, I walked in and found my way to their sitting-room. That's the one right opposite this one, across the corridor. I still didn't know what to expect, of course, or what'd been going on, but I could hear her inside the sitting-room, sort of sobbing, and when I looked in she was sitting with the phone in her lap. She'd made a 999 call, but not about a break-in. No. About a shooting incident – when I could get any sense out of her. My sudden appearance seemed to send her over the edge. I mean ... you make a phone call asking for help from the police, and you've barely put the phone down when one walks in. Just like that. She – '

17

'I do get the point, Oliver.'

Why, I wondered, was he sounding apologetic? No – he wasn't being apologetic, he was trying to justify her reactions.

'She just stared at me and passed out,' he went on. 'I managed to bring her round. At that stage I knew nothing about what had been going on. What was so strange was that she was wearing her husband's waterproof shooting jacket, and she was soaked, drenched, dripping.'

'Hadn't she got any live-in help?'

'No. Let me get on with it, Phil, please. He'd been out shooting, I gathered. Harris Steadman, that is. And he'd been caught in the storm. When I could get one sensible word out of her, all she could say was that she'd shot him. She used the word "killed". And she told me he was dead in the gunroom – this room. See the cases all round the walls? They're gun cases. Each one held two guns at that time, and there're twenty-one cases. That's forty-two shot-guns – and loads of cartridges in that cabinet over there. And each gun was a collector's piece. All hers, inherited from her father. Put together, they were probably worth more than the house. And there was also a shot-gun that Steadman owned. We found that one lying on the hallstand.'

'There're no guns here now,' I pointed out. 'The furniture's here, but no guns.'

'No. That's true. We ... the police forensic squad, that is ... took them all in for examination. They've been stored for her. Free. They still belong to her. But Harris ...' Oliver had begun to use his Christian name, so must have known him. 'Harris treated the collection as though it was his own. I don't mean he used them. No – he had his own gun, as I said, for his own personal enjoyment.'

'Enjoyment?'

'Oh yes. He thoroughly enjoyed shooting birds out of the air.'

'I'm beginning to hate him.'

'But he'd have justified it. He'd have told you it was only like farming, though this was grouse and partridge. The only difference was that pigs and cattle and sheep went to slaughterhouses, but shooting was the only way to kill gamebirds.'

As Oliver seemed to be supporting this point of view, I flared in abrupt anger at him. It was out before I could trap it. 'But the slaughterhouse people don't *enjoy* it, damn you.'

He raised his eyebrows at me. 'I'm expressing his attitude to it, Phillie. So that you'll understand him.'

'And understand her?'

'If you like.'

'You mean she enjoyed the same pastime?' I couldn't bring myself to call it a sport.

'No. Her father taught her to shoot when she was very young – took her on shoots in her teens. But she never hit anything. She hated it, and aimed elsewhere. But she *could* handle a gun. It was just that she'd never been able to bring herself to kill anything.'

'Anything, as you put it, except her husband? Didn't you say she shot him?' I nodded at him reprovingly. He was being too supportive towards her.

'Not purposely,' he assured me.

'No?' I was beginning to dislike this Clare Steadman, who had Oliver's stubborn support. 'But all the same ... you say she's in prison for it.'

'I'm quite certain she didn't murder him. Shoot him, yes. By mistake. Murder, no.'

'So why ... what *is* it you know, Oliver?'

But he wouldn't allow himself to be tied down. I'd never known him so terse and evasive. Now he seemed to head off on a different line altogether, changing the direction of it with an almost insulting rejection of my protests.

'They'd had a row ...'

'Not in cold blood, then,' I said acidly.

He ignored that. 'They'd had a grand row in the sitting-room opposite. He'd come home, all wet and cold and in a foul mood, and the storm was still crackling all around the house. We discovered he had a good reason for his anger, because a friend of his he'd met on the shoot had told him he was about to instruct his solicitor about some debt or other, which Harris couldn't repay. He was a partner in a company, not large – only twenty-three employees. But he was on the sales side, and the profits had been poor recently. He'd got his life in a financial tangle. He was a lousy businessman, a rotten employer, a liar, a cheat and a bully. That night, he'd apparently come home with some idea that Clare would sell some of her guns to help him out. Or something like that. They got to shouting at each other, she accusing him of throwing money around on his women – which was true. I knew that. And he was shouting at her that she had a man of her own as a lover, and he knew about it, and if she wouldn't help him out he would spread it around ... stupid, really. What would it signify, these days? But all these things came out when my superintendent got her to the point of making statements. The causes of the quarrel

19

I heard second-hand. But the details of what happened that evening I knew first-hand, because I was here, on the spot, that night.'

'Now wait a minute. Wait, Oliver. What did *that* mean? Heard it second-hand? If you were a CID sergeant, surely – '

'They took me off the case. Personal involvement.' He shrugged, staring past my shoulder.

'You mean – '

'One of the first things she told the superintendent was that I was the lover that Harris Steadman had been referring to.' He pouted. 'Gentleman friend, she called me.'

2

I had not examined the room in any detail, my attention having been concentrated on Oliver. This seemed the time to do it. What he had said was as good a reason as any to apply myself, now, to a more careful survey. Not that I would be able to concentrate on it, not after his flat statement. That there had been previous women I had begun to realise – it would have been surprising if there hadn't been – but here, at last, had appeared one with a more solid background, one who might have earned the courtesy title of mistress. Which was what he wanted me to be. After all, if one mistress was in prison, he might be expected to fill the empty space with another, if only until the first was released. Good heavens, I thought, was that why Oliver was reluctant to marry me? Because he was waiting for the genuine loved one to be available again? *Then* he would live here ... but not with me.

At this infuriating thought I whirled on him, angry words jostling for position, to be hurled in his face. But casually he was standing with his hands in his trouser pockets, staring out over the terrace at the recently mown lawn.

'Wouldn't it be splendid,' he said to the glass, 'if you could prove her innocence for her? How grateful she'd be.'

'You must be insane.'

'You've been successful two or three times in sorting out other people's problems. A true daughter of Chief Superintendent Lowe. Philipa Lowe, the lady sleuth. Apply your brains to this one, my pet, why don't you.'

It was not a question, not even a request – a challenge to something. To my understanding and tolerance? He was being remarkably cutting with his tone, a surprisingly new Oliver Simpson. Was he angry with himself for not having been able to save her? But, to apply for me for assistance, that was grotesque.

'You're making yourself decidedly unpleasant, Oliver,' I said to his back, a certain amount of coolness entering my voice. 'You've never used that cold and sarcastic attitude with me before. Damn you, if you want to get her free, do it yourself.'

I was reaching back for the door handle, intending to march out of there and back to the car and drive off and leave him, if my fury hadn't eased a little before then. But he turned, and there were lines of pain in his face, such as I had not seen since the incident that had almost lost him his arm, and misery in the line of his mouth, distress in his eyes.

'I wasn't being sarcastic, Phil. I was asking for your help.'

'My help ...' I whispered. 'For her?'

'I tried.' He raised his shoulders, then allowed them to slump back. 'I couldn't find the truth. There was something I couldn't quite get a hold of, and I couldn't make sense of anything.' He wouldn't quite meet my eyes. 'All I'd got to back up my instincts was what I knew of her. Oh, I'm not arguing ... the evidence of a deliberate killing was all there. But I was certain she couldn't have killed him. She'd already severely disabled him – no, don't interrupt, Phil, I'll explain in a minute. She'd come out on top, you could say. So there was no reason, even in the state he'd brought her to, for her to deliberately kill him. I knew her, Phil. She would not have fired that second barrel at him, not face to face, and when he was completely helpless.'

I couldn't understand what he was trying to impress on me, nor why he was laying it out in such detail – this sympathy he had for her. To appeal to me ...

'After all this time,' I stalled, 'what could you expect me to do about it? Talk sense, Oliver. And why should I? Why should I try to get this woman released, when she'd return straight to you? You must be out of your mind. Even to *ask* it! Damn it, that's bloody well insulting, Oliver, now that I come to think about it. No. Don't say another word. Let me finish. If you think I'm here just to be used as a stop-gap, to sleep in your bed until the time comes when I can restore her to it ... pre-warmed ... that's so insulting that I could kill you myself, before – '

'There!' he cut in. 'You see? *You* could kill. You just said it. So you could probably be the one to understand how *she* could've killed. Or not. Phil ... Phil, in court, when she was sentenced, she turned and looked directly at me. Into my eyes. With sorrow and disillusionment. I'd let her down, and hadn't been able to help her. I've never got over that. Do that for me and ... and Phil, I'd marry you. There.'

'What!'

Didn't he realise what he was saying? He made it sound as though he would sacrifice himself in marriage to me, if I'd assist the woman he really loved! It was disgusting. And oh – how he was suffering at having to say it!

'You can just go to hell!' I shouted, and I turned to the door.

He was beside me in a second, had caught my shoulder and twisted me back to face him, and this with his right hand. It must, I thought, have hurt him terribly.

'Phil, Phil, I'm sorry. I said it all wrong. I don't love her now. Never from the moment I met you . . .'

I had a flash memory of him raising his tweed hat. Of his later comment, 'Never trust a man wearing a tweed hat, that was why I raised it.' The image almost choked me. He wasn't wearing his hat now, but could I trust him?

'You're hurting my shoulder,' I whispered.

He released me at once, as though my flesh was suddenly red-hot. 'Silly Phil,' he said softly. 'When you know it's you I love. But I feel I let her down – and I can't forget it.'

'You hated that?' I was trying my own brand of sarcasm.

'It's like promises. You make a promise – you keep it. I felt I'd made her a promise – though nothing was said – and I've broken it.'

'They mean that much?'

'Promises? Yes, they do.'

'Then promise to marry me.'

He shook his head. 'No, Phil. That's blackmail. A forced promise is automatically self-cancelling.'

'But you *did* say you would promise – '

'And you spoiled it by telling me to go to hell. That's where I am right now. So that promise is null and void.'

'You', I said, 'ought to have been a barrister. You'd have twisted the Lord Chief Justice round your little finger.'

'Then do it as a cold and unemotional mental exercise, like Sherlock Holmes. Or Philip Marlowe, without the mister. But do it for me, and get her released, and *then* we'll talk about marriage.'

'The "we" in that statement meaning you and this Clare woman?'

'No. You and I.'

'But Oliver, if I managed to get her released she'd no longer wish to sell this house. And I want it. I've never wanted anything so much in my life.'

'You never know . . . she might be so grateful that she'd give it to you.'

'Hah!' I said in disbelief.

'She'd still have her guns, you see. A fortune in guns.'

I nodded knowingly, and tried a small smile. 'And if I married you, Oliver, it'd be me she'd be gunning for next. With all forty-two of them.'

Then at last he broke the fine thread that remained of the tension, by grinning at me. 'No, she wouldn't. If she did that, she'd need you again, to save her a second time.'

It's very difficult, I found, to kiss satisfactorily when you're both laughing.

Then at last he said, with quiet sincerity, 'May I tell you what happened?'

I fluffed up my hair, as much as it will fluff, as it's more like copper wire than hair. 'If you must.'

He pouted at me. 'It does seem that I'll have to.' And he did.

It had been in early September, almost six years before. Harris Steadman had been out shooting and returned in a foul temper, as Oliver had said, and Clare had found herself facing his anger and his wild accusations. Harris was more than a little drunk, having taken a large brandy flask with him to keep out the damp. It had begun to rain even before he left the house. He'd put on one of those waxed green Barbour waterproof jackets, with plenty of pockets. This jacket he left lying on the old black hallstand, when he got home later, with no respect for its venerable polish.

At that stage there were two twelve-bore cartridges in one of the pockets.

Clare was in the sitting-room, the one immediately across the corridor from the gunroom, though the doors weren't opposite each other. It was in there that Harris faced her, and provoked a bitter quarrel. She heard for the first time, she said, how deeply he was in debt, even to the extent of having fiddled money from the company in which he had a small shareholding. He'd already convinced himself that it was all Clare's fault, when she could easily have covered his debts.

'Fiddling?' I cut in. 'You mentioned the business – what kind of business?'

'They made lampshades. Still do, I suppose, without him.'

'Lampshades!' It seemed perhaps a rather ladylike pursuit for a man who was rapidly sounding more and more like a rip-roaring macho thug.

24

He smiled at my expression. 'I think Clare must have fed in a little capital afterwards, because it's still going strong, under its original founder. A cousin of Clare's, I think. She does all the designing herself. Josie Knight, her name is. Anyway ... Harris wanted Clare to help him out. Apparently he thought she might sell some of her father's collection of guns. The very idea would've infuriated her.'

'If she'd got money ...' I began, but then I saw that it would have been irrelevant. The guns would have been symbolic – *her* guns. Harris had clearly been needling her purposely.

'They shouted at each other,' Oliver continued, when he saw that I wasn't going on with it. 'Clare threw a glass ashtray at him, and he, completely beyond control, stormed out of the room, shouting something about her guns sitting there doing nothing, so they might just as well be where he was – out in the cold.'

'Hmm!' I said, nodding. So far I was on her side.

'It was only when Clare heard the gunroom door slam,' Oliver went on, 'and the lock being thrown over, that she even began to guess what he intended to do, but at the very worst she thought he might be intending to grab three or four of her guns – as many as he could carry – and run off with them. So she went after him into the corridor, and started hammering at the gunroom door, and then she realised it could well be worse than she'd imagined, because Harris wasn't even taking the trouble to get the keys from the drawer in order to open the showcases. She could hear him smashing the glass fronts, and bellowing at the top of his voice.'

Oliver was narrating this in the unemotional voice he would have used in court, but I had to bear in mind that he would have encountered many domestic disputes, and become hardened to the bitter furies these always created.

'She must have been terrified,' I ventured.

'Yes.' He paused, clearly thinking about the extent of Clare's terror. 'But she wasn't what you could call petrified with fear. Not Clare. We found the remains of a small occasional table outside this door. She'd pounded it to pieces, trying to get in at him, with Harris laughing like a maniac because it was locked, with the key inside, and Clare's father had known what he was doing when it came to buying locks, and if you'll take a look, Phillie, you'll see the doors are solid oak.'

I didn't trouble. Now I was paying more attention to the room and its layout, wandering around as Oliver talked. The door was not central in the long wall behind me, and the french windows were not opposite the door, but off-set. For french windows they seemed huge, and there were no curtains to them. Almost central in the room was a long table, its surface battered and scarred. I had to assume that this had normally been used for stripping and cleaning the guns, or whatever had to be done to them. There was a tall chest of drawers against the wall facing me, beside the french windows. The drawers held boxes of cartridges, I discovered, in different bore sizes; that information was on the box lids. There were also cleaning materials. Next to it was a tall cupboard. It wasn't locked, but when I glanced inside I saw that it held nothing but various items of clothing thought essential to the practical shooter. There were only two chairs, one at each end of the table, utility chairs and not designed with any consideration of comfort in mind.

'Then,' Oliver was saying, 'after the glass-smashing bit, Clare heard a clattering sound, which would've been Harris flinging her guns on to the table. And he shouted something about how much they'd be worth after a dose of rain. She said later that it was only then that she realised what he intended to do. Which was to throw her guns out on to the lawn. The storm was at its height at that time. As I told you, it delayed me, and also the local squad car, which was on its way almost as soon as I was. But I had to back out of three flooded lanes and do circuits.'

'And how long, would you say, did it take you to reach here?'

'Oh ...' He wagged a hand vaguely. 'Ten minutes or so. Fifteen at the outside.'

'So the important episode you're coming to took place in those few minutes?'

'It was over when I got here, but a lot can happen in a few minutes.'

'Yes. I take it that her first action would've been to run through the house and out at the front.'

'That's as she told it. She reached the entrance hall, and then, when she threw open the front door, she realised how bad the storm was. But Harris's green jacket was there, where he'd thrown it on the hallstand. She put that on – and in that way armed herself with two twelve-bore cartridges. It's uncertain whether the opening of the front door or the french windows came first, but it hardly matters. One of them triggered off the burglar alarm.'

I could visualise it all, up to that point, and very clearly, she having to run through the house – what shoes had she been wearing? – then all round to the back and to the lawn. Was the grass long, or mown short at that time? And she would have found the french windows flung wide open on to the terrace ... and Harris? What was *he* doing, with the storm cracking all round them and the rain streaming down?

'Do you know exactly what happened, Oliver?' I asked.

'Only from what she said to me, and to the super later. But it all sounded very real and true.'

'So ... ?'

'Harris had begun to throw the guns out on to the lawn,' Oliver provided. 'He was a big, strong man. A shot-gun in one hand wasn't a great weight to him. He threw them as far as he could – bellowing in anger and throwing filthy language at her. And Clare ... sobbing and screaming and scuttling about, with no more than the spilled light from the french windows and the flashes of lightning to guide her, finding the guns, running to the terrace with them one at a time to throw them back to safety inside ...'

I could tell by his tone, and the way the words streamed from him, the extent of his sympathy with her in this. Harris had been throwing them out and down. Easy for him. Clare would be weaker, and couldn't possibly match him. More would go out than could be thrown back, and those would be thrown out again at her at once. Quite frankly, with a storm raging round me I would not have liked to stand out on that soaked lawn in a vertical stream of rain, waving a metal lightning conductor in my hands.

But would she have cared about that? Would she have heard one crash of thunder, seen one fork of lightning? I thought not. It could simply have continued until she collapsed from exhaustion, with the whole collection strewn around her on the sodden grass.

At what stage, then, had she realised that she had two cartridges in her jacket pocket, and the choice out of possibly forty-two guns into which she could load them? Yet Oliver had mentioned that Harris's death could well have been an accident. A provoked accident? But what, in that event, had she been protecting? Her guns? Not herself, certainly. So murder it would have been.

Yet my mind had galloped ahead of Oliver's story, so that by that time I was right behind her, whatever she had done. She had won herself a champion, though she couldn't have known it, with her guts and her persistence.

'And how did it all end?' I asked quietly. I could imagine no termination to it other than her collapse or Harris's death, as he'd held the stronger hand.

Oliver laughed shortly – a brief expression of disgust. 'It was

Harris himself. A queer cuss, he was. Unpredictable. His furies were enormous, and his sense of humour on the banana skin level. There he was, just inside this room, dry and warm – and what would Clare have looked like, out there on the lawn, bedraggled, wet through, her hair plastered round her face and her clothes clinging to her, weeping and swearing at the same time, and almost on her knees from exhaustion? It struck Harris as funny. He stood there and roared with laughter, and simply stopped throwing them out at her. She knew him. She ought to have understood him through and through. In effect, he'd abdicated. If she'd simply called him a dirty name and asked him to come out and help her, he'd probably have done it. But no. Not Clare. She called him a dirty name, right enough, and told him he'd had it, and he could just start packing and could sod off out of her life with any one of his women. And while she was telling him, she was still tossing the guns back inside. By that time she'd barely got the strength to do any tossing, and she was piling them – the guns she could locate in the dark – on the terrace. He just watched her for a minute or two, then he got fed up with it – and simply closed the french windows, and locked them.'

'Oh,' I said emptily, trying to decide what I would have done in her place. But my sense of humour's a bit warped. I find I can laugh at myself from time to time. Not Clare, apparently. She'd been way beyond laughter. 'What did she do?' I asked.

'Well – it seems – the first thing she tried was to smash the glass. She threw a couple of the guns at it, but they just bounced back.'

'By this time,' I suggested quietly, 'having forgotten how precious they were?'

'Seemingly. But you know about double-glazing. It's difficult to smash, with that air-cushion between the two layers. People have died in fires, unable to break their way out. And these windows, being so large, are of plate glass. I suppose you might drill a hole through, and then possibly smash them. Or chip a way through with an ice-pick. I don't know. What she did, anyway, worked. She found she had cartridges in her pockets. She loaded both barrels – she was clear on that – and let the window have a blast. But she fired only one barrel, she insisted later. What she aimed at was the central frame itself, where the lock was. What she hit – and heaven knows she was exhausted and could barely see what she *was* doing – was the glass to the left of the lock. It was just on the edge of the blast that she got the lock itself.'

I could appreciate that at that stage she wouldn't know exactly

28

what she was doing, but the idea had been sound. I would probably have done that myself.

'But the windows open outwards, Oliver. What did she expect?'

He shrugged. 'I don't know. What she did get was a jammed lock. It was jammed when our lot got here. And she'd blasted a hole a foot across in both thicknesses of glass to the left of it.'

'A shot-gun would do that?' I asked.

'It *did* do it, in any event. But she'd thought she could put an arm through and unlock the windows. It would have been hopeless. And she told us there were chunks of glass still dropping round her feet. So she'd gained nothing.'

'And Harris?' I had to clear my throat. 'Where was he?'

'She couldn't see him at first. That whole window was starred and impossible to see through. The other window was cracked, too, but not so bad. She couldn't make out anything, then she peered through the hole – not getting too close – and there he was, sitting slumped against the opposite wall, just a few feet to one side of the door you're standing by, Phil. She couldn't see much because he wasn't opposite the window, and part of the table got in the way. You can see that yourself. Nothing's changed. But she could see enough to realise he was covered in blood and wasn't moving.'

'She'd shot him through the glass,' I said, drawing my breath in sharply.

'But no. If she had, that would've been all right.'

'All right?'

'It would have been accepted as a tragic accident. But it wasn't like that. The pathologist and the forensic team had a grand time with it, and they came up with the fact that the blood she'd seen, at that time, had been from flying glass. They picked about eighty bits of glass out of him.'

I took a deep breath. 'He'd been too close,' I said quietly.

'Not necessarily. There was glass everywhere, bits stuck in the wall, that door, the ceiling.'

'But ... eighty pieces! He *must* have been too close.'

'Wherever he was ...' Oliver sounded a little weary of my emphasis on detail, though he'd asked me to help. A woman's eyes to consider it; a woman's point of view. What would I have done, in those circumstances?

He seemed to realise this, cleared his throat, and started again. 'Wherever he was at the time of the shot, Phil, he must have staggered back against the rear wall, and slumped down until he was sitting with his back against it.'

'And what did Clare do then?' I asked, as he'd paused, and didn't seem inclined to continue.

'She dropped the gun on the terrace and ran round to the front. Then through the house to the sitting-room opposite, then she picked up the phone, dialled 999, and reported that she'd killed her husband. That was what she thought at the time, you see.'

'And where were you at that time, Oliver?'

He walked round a little, apparently to stimulate his memory. 'I worked it out later. She must have got back inside just a minute or two before I arrived. Don't forget – I'd come on a burglar alarm call. So I didn't go straight in, but had a quick scout round. I spotted the shattered window, and that seemed to fit the general idea of a burglary, so I knew I had to move carefully. I walked all round the house, saw nothing else unusual, so I walked in at the front door and quietly along to where I guessed Clare might be – that sitting-room.'

'And?' I had to prompt him. He seemed locked in the memory.

'She was there – sort of in shock. I had to shout at her to find out what had happened, and she started babbling about the gunroom, and Harris being dead against the wall. Five minutes later a squad car got here from the station, also in response to the burglar alarm warning, and only ten minutes after that, a CID team, in response to her phone call. It was chaos, with a lot of misunderstandings – until we sorted it out. But Harris was dead, sure enough, and from gunshot wounds, as would have been inflicted by a shot-gun.'

'So she *did* kill him by accident, when she shot the hole in the window.'

'It was no accident, the way he died. Harris Steadman was found leaning back against the wall, as she'd described it. But there were shot-gun pellets in that wall, in a pattern all round him . . . but not behind him. And his body was peppered with them.'

I gripped his good arm firmly, in order to stop him. He was going too fast for me, or my mind was too slow.

'Now hold on. Wait a minute. You said earlier, Oliver – though I thought it was a slip of the tongue – you said she thought she'd killed him, because he was covered with blood. It doesn't hang together. Are you saying she shot at him – a second shot – through that hole in the glass? Surely that would've been nearly impossible.'

He smiled. He'd slipped it in as a kind of trap, to see whether I was on the ball and my mind reasonably active.

'That was not only damn near impossible, it simply wasn't done. Shot-guns have a certain spread, you know, according to the machining of the barrel, and they had the actual fired gun to work with. Those forensic people know their stuff, and they could calculate reasonably accurately the actual distance from which the second shot was fired. They simply collected her gun from outside the french windows and took it along to their lab. The result was that they were certain Harris had been killed by a blast of shot-gun pellets from a distance of no more than four feet. It damn near took his head off. And only Clare could've done that.'

'Now hold on a minute. She'd left the gun on the terrace?'

'So she said.'

'And you've been saying Harris was killed by a second shot. Clare fired one at the glass. She said that ... surely she said that. And she dropped the gun outside on the terrace. Now you're talking of the second shot being fired inside the room – inside here.'

He shrugged, turned away, turned back. 'When the gun was found, outside on the terrace and just beneath the hole in the glass, both barrels had been fired.'

'Not both from *there*...'

'No, love, not both from there. The forensic evidence was that the second one must have been from inside, and close to him.'

'With the door locked and the french windows jammed?' I asked with scorn.

He seemed to ignore that. 'She kept saying she'd killed him, with her shot through the glass.'

'So she ran round to the front and through the house to the room opposite here, and grabbed for the phone?'

'You've got it exactly.'

'But you ... didn't you even come to take a look in here?'

'I told you. I'd come about a burglar alarm warning. I'd had a quick scout around the back, and I'd seen the shattered window. It didn't look good – the situation. Then I went back round the house, and through the front, and managed to get some sort of sense from Clare. So naturally I looked in here.'

'But she said the door was locked.'

'That's true. She said that.'

'You told me she'd smashed a table against it, trying to get in.'

He was smiling gently, no doubt at my persistence – or more likely at the fact that he'd clearly captured my interest.

'Well ...' he said. 'It certainly wasn't locked when I tried it, so I looked in.'

'You're sliding over it,' I accused him. 'And it's important. She said he'd locked the door, and she'd smashed a table against it, trying to get in. So how could it – all of a sudden – be unlocked?'

He shrugged. It was clearly a point on which he'd been worried, and now he was having to face it again. 'Perhaps Clare was lying about that.'

'What! When she desperately wanted to get in and stop him before he started playing games with her guns? Talk sense, Oliver, please.'

'That door was unlocked when I tried it,' he said quietly.

'So tell me how that could have come about?'

'The super decided that Harris must've unlocked it. How else?'

'When did he do this unlocking, then?'

'When Clare started bashing a table at it,' he suggested.

'And she didn't realise he'd unlocked it? Nonsense. It was what she was trying for. So she'd try the door handle. That'd be natural.'

'Or perhaps he unlocked it after all the throwing.' Why did he have to say that with a little smile on his face? 'When he was hurt. Realising that he would need help.'

'Rubbish.'

I watched him nodding to himself, staring beyond me at the wall. He was trying desperately to remain neutral. Or to give that impression.

'Whose side are you on, Oliver, for heaven's sake?' I demanded.

'Hers, yours, ours. Put it how you like. I'm just letting you see the snags when it came to her defence in court.'

'You mean they claimed she'd lied about the door being locked?'

'Exactly. Because there's no other answer.'

'Oliver, Oliver! If you want to help her, you've got to believe she told the truth.'

He sighed. 'You haven't met her, Phil. I wish you could. But let's not jump the gun on this. Shall I tell you what the Crown's case was, and you can try picking holes in that.'

'Tell me, then. But not in here, please. It's too quiet and bare, and I can't *see* the thing you're talking about. Outside. Let's go round and look at it from outside. Maybe I'll get a better impression.'

'All right.' He seemed pleased to be able to get out of there himself. 'We can simply walk out on to the terrace.'

32

'Yes, yes. Stupid of me. Of course.'

He turned the key and pushed open the french windows. There was a bolt top and bottom for the left-hand one. They opened with a creak. Outside was the terrace, a plain spread of paving slabs, eight feet or so to their edge and running the whole width of the house. The drop to the lawn was about three feet, and there were steps down to it, though not, with this house, opposite the windows. The grass was dry at this time.

I walked down on to the lawn. The french windows now seemed quite a long way away, and above me.

'How much does a shot-gun weigh, Oliver?' I asked him.

'Oh, I don't know. Anything from about seven to ten pounds, I'd reckon.'

'Say eight pounds, then. That's equivalent to four bags of sugar. I wouldn't reckon to throw that weight from here into the gun-room. Once, perhaps, but not on and on. And certainly not in a raging thunderstorm.'

'Phil, Phil, this must certainly be amongst the thousands of things your father told you. In times of great emotional stress, people can do the most remarkable things. You'd be surprised. In any event, she did do it.'

My respect for her grew another few notches, but I told myself that I had to remain uncommitted.

'So ... under this stress, you're saying, she would be capable of walking into that room, when the hall door was supposed to be locked, and calmly shooting her husband from a distance of a few feet?'

'I'm saying she wasn't,' he pointed out. 'My superiors claimed she was.'

'What, exactly, did they claim?'

He took a deep breath, and let it out slowly. 'If we must...'

'Most certainly, we must.'

'Very well. They said she fired only one barrel at the window, and there was no argument about that. They said that Harris, realising he was badly hurt, managed to unlock the door before he collapsed.'

'I've already said all I'm going to about that. It's ridiculous.'

'All right, Phil. But, however it happened, they said that she did do that, walk in, that she was still carrying her gun, and that she fired her second barrel directly at him. She then put the gun out through the hole in the glass that she herself had blasted in it, and

33

dropped it on to the terrace, with the intention of claiming she'd fired both barrels outside and shot him by accident.'

'But she *didn't* claim that?'

'No. I think the jury felt that she'd realised she couldn't, because of the forensic evidence of the second shot, fired at him from close range. They made a special point of that, the Crown did.'

They, they! Oliver had previously dissociated himself from his immediate superiors, now he was challenging the Crown's claims. They'd been quite correct in taking him off the case.

'In any event,' I said, 'she'd admitted having fired it. She didn't deny that.'

'No. But she wouldn't budge from claiming she'd fired only one barrel. She said she *knew* she'd fired only one barrel. You can't fire both without knowing. And that she'd dropped it outside on the terrace. The gun was found there, where she'd said, but with both barrels fired – and the empty shell cases still in the breech.'

'So the case against her was that she fired one shot outside, then ran round and into the gunroom – and fired the other?'

'Precisely.'

'And you're convinced she couldn't have done that – would have been incapable of it?'

'That's it.'

'Even when you've explained so carefully that people can do literally anything, when under emotional stress.'

'I still think she didn't kill him.'

'Then don't you see that you're claiming somebody else did? Just imagine it. They'd have had to pick up her gun from where she'd dropped it – assuming she *did* drop it – go round to the front and follow her into the house, enter a door that had to be locked, whatever you might say, shoot him, put the gun out through the hole in the glass ... and simply walk out of the house again.'

'I'm not saying that.'

'Then what?'

'I don't know. If I did, why would I ask for your help on it?'

'All right. Is there any evidence for such a thing? Did Clare, for instance, hear such a shot?'

'She said she did hear something like a shot. But the storm was still going at full tilt.'

'And she took it for a clap of thunder?' I asked with sarcasm.

'The police aren't exactly stupid, Phil. What about your own father? He wasn't stupid, was he? No. My super as good as offered her that. He suggested that if there'd been another shot, while she

34

was in the living-room, she'd certainly have heard it. As you've just suggested.'

'Ha!' I said. 'If she'd been guilty she'd have claimed that, without any prompting. The fact that she had to be prompted as good as proves she wasn't guilty. Did she *say* she'd heard it?'

'When prompted,' Oliver said. He was watching my reactions gravely.

'She claimed it then?'

'Not exactly. What she did say was what convinced my super she was just plain guilty. She overdid it, Phil. She claimed she heard two. Two, not counting her own. One close to, one further away.'

'Oh!' I groped for a way out. 'The final one being a clap of thunder?'

'The super suggested that, too. He was very careful with her. But she was quite indignant. She said she knew a thunderclap when she heard one, and a gunshot, and what she heard was two gunshots. And she stuck to that.'

Then he turned and began to walk back round the house. 'That's the wrong way, Oliver,' I called after him. 'The french windows...'

'You can shut 'em,' he called back. 'I don't want to go inside there again.'

It was only then that I realised the dislike he felt for the house, and therefore what a strain I'd put on him. Dear Oliver, he'd carried it through very well.

But for whom? For me – or for Clare Steadman?

I was beginning to wonder whether Clare could be one of those annoying people who always tell the truth, either from a mental laziness that precludes the effort necessary to compound a lie, or from the false belief that the truth is always more practical and acceptable. They are not universally popular. They must also be a little stupid, or at the best naïve, as a small lie can so easily smooth the social progress through life. 'How d'you like my new slacks, dear?' 'They're awful.' The truth, perhaps, but not welcome.

I couldn't wait to meet her.

But if, then, Clare had told the truth about the extra shots, I had to accept that she had heard two of them. Not one, as the super had offered to her. To have admitted to hearing a single shot after her own – to have claimed it – would at least have suggested another killer in or about the house. Most people would have pounced on the offer. But no ... she'd insisted on two. Yet the forensic experts could not have been mistaken about the discharge that had killed

35

Harris Steadman. Even if they'd had to count and weigh the recovered pellets, either in or surrounding Harris (which they probably had), they would have been certain that only one discharge had ended his life, there against the wall, and helpless.

Consequently, if Clare had fired only one barrel at the glass, and one barrel had been fired, separately, at her husband, her gun, found with both cartridges fired, exactly fitted the scenario that she had fired both.

Yet it was beyond reasonable acceptance that another person had whipped up her gun, run round the house, and finished off Harris Steadman after having seen him sitting there against the wall and covered with blood. But the superintendent had offered Clare this possibility, suggesting she might have heard a single shot. Craftily.

And then she had claimed she'd heard two shots. That was where the scenario splintered into fragments, like the french window.

It was because of this, and the fact that the french windows had to be locked again from inside, that I chose to walk back through the house. I had to check the possibility of an outsider having got in. And out again.

I locked the room door behind me and stood in the cross corridor. It ran in both directions. The door to the sitting-room was as Oliver had said, not quite opposite. I walked along to it. This door was also locked, but the key was on the outside. I opened it and looked inside. We had already seen this room, in passing, but I hadn't paid particular attention to it. Now I did, and there was the settee where Clare had collapsed, there the small round table with the phone on it. I went across and picked it up. The line was dead, the phone disconnected.

I then went out again and investigated the cross corridors, and the alternative routes to the front. It would, I decided, have been just possible for an outsider to have followed Clare inside, shot Harris Steadman with Clare's gun, and retreated without being observed. But what a risk! What a reliance on chance!

It was with some surprise that I realised I was already caught in the web of the mystery, my senses stretched and my mind racing, and with even more surprise that I found I was assuming Clare had told the truth.

Yet ... if I accepted her veracity, I would also have to accept that the gunroom door had been locked. In that event, nobody would have been able to get in and fire that second killing shot. But Oliver had been able to get in. The squad had been able to get in. So where did that leave my belief that she had told the truth?

I damned Oliver firmly for having embroiled me in this, though I had to concede that he had been reluctant to come anywhere near the place.

Consequently, in a contrite mood, smiling to show I forgave him even if he couldn't know for what, I opened the front door, remembered that Oliver still had the keys to both the door and the alarm system in his pocket, and closed it behind me.

The little green light in the alarm box was no longer blinking at me; a little red light had replaced it and was glowering warningly. Duly warned, I turned to face the steps.

A battered red Porsche was parked this side of the maze. The nose of a police car – I could just see its blue light on the roof – was parked to the right of the maze, and the bonnet of what must have been a second one was just visible on the left. I knew what that meant, and I found it a stimulating experience suddenly to feel like a criminal, caught in the act.

Oliver was at the foot of the steps, chatting to a short, slim firecracker of a woman of about my own age, with close-cut black hair and huge brown startled eyes, dressed in blue denim jeans and a short russet jacket over a cream shirt. Oliver raised his eyes to me, his face caught in the half-embarrassed and half-enchanted expression of a man with two women to reconcile.

'Ah, Phil!' he cried, his voice too hearty. 'Here you are, then. This is Clare Steadman. Clare, I'd like you to meet Philipa Lowe.'

3

I stood at the top of the steps, not willing to surrender this minimal advantage. She would have been about three inches shorter than me, I reckoned, and two-thirds of my weight, but she was crackling with the outrage of encountering a strange woman walking from her own home to welcome her, and her present control was perhaps maintained only because she was in the presence of what seemed to be a considerable phalanx of policemen, who might be poised to observe any breach of the peace by a convict, possibly out on licence. That they'd appeared so rapidly and in such strength indicated that they'd expected trouble.

But I couldn't stand there all day. I advanced slowly down the steps. Oliver eagerly explained.

'Clare saw the green light was on, so she switched it to red. As we'd got the french windows open – '

'I get the point,' I assured him. 'How do you do?' I asked Clare, offering a hand.

She touched it. 'How the hell d'you think I do?' she demanded. 'Finding strangers in my own house!'

'Oliver's surely not completely strange,' I suggested, trying to establish a proprietory interest, and at the same time expressing a certain amount of knowledge of how strange he could be.

'Might just as well be,' she snapped. 'The bastard's never been to visit me.'

'Now, Clare...'

He was afraid of her! Yet he glanced at her now with a tentative smile, fondness in his eyes, and, I thought, a certain amount of annoyance that he couldn't in the circumstances whip her up into his arms and welcome her, like a noble welcoming his warrior lady back from the crusades. For this woman could have outraced Boudicca in a chariot; outfaced Helen to the tune of a few hundred ships. I was now convinced that if she did always confine herself to the truth, it would not be for the reason I'd guessed. No. It would be based on pride, from a certain amount of arrogance. 'That's the truth, damn you, and you can take it or leave it.' She would feel it degrading to have to resort to a lie, or at least resent the pressures that forced her into resorting to one.

And yet ... there was, when she turned to face me, a light in her eye indicating that lurking behind it was a wicked sense of humour, which itself might produce a whole string of lies, if only for the fun of it.

'And you ...' She left it hanging.

'Philipa Lowe, a friend of Oliver's. We're here to see the house, as I was considering buying it.'

'What idiot let you have the keys?' she demanded. 'I wrote to them six weeks ago, cancelling the whole thing. That was when I was told I was coming up for release on parole.'

'You beat me to it,' I told her.

'Beat you? In what way?' She cocked her head, interested, but with her lips twisted in a sceptical manner.

What was now proceeding between us, though expressed as idle chat, was in fact deadly serious. We were probing each other's intentions and involvements.

'The possibility was,' I explained, 'that I might be able to prove your innocence, and get you a pardon.'

'Well ... I suppose I ought to thank you. But I can manage very nicely myself, if you don't mind.'

'Oh ... I see.'

She eyed me with suspicion. 'You see what?'

'Your lawyers have put in an appeal. It's quite the rage, these days. They show that the original verdict wasn't safe, as they put it, and your conviction gets quashed.'

'Oh ...' she said, flipping a hand and dismissing legal confrontations. 'I don't need *them*. Look what a cock-up they made of it last time! No, thank you. I'll handle it myself.'

Oliver cleared his throat in the background. As far as we two were concerned, this being intensely personal, he might not have existed.

'You think you can discover the truth yourself?' I asked, making it sound quite unreasonable. 'I've at least had *some* experience.'

'I don't need experience. I already know who killed Harris. It's just the question of doing something about it.'

'You know?'

'Certainly.'

'Then why haven't you said something?' Was the woman insane?

She lifted her shoulders fractionally. 'Nobody would believe me.'

'I would believe you.'

'You would?' She tilted her head at me. 'How very strange.'

'Excuse me, ma'am.' A sergeant was standing suddenly beside us. He might have been there a long while; we wouldn't have noticed him. 'Is everything all right now?' he asked.

'Oh yes. Yes, thank you. I do apologise for bringing you all the way out here.' She raised her voice, looking, as well as she could beyond his bulk, towards his fellow officers. 'Thank you, gentlemen. You were very quick off the mark. Nine out of ten for efficiency.' Then she laughed lightly, a tinkle of a laugh, and watched them leave, watched till the last vestige of them had disappeared. She then returned her attention to me.

'You can't imagine what it's like – walking away from that place – driving away from it, rather. What a good thing I'd got Porky here. So I drove away. The head wardress waved. I'm so glad I'd left it garaged quite close . . .'

'They let you drive yourself to prison?'

'Not alone, of course. A big, fat policewoman sat beside me, and there was a police car on my tail. They thought I was a bit eccentric, but I found it amusing.'

'You did?'

'Indeed. And now all I've got to do is decide how to do it. I know *who*. It's just a matter of how I'm going to go about it. And this time I'll know what to say in court.'

I wasn't sure I understood her. She surely couldn't be meaning what she seemed to be saying. It was part of what she might consider a bit of a laugh. Calling her Porsche 'Porky' was probably in the same spirit. Perhaps the whole thing had been untrue.

'But you must come in and share a celebratory drink,' she said. 'After all, you've been put to a lot of quite unnecessary trouble. Come along.' And she led the way back inside, remembering to switch off the alarm.

I had walked out of that door with the feeling that I might be returning as the owner. I followed her inside feeling lost and useless, and an undesired guest.

'But the house is empty, Clare,' said Oliver. 'I saw no sign of anything to drink – and you've got no food in.'

'Oh, I expect I'll manage. I'll pop into Asherton later . . . and have a pleasant word with that blasted estate agent.'

She marched with me, ahead of Oliver, not along any of the corridors but by way of a maze of doors, each of which needed to be unlocked, and through an assortment of rooms. She was telling the house she was back. There was no doubt as to each one's purpose – a television room with a huge screen and soft, comfortable chairs arranged facing it; a lounge, as opposed to the sitting-room we'd seen, with luxurious lounging facilities; a library packed with books; even a bedroom or two – and eventually we were back in the sitting-room we already knew.

'Father laid down a cellarful of wines,' she told us. 'Harris stocked it with spirits.'

'I'll help,' said Oliver quickly.

'No, no.' She nodded to chairs. 'Shan't be a tick.' Then, abruptly to me, she said, 'You said . . . prove my innocence. What makes you think I'm innocent?'

'If you'd been guilty,' I told her, 'you'd have invented another shot after your own, but you had to be prompted by the superintendent.'

'True,' she conceded. 'He *did* try to help, the dear man.'

'And when you agreed to a shot, you wouldn't have doubled it up, for luck, and said there'd been two. That's what got you sent down, I wouldn't be at all surprised.'

She stared at me with wide, shocked eyes, her eyebrows climbing. 'But it was the truth,' she said. 'You wouldn't have had me telling a lie, now would you?'

'A guilty person would have stuck to one extra shot.'

'There you are, then. You'd still prefer brandy, Ollie?'

Ollie? And I didn't think he ever touched brandy!

'If you've got brandy.' He seemed restless.

'Of course there's brandy. Make yourselves at home.' And she frisked away, her hair dancing and her pretty little bottom dancing with it. Mine doesn't bounce, it just stays put. My hair does too. Oliver gazed after her without any expression that I could detect.

'Well?' he said, when the door closed behind her.

'Well what?'

'What d'you make of her?'

'She's a woman you can't make anything of, Oliver. You never know whether she's laughing at you or at herself. Everything's a game, and nothing counts.'

'The guns counted, otherwise there wouldn't have been that performance on the lawn.' He seemed very serious about that.

I tried for an easy laugh, but it sounded a little sarcastic to me. 'If it *did* happen. If she didn't make up the whole thing. Rigged it as a background for a cold-blooded murder – for a bit of a laugh.'

'Then the laugh was on her.'

'She'd enjoy it, just the same. She gets it from her grandfather. Perhaps we'd better switch intentions, and try to prove she did do it. That's the only chance I can see of ever getting my hands on the keys to this house.' I nodded firmly, as though this could be a practicality.

'Perhaps she *was* guilty,' Oliver said moodily.

'Oh no,' I replied. 'No, no. The jury just didn't understand the significance of the three shots.'

'And you do, Phil?' He didn't have to sound so sceptical, I thought.

'I wish I did.'

'Then when you get round to it ...' He sounded remote, and there was a little acid on his tongue. 'When you do, maybe they'll let you appear for her in the Appeal Court. It'd save paying a whole team of barristers.'

'My fee would be calculated accordingly.'

'Maybe you'll even be able to prove she fired all three shots.'

'Now, Oliver...'

He gave me a sidelong, leery smile, then the door was kicked open and Clare swept in, her arms clasping a number of dusty, cobwebbed bottles.

'Something else', she said, 'that my father collected. And while I remember, Ollie – where *are* all my guns?'

He was helping her with the bottles, lifting them from her arms, an operation that required a far-too-intimate contact with her rather insignificant bosom.

'They've got them at the County HQ, in their Black Museum. Made quite a good show of them, I believe.'

'Well ... of all the nerve!'

'You ought to be pleased,' he assured her. 'Who else but the county firearms expert could've cleaned and oiled them properly? It was logical. You can collect them any time.'

'Now,' she decided. 'I had a quick look in the gunroom. It looks bare. They made a good job of reglazing the cases, I thought. I got old Chas Wright to do that. From the village.'

'Now?' Oliver asked, raising his eyebrows.

'After we've had a drink.'

'It's coming up to lunch-time,' I pointed out.

'Then we'll have lunch on the way. Is she always like this, Ollie, seeing problems at every step?'

'Not always. She usually takes them in her stride.'

I could have wished he'd said that with a hint of pride, not ruefully and with a grimace of distaste, though this, I reassured myself, might have been caused by the sip of brandy he'd taken. I'd been certain he hated it. She had been wrong, and I treasured the thought.

So, after the drinks there was once more the securing of her fortress. (I wasn't sure I'd be so fussy about security if I took over.) Then we went out to the cars, hers this side of the maze, my BMW round the other side. At once it was clear that there would be difficulty over whose car Oliver would grace with his presence. He was with me, but Clare, with an expression of mischief on her face, went to her Porsche and unlocked the passenger's door first. It was a proprietorial gesture, and I resented it. Accordingly, I tossed my keys to Oliver and called out, 'You follow us, Oliver, and watch you don't scratch it. We want to talk, Clare and I.'

'Do we?' she asked.

'I'm sure we do.'

I expected her, after that, to drive furiously and dangerously, partly to scare me and partly to vent her annoyance. But that soon evaporated. She slowed, driving well, enjoying the car.

'You timed it beautifully,' I commented.

'Timed what?' But the lift of her chin indicated that she was ahead of me. She darted me a minimal glance.

'Your arrival. Quite a coincidence, Oliver and I being there.'

'Oh ...' she said, lifting one hand from the wheel and flipping it. 'It wasn't quite like that. To tell you the truth ... shall I tell you the truth?'

'Tell me, and I'll guess how much truth there is in it.'

She allowed a little silence to build up, then she went on. 'I've been out a week. More – ten days. Just been touring around, stopping nights wherever I found myself. I mean ... there I'd been, yearning to get out of that place and back to my own home – and when I finally got the chance ... I couldn't face it. Strange, that was. I was nervous. Don't you think that was strange?'

'Not really.'

Once more I was aware that she'd glanced at me, but I kept my attention ahead.

'Hmm!' she said. 'Anyway, I phoned Evelyn – that's the estate agent at Asherton...'

'I know.'

'Phoned her this morning to tell her I was... free, sort of, but that I was taking a holiday, and she said she'd given the keys to a couple... that'd be you and – well – him.'

There was a pause. I knew what she wanted to hear.

'Oliver,' I said. 'Yes.' Giving away nothing.

'I was furious. I mean, I'd ... but never mind that, now. So I drove back. Fast. I've covered fifty miles in the hour.'

'Less time than that.'

'Whatever. And as it happened, I got there just in time.'

'To trap us?'

'Put it like that, if you like. To see Oliver again, if the truth be known. Just to *see* him. What's the matter with his arm?'

She was very quick, very observant. I wondered in what way he'd demonstrated the weakness or strength of his arm.

'He tried to take a gun from somebody,' I told her.

'Typical,' she said in disgust.

'A shot-gun.'

There was a pause. 'They keep cropping up in my life.'

But Oliver wasn't in her life now. Oh no. 'It cropped up in mine, Oliver's shot-gun.'

There was a pause as she scrambled down through the gearbox for a fast corner on a hill. I glanced over my shoulder. Oliver was keeping station meticulously.

'You're sharp, aren't you,' she remarked at last. 'I do believe you could do it, after all.'

'Do what?'

'Find out who killed Harris.'

'But you told me you already know that.'

'Tcha!' Then she added a tiny laugh. 'It might amuse you to confirm what I believe.'

As I couldn't understand that, I ignored it. 'You said you knew who'd done it, and you knew what to do about it. Was there a hint of violence, there?'

'Perhaps there was,' she said. 'They prepare you for the outside world, where I've been. They put me in a cell with a raving dyke, and I thought I'd go insane. So I took lessons in the gym on karate. The instructress was a slim little Eurasian lass, who was at Benfield for breaking her husband's neck when he tried to stifle her baby with a pillow.'

'They put her away for *that?*'

'Yes. It wasn't self-defence, you see.'

'Wasn't it?' I mumbled. 'And the baby...'

'It's with her mother. I promised to visit her when I got out.'

'And will you?'

'Of course. I have, already. Anyway ... do you always do this, Philipa Lowe?'

'Do what?'

'Distract people when they're trying to tell you something. We turn right here, I think.'

'We do. We ought to have let Oliver lead.'

'It was you told him to follow.'

'So it was. Finish the bit about the Eurasian girl, Clare.'

'Oh yes. She taught me how to do it, you see. I know lots of very painful and incapacitating things now. I can't wait to try them. But ... the first time that dyke came near me after that, I showed her how it worked, too. Not actually *broke* her neck, you know, but she passed out, and asked to be moved. She said I was dangerous, of all things.'

'Hmm!' I commented cautiously. 'So all that rigmarole was to tell me you'll be breaking somebody's neck if and when I can tell you ... confirm for you ... who killed your husband?' If it wasn't all a flight of fancy.

She didn't immediately answer, but silently drove another mile. We were on an open main road now, two-lane and not busy. The speed mounted. My BMW maintained a steady distance behind.

'Well, yes,' she said at last. 'I'll probably do that, Philipa, but not for the reason you're thinking. Not because he – or she, I'll say – killed Harris. No. He was due for it. He'd been asking for it for ages. Begging for it. For landing me right in it, that's what.' She turned her head and glanced at me, not what I would wish at something over eighty. For one moment, I'd swear, she had forgotten she was driving.

'Watch the road, for God's sake!'

'You're not listening. Landed me right in it, by using my gun. I *know* I fired only one barrel. D'you think I don't know how to handle a shot-gun! I fired one barrel, and dropped the gun outside the french windows. Somebody fired the other one. I mean ... must have done, because they'd both been fired when they found it.'

'Where you'd dropped it – outside the french windows?'

'Yes. Exactly.'

'But how could anybody have done that? Just think. They would

45

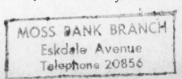

have had to pick up your gun from where you'd dropped it and run round the front after you, sneak inside the house, and when you were safely inside the sitting-room they'd have gone into the gunroom...'

I left that hanging, waiting for her objection. She made no response. She didn't even nod.

'In spite of the fact that the door was supposed to have been locked,' I added.

'It *was* locked.'

'So you didn't glance inside there, in order to check – '

'I didn't go near the gunroom,' she said sharply. 'I wanted to get to a phone.' She jerked a quick, angry glance at me. 'I thought he was dead already, from what I'd seen through the hole in the glass. I didn't *try* to get into the gunroom, because I knew the door was locked. It was *they* who said it was unlocked, the police, *they* who said they could just walk in when they tried it. They said I'd gone in there and ... and finished off what I'd started. That was wrong. That was a damned lie. Oh hell, now I'm lost. What's the way from here?'

'Why don't you pull over and wave Oliver past, and he can lead?'

'How clever of you,' she said acidly. But she did it. Oliver hummed past, and settled down to a more reasonable speed.

'Keep to the point,' I said, once she'd relaxed. 'This man – assume a man for now – he would have had to follow you into the house and wait until you went into the sitting-room, then somehow get into the gunroom, shoot your husband ... then he must've run out smartly, because Oliver was there moments after you'd put the phone down.'

She was silent for a long while, as though wondering whether to trust me with a morsel of truth. Then she said quietly, 'Nobody could have got in after me. I ran round to the front – dropped the shot-gun on the terrace and ran round. And I slammed the front door after me. Then Oliver came. The door's got a Yale lock, and locks itself. Like all front doors, I suppose. I had to unlatch it for Oliver to get in.'

'But he said ... said he found you in a state of collapse on the settee.'

'Well, yes ...' She grimaced, then flashed me a quick grin. 'I was waiting, see. Waiting in the hall with no light on, looking out from the stained glass windows. As soon as I saw it was Oliver getting

46

out of the car, I unlatched the door for him. Then I ran back to the sitting-room.'

'He told me you were on the settee, by the phone, almost passed out.' I insisted on getting this correct. It was necessary to extract every item of truth meticulously.

'Well . . . I would be, wouldn't I! For Oliver. To give him a chance to revive me – make him feel all big and masculine. Once I'd seen it was him, I ran back quickly.'

'You're a wicked woman,' I told her severely, watching her profile, and catching just a hint of a self-congratulatory smile.

And a woman, I thought, who, believing she had shot her husband, had been remarkably calm and with everything in control.

'So nobody else could've got in?' I asked, tying it down.

'Oh no. I can't see how it would've been possible.'

'But if . . . I only say if, you realise . . . if you didn't enter the gunroom and shoot him yourself, how else could it have happened? You'd dropped your gun outside . . . I suppose *that's* the truth?'

'Oh yes.' It was a plain statement. She didn't even trouble to nod in emphasis.

'And nobody could've picked up your gun after you'd dropped it, followed you in, and fired the shot that killed Harris?'

'I don't see how they could,' she commented casually.

'But you said you *heard* the shot.'

'Yes. That was while I was phoning.'

I sighed. It was no wonder the police hadn't believed her. She tied her own story in knots.

'*Not* while you were phoning,' I said. 'No – don't interrupt, just drive. You'd already done your phoning. It was the first thing you did after getting back inside. Otherwise, you wouldn't have been peering out of the stained glass window, expecting a police car . . . and pleased to see it was Oliver.'

She kept her eyes on the road, but I saw the same quirk at the corner of her lips.

'You're quick, aren't you!' she said. 'Perhaps you *can* find out the truth.'

'Please don't try to distract me. You said you heard a shot. Do you mean while you were genuinely phoning, or when you were pretending to, for Oliver's benefit?'

'The second,' she said firmly. 'While I was sitting with the phone

47

in my hand, pretending I'd just phoned, waiting for him to walk in.'

It was not surprising that the police hadn't believed her. The actions she'd described didn't seem to fit the image of a distraught woman who'd just experienced a traumatic experience on the lawn in the pouring rain. But perhaps *that* hadn't been entirely true. She seemed always to produce whatever best fitted her self-image.

'You heard one shot?' I asked. 'Singular? That means: not two.'

'Yes. It usually does. One shot. Somebody else fired that.'

'All right. One shot. *That* might just have been acceptable. Crazy, but somehow valid . . . if *you* didn't fire it. It'd be a kind of alibi for you. But you went and spoiled it, Clare, you really did. You must have realised that, surely.'

'I didn't realise anything. How much further is it, for heaven's sake? How did I spoil it?'

'By telling them you'd heard two shots after your own.'

'Yes . . . well . . . that's because there *were* two, one I've told you about, and one when Oliver was there with me in the sitting-room. Comforting me.' She shot me one of her short, searching glances. 'I was surprised he didn't back me up on that. It was kind of more distant, that last shot, as though it was outside the house.'

'Thunder – '

'No!' she cut me off sharply. 'I know a gunshot when I hear one. My father tried to get me out on shoots. I heard plenty then, close and distant. That night – I heard one close and one distant.'

I considered this, not knowing what to think.

'But Clare,' I ventured, 'how could there have been two, after your own first one? Even if you fired the second shot yourself, that'd be only two. Even if you fired it directly at him – oh, you'd hear that one right enough – how could there have been a third? They don't make three-barrelled shot-guns, do they?'

Silence. Oliver was slowing for traffic. We hadn't done any stopping for minor details such as lunch.

'There were two,' she said at last, stubbornly shaking her head.

'But that was what led to the guilty verdict. I'll bet it was. They'd have assumed you were lying. There would've been no point in a third shot. For no reason? At nothing?'

She was silent.

'So you gained nothing by lying about a third shot.'

'It wasn't a lie.' She thought a moment about that, then she added, 'But I would've done.'

Then she clamped her lips tightly together, and her jawbone became prominent, as though she had revealed a wondrous truth, and already regretted it.

I considered her profile thoughtfully. She was frowning now. Then, abruptly, and with a shock that made me dizzy for a moment, I realised what she meant, and a whole tangle of tiny details suddenly unravelled in my mind.

'Good grief, Clare! You can't be thinking that!' There was no response. 'Are you telling me ... but he couldn't have had time ... he hurried to you...'

'He had plenty of time. There I was, on that settee. I'd unlatched the front door for him, and run back. He knew where I would be – but he didn't come. Not straight away, he didn't. Not rushed to me. I waited...'

'How long?' I whispered.

'I don't know. Two or three minutes. Perhaps four. *Then* he came. Philipa, you're forgetting something. He didn't come because of my phone call; he came because of the burglar alarm going off, when Harris opened the french windows, I suppose. He told me that – sort of – when he came in and saw me half collapsed on the settee. Said he'd had a look around, but whoever it was who'd broken in by way of the french windows, they'd hopped it. I suppose, at that time, he thought that was what the hole in the glass was all about. I'm sure he must have...'

She bit her lip to silence. Ahead, Oliver was trying to juggle with the traffic, and at the same time not lose us. Clare concentrated on her driving.

I waited until we were again in the clear. Then I said, 'But Clare ...' It was a croak. I cleared my throat. 'Clare, when did you hear the shot? When, exactly – the first of the extra two you said you heard. When did you hear it?'

'Only ... only a minute or so ... less, perhaps ... before he walked in on me.' She flashed me a quick, desperate glance. 'And I wasn't really ready for him!'

'You heard a shot, then he walked in. Did *he* say he'd heard one?'

'He just stood and stared at me. I didn't ask him about a shot. He didn't say anything about hearing a shot.'

'Oh Clare ... you heard a shot, and then there he was in the room with you, and in next to no time. So you assumed ... oh my God, Clare, are you telling me you *invented* another third shot, to fit in with the time he was there, with you, in the sitting-room?'

She shook her head violently. 'I didn't invent it,' she persisted. 'I *heard* it.'

'But there was no point in a third shot. It doesn't come into it. It didn't *do* anything. You were ridiculously stupid to say such a thing.'

'I didn't invent it,' she stubbornly repeated. 'It was just ... that I *said* it and I didn't have to. That was all I did for Oliver, because, of course, he couldn't have fired *that* one, because he was with me. So I said it.'

'And landed yourself in prison, with a raving dyke for company.'

'As it turned out.'

'Oh Clare ... Clare ...' I mumbled, and hell, how she must have loved him!

'But I *did* hear it.'

'Get it into your head, will you, Clare: *there was no third shot*.' I shouted it, competing with the Porsche's engine.

'There was. Mine and two more.'

I could see no point in arguing with her about it, but had to consider what she had said about her intention to deal with her husband's killer. I had to consider it in the light of the fact that she seemed convinced that the killer was Oliver. Did she intend to kill him with her treasured head-lock, or did she hope to kill him with kindness – to love him to death?

'It looks as though we're here,' she told me.

I hadn't noticed; didn't know where I was.

I had expected something resembling a large police station, as I knew them. But this place more resembled a barracks, with a multi-storey concrete building jutting up behind it. The building was the County Police HQ, I discovered. The barracks housed a police training unit, a forensic lab, and the Black Museum.

It was to this last that Oliver took us.

'Look at your guns first,' he suggested as we stretched our legs. 'And we might scrounge a lunch in their canteen afterwards.'

It suited me. It suited Clare. We entered a lobby, manned by a civilian, or at least, by someone in a smart double-breasted suit and a flowered tie. Oliver said we wanted to see Charlie Green, and to tell him it was Oliver Simpson with two ladies he'd be pleased to see.

The clerk winked. Charlie probably had a reputation for being pleased to meet ladies, singly or in multiples. He took up a phone, and in two minutes Charlie was with us, a large, bustling, beaming man.

'Oliver!' He came forward with both hands thrust forward, one to grip Oliver's, one to beat him on the shoulder. 'Heard you got hurt. This arm, is it? Serves you right. You forgot what I'd taught you. And these dear ladies are...'

We were introduced. His eyes dwelt on Clare, admiring her pert beauty, no doubt, and perhaps her expertise with a shot-gun, as he'd heard it.

'You've come to see the Collings collection,' he guessed, inaccurately as it happened.

'I've come to take them away.'

In the Porsche? How many shot-guns could be slid behind the twin seats? He smiled knowingly. No van was parked outside, where we might have left it.

'You've come to claim them, and I'm desolated,' he told her. 'The place will seem empty without your guns. But you simply sign a receipt when we deliver them in our van. How's that?'

'That will be ideal,' said Clare, who, I saw, was quite impressed by him, though he was a little overpowering for my taste.

'Come through to our museum,' he invited, half raising one arm as though to place it round her shoulders. But she flicked him a smile that the Eurasian girl had probably taught her, and he backed off a little.

Charlie Green was, Oliver told me later, the firearms expert for the county. He trained the teams authorised to be issued with firearms as necessity dictated. He *knew* guns, from pistols to howitzers. What Charlie Green didn't know he couldn't look up in learned treatises on the subject, because he'd written most of them himself.

He took us round his collection of weapons, which had all been used in crimes. Most were permanent acquisitions, as they dated back to the times when their users had been hanged, and thus couldn't reclaim them, or because their original users wouldn't want to see them again under any circumstances. But some, such as Clare's collection, they treated as loans, as their value guaranteed that eventually they would be claimed. Clare's were different. Only one of them had been fired, and thus could claim a legitimate place in the Black Museum section. The rest Charlie had appropriated after the forensic squad, wild with enthusiasm, had drained from them the last morsel of evidence usable at her trial. These had their own special separate display.

She was lucky, he was not too shy to mention, that they had fallen into his hands: there was nobody who could have better maintained them, and restored them to their pristine beauty.

And indeed, they were beautiful, considered as the result of dedicated attention from craftsmen, even artists, in that field. Their ultimate ugly purpose one could overlook. The craftsmanship was awe-inspiring.

They were not, as at Clare's, kept in cabinets, but nearly covered a whole wall, and were mounted at identical angles – military precision, one assumed, being appropriate. They gleamed, they shone, their delicate engraving could have been, cumulatively, a life's work.

We walked slowly along the display. They were mounted in chronological order, the earliest being in singles, as these dated from the seventeenth century, but I saw, as we came closer to modern times, they were more often in matched pairs, which I supposed added to their value.

The critical shot-gun was separate from the rest, and had its own place of honour, lying on a shaped pad of black velvet on an inlaid table. A brass plaque mounted on a walnut base was engraved with the information that this was the weapon with which Clare Steadman had killed her husband on 5 September 1986. It was a Winchester model 97, we were informed. To make the point, two discharged cartridge cases lay beside the gun.

'Of all the nerve,' said Clare. 'It's a disgusting display.'

'It *is* the one, though?' I asked.

'How do I know that?' she demanded, angry with me because she had to be angry with somebody. 'It was nearly dark, pitching down with rain. I just grabbed one up, and as there were two unused cartridges in Harris's shooting jacket ...' She shrugged.

Oliver and Charlie strolled over to join us. I expected an explosion from Clare, but she was mercifully silent, so that Charlie was able to display his learning by launching into what was obviously a prepared lecture on the display. I could sense that Clare was simmering beside me. He was preaching to a woman who already knew the most intimate details of her guns (her father reminded me a little of mine; perhaps he, too, had wished for a son) and to two people over whom his enthusiasm washed with barely a ripple. From Durs Egg to Browning, from Winchester to Purdey, and Holland and Holland. I walked, awestruck, in front of a fortune. My so-called wealth might have purchased a dozen of them.

'Wonderful, wonderful,' Charlie murmured. 'Your father, dear lady, knew what he was about.'

'I'll thank you for taking care of them,' said Clare, not, I thought, with too much conviction. 'I was terribly worried that the rain...'

'People shoot in the rain,' Charlie pointed out.

'But – the throwing about...'

'In foot-pounds, the impact in a shot-gun breech is a hundred times greater than what the odd toss around a lawn would generate.'

He beamed at her. She knew her guns. He would concede that. But she was, nevertheless, a woman.

'And there's one short,' she said, in a voice that chopped the complacent smile right off his face.

'One – '

'Short,' she snapped. 'I've counted forty-two. One's missing.'

'There *were* only forty-two,' he protested.

Oliver was staring at Clare with horror all over his face, like a murky veil, because she was arguing with the great Charlie Green.

And I felt a thrill run all up my spine and finish somewhere in the back of my head. My cheeks were suddenly flaming, then were chill, the skin tight. I held my breath.

'Forty-two in the collection,' said Clare firmly, 'plus my husband's own Browning over-and-under.'

'That's here.' He waved a hand to embrace the whole display. It was an angry, dismissive gesture.

'He left it on the hallstand,' she declared. 'When he got home, that night. *That's* here. Yes, I noticed it. So it's one of my collection that's missing.'

Charlie didn't look well. It was not, I guessed, that anybody was going to dare to blame him for having mislaid one of the guns. Who would face him with such a suggestion? But rather that it meant that the forensic lab, who would surely have noticed the odd gun lying around, must have examined only forty-one guns out of the collection of forty-two. The court evidence, based as it had been on the available guns at that time, was now in danger of attracting that unwelcome word: unsafe.

'But my dear lady – '

'There's no dear ladies about it. I'm a furious lady. I'm going to have another look.'

Which she did, walking slowly along the display and muttering to herself, and I'll say this for her, she must have had a very good mind, both to be able to recognise them and to be able to catalogue them from memory.

'Yes,' she declared, at the end. 'There's a rare Darne with a sliding breech missing.'

'Are you certain?' Charlie asked cautiously. 'Your memory ... after such a lapse of time...'

'Damn it!' she said, holding back an anger that had spurred her to the pitch, that terrible rainy evening, of hurling shot-guns through the air. 'Don't you think I know a Darne when I see it! Or when I *don't* see it. There was a Darne in the collection, and it's not here now.'

'I didn't know ...' Poor Charlie was bereft.

'Then you ought to have known. There's an inventory at the house.'

She looked him up and down with painstaking contempt. 'You can't know your job very well, you great oaf. Admit it.' And she turned away before he had a chance to.

Charlie seemed unable to speak.

4

All the same, he managed eventually to make a solemn promise that all the forty-two guns (which included the murder weapon) would be returned to her as soon as it could be organised. We left, and stood by the cars for a few minutes, as Clare walked round in circles, recovering her composure. Oliver watched her with concern. I just watched her. Clare was an exhibitionist, and she was enjoying every moment of it.

It now seemed that we would not be welcome to lunch at the police canteen. No doubt the word would get around that somehow they had mislaid a gun, either in a physical sense, or from a list. The buck would already be moving in all directions – mostly away from Charlie, no doubt – and we didn't want to get in its way.

Eventually, Clare seemed to come to a decision. 'I want to go home,' she declared, like an exhausted child seeking her bed.

It didn't seem a good idea to me. She couldn't simply move in. There would be no food, bed linen would probably be lying a little musty in drawers, and her clothes very much dated in moth-haunted wardrobes. An hotel, I'd have thought, then a shopping spree, and hired helpers to restore the place to welcoming normality. But Clare wanted to go home; Clare had to have her way.

She said nothing about our accompanying her, as we no longer figured on her agenda. Oliver seemed hurt as she drove away.

'She'll need help,' he murmured, but I urged him into my BMW, and we set off after her, allowing her a comfortable lead.

There was now no expectation that Collington House could ever be mine, so that theoretically our involvement was at an end. But quite apart from the fact that my mind and my curiosity, even my emotions, were now captured, there was also the question of Oliver to be resolved. He didn't seem to realise this. Strangely, he was annoyingly silent. Clare was now well ahead, and there was no point in trying to overtake her. Besides, I needed time with Oliver. I drove sedately, and still he was silent.

After a few miles he looked around him, at last opened his mouth, and commented on the fact that we didn't seem to be heading back to our homes in Penley. I said no, we were going to Collington House, if for no other reason than that he had a set of Clare's keys in his pocket. He mumbled something ridiculous about sending them by post, but without enthusiasm. So I reminded him that it was he who had suggested that I might try to find an answer to the meaty problem surrounding the killing. It was no good his claiming that it was now irrelevant. I wouldn't get any sleep, I told him, until I knew the truth, and he wondered how I could ever sleep soundly at all in my isolated little cottage, though perhaps, with him beside me ... The same old thing. I agreed that I would indeed be able to sleep soundly with him beside me, but he wasn't to worry about me because I wasn't going there, anyway, not in the immediate future.

'Then where?'

'You know the district, Oliver. Haven't they got a pub or an inn or the like in the village of Lesser Collington?'

'There's the Wounded Cavalier, but they'd have a job finding even one bedroom.'

'What about Greater Collington?'

'There isn't one. Only Lesser.'

'Less than what?'

'What it was, I suppose, before Cromwell moved on, heading for Bridgnorth.'

I think we both realised we were avoiding the issue. And the issue was himself.

'You *are* in a rotten humour,' I remarked. There hadn't even been an optimistic tone in his mention of a sole bedroom. 'If necessary, we'll try Asherton. That's not too far away, and big enough for a real hotel. I think I noticed one.'

'It's as you wish, Phil. But what you expect to *do* ...' He left it hanging, himself uncommitted.

I drove on. We ran slowly through a small township whose name I didn't notice, as I was alert for a genuine hotel. We were now only six miles away from Collington House.

'There,' he said suddenly.

'What?'

'A café. I'm starving.'

It was, indeed, well after two o'clock, but my mind hadn't been involved with food. I parked. There were no signs of yellow lines, even single ones. Not much sign of inhabitants, either. We walked back to the café.

It was after any normal person's lunch-time, and there seemed to be only one young woman in charge. But she came up with fried eggs on fried bread – how many years had it been since I'd enjoyed that gourmet's delight? – followed by freshly picked strawberries covered with clotted cream. Usually, I have a light meal around that time, but to hell with it. We ate. We barely said a civil word to each other.

'You knew about this place, Ollie,' I challenged, as we got back in the car. I drove away slowly.

'Oliver, please,' he said. 'I hate that name. It makes me feel fat. And of course I knew. You know it was my district. In fact, it was only a mile from here that I had that fence dispute with the two farmers.'

'Ah yes. That bad night of the shooting.'

'Yes.'

I'd been wondering how I could get round to this without being too obvious. He'd done it for me.

'Different weather, though,' I commented casually.

'It was a bit later in the year. It'd been a grand summer – like now. Several weeks of almost unbroken sunshine, and hose-pipe bans everywhere. It had to break sometime, and that was when it chose to do it.'

'And you got that burglar alarm call to go to Collington House? I bet you weren't pleased.'

He was relaxing now. His laugh was easy and unforced. 'Not really pleased, but I wasn't taking it too seriously. Clare had always been a little vague about that alarm system. She'd forget she'd put it on, then go out with a torch to cut a few flowers or something.'

He didn't have to mention her peculiarities in such an affection-ate tone, I thought. 'Silly woman.'

'Even . . . you'd never believe this, Phil . . . she more than once set it off on purpose, times when Harris was away on business, just because she was lonely and wanted company.'

'She must've been desperate if the best she could hope for was a policeman,' I observed.

'Once, she got a policewoman, who told her off very firmly, I heard.'

'But more often she got you?'

'Well . . . yes.'

'Such as on that particular evening.'

'But that was different. I knew Harris wasn't away. I'd seen his car earlier in the day, in the village. So I had a feeling that this time the alarm was genuine. And I *knew* it was, as soon as I got there.'

'How did you know that, Oliver?' I was being pedantic, picking my words with care, and thus using them awkwardly. And I was trying to sound as though I didn't consider his answers to be of any importance.

'Oh ... because the front door wasn't open. It was a habit she had, with that door. If she was expecting me, it would be left just a little open, for me to walk right in. That night it was closed. So I had to allow for the fact that this time it could be a genuine break-in alert.'

I wasn't sure I wanted to hear any more of this – but I knew I had to. 'You'd find that disappointing, I'm sure.'

'It jolted me, I must admit.'

'So what did you do then?'

'Went and had a quick scout round.'

'Outside?'

'Yes.'

'In all that rain?'

'I'd got a job to do. Can you imagine me reporting to my inspector: "No sir, I didn't look around, I might've got wet." Oh, lovely!'

'So you scouted?'

'Why all these questions, Phil?'

'It'll soon become clear. *Did* you scout?'

'Yes. Yes, if you must know. What the hell – '

'Round the back?'

'Of course round the back. Drop it, Phil, please.'

'No, Oliver.' I stopped the car abruptly. We had entered a small village and the sign had indicated that this was Lesser Collington. It all seemed very quiet, with not a soul in sight. 'We're nearly there. I've got to get this clear.'

He opened the door and put a leg out. 'I refuse to – '

'Get out of this car, and I'll drive on and leave you here.'

'I refuse to be cross-examined – '

'Shut that door, sit still, and listen. This matters. To you.'

He was angry. It was our first serious dispute. He slammed the door and stared morosely at the deserted village. 'Say it then.'

So I said it, putting together what I'd discovered and laying it out in front of him. I asked whether, when he'd got round to the

58

back, he'd seen the gunshot hole in the glass. He replied that of course he had, as the light'd still been on in there. As far as he had been concerned, this had to be linked with a break-in, as he'd known nothing at that time of the gun-throwing episode. I assumed he'd peered through the shattered hole in the glass, and he said he had. Harris Steadman had been dimly visible against the facing wall, slumped down and covered with blood, and giving every appearance of being dead. I asked whether he'd then run back to the front door, which he confirmed, rather like a talking dummy. He claimed he'd been in a tricky position, being alone until the back-up arrived, and obviously there'd been violence on a grand scale. So he had eventually entered the house with caution and quietly, as he'd discovered that Clare had left the door un-latched, almost as though this might have been a social visit, as he put it. He had then made his way through the house to the rear, to what he knew she called her sitting-room.

And there she'd been, Clare, looking at her most dramatic best, a terrified woman who'd just put down the phone (apparently) after phoning the station to report that she'd shot her husband.

'She'd heard a second shot, not long before you got to her, Oliver.'

'She said that.' He was more compliant now, realising that what I had to say was very relevant to himself. But he was still cautious.

'Did *you* hear one? You'd have been somewhere outside at the time, or perhaps just be going in to her.'

'I didn't hear it.'

'Maybe it was just before you got there – when you were coming up the drive, say.'

'Whenever it was, I didn't hear it.' His voice was toneless, and there were deep frown lines on his forehead. Not only didn't he understand what I was getting at, he also didn't approve of the way I was searching it out.

'But her gun was definitely fired twice, and she's always said she fired it only once.'

He sighed. 'D'you think I don't know this, Phil?'

'But I'm sure you don't know what *she* made of it.'

'She didn't have the chance to tell me.'

'All right, then. We'll assume it was as she claims, that there were three shots in all – her own at the french window, and two more. Of course, those two . . . no, don't interrupt, Oliver, please . . . of those last two, the first one came when you could have been somewhere inside the house – or just going round to the front – or even before you'd actually arrived, as I've said. And the last of the three shots, she claims, was when you were actually with her in the room. Didn't you hear either of these two shots?'

'No.' His fist was clenched on his knee. 'No, no, no! How many times . . .' He controlled himself and took a deep breath. 'There was a lot of storm noise around. Have you taken account of that?'

'But she swears she did. Heard both the last two. Storm or not.'

'Ah well . . .' He shrugged. 'What you're forgetting . . . my mind was tuned to the storm, so I'd naturally assume any sudden noises were the storm. Her mind was tuned to gunshots, so whatever bangs *she* heard she'd hear as gunshots.'

I turned and stared at him. 'How very clever of you, Oliver. You could well be correct. But she *says* she heard a shot just before you got to her, and later a third. That's the big problem. There couldn't have been a third. It just doesn't fit in. And nobody's produced anything that was shot at.'

'So?' He was naïvely unaware of what I was leading to – or manoeuvring round.

'Oliver,' I said flatly, staring ahead through the windscreen, 'she believes you went round to the back and saw what'd been going on, and you put two and two together. Heavens – I've only just realised – she could have thought you got there early enough to *see* what was going on . . . when it was actually happening.'

'If you think I'd stand there and watch – '

'I'm talking about what she could have thought. In any event, she believes that you picked up the gun she'd dropped and took it round to the front and into the house, directly into the gunroom, and finished what she'd started . . . by shooting Harris where he lay against that wall.'

'But . . . but . . .' A look of wild disbelief was freezing his expression, as he tried to force his mind into accepting it. 'That's . . . that's just stupid – '

'Do shut up, and listen, Oliver. She claims she later heard a third shot, while you were actually with her. I believe she was lying about that. Did *you* hear it?'

'No. Didn't notice it, anyway. But Phil . . . you can't say . . .'

Not waiting for him to rationalise it, I went on quickly.

'I think she invented that third shot. You were with her, but there's nothing at all to support a third shot. Why would a third shot have been fired? What could have been achieved? And if she invented it . . . why? I've tackled her on this, Oliver.'

'You've *what*?'

60

'We've discussed it. And while she – '

'You've been discussing me! You two women, taking me to pieces – '

'Will you stop being stupid, Oliver! Of *course* we discussed you. And although she stuck to the fact that she did hear a third shot, she really knew it would do her no good to say it at that time, because it would have seemed to be a lie. But she *did* say it, you great fool, because she thought it gave you some sort of an alibi – at least for the third shot. So she thought it might cover you for the second, too. I must admit I can't always follow her peculiar reasoning. But that's what she did.'

'Oh my God!'

'And as a third shot went against all the evidence, it must surely have influenced the jury. It would seem to be a blatant lie – as it probably was – and if she could lie about one thing, she could lie about others. So they brought in a guilty verdict.'

'Is this true? I can't believe ... What the hell do you women get up to, when you're together? I've never heard anything – '

'Do stop moaning ... and listen.' I was impatient with his childish objections. 'Can't you see how important this is to you ... to us?'

'I'm damned if I can. Why? Why is it? I just don't see – '

'The point, you idiot, is that anybody who used her gun in order to kill Harris would have been planting the crime on her, because it was left where she'd dropped it. Not purposely, perhaps – maybe only in self-defence ... thoughtlessly. But in any event, it was catastrophic for her. And she thought that person was you. Oh Oliver, don't you understand her at all? There's something special about that woman. Or something quite terrible. And I've got to know what and why.'

And if he cared to believe I wasn't suffering agonies to offer him this solace – if that was what it was – then he had far less imagination and compassion than I'd credited to him.

But poor Oliver was lost. For the moment, any pain I might have felt in having to explain all this was swamped for him by an uncertainty as to whether he should rush to the side of a woman who must love him desperately – or have done so – or to the same one, who might be nursing a bitter hatred which she had been keeping at boiling temperature for six years.

But Clare, I was beginning to understand, was a rampant romantic, who would treasure to herself the knowledge of a noble sacrifice she had made for her lover. At the same time, romantics usually harbouring a masochistic streak, she would hug to herself the pain she'd suffered, and keep it alive until she could possess him, love him, and systematically destroy him with minutely contrived distresses and obscure deceits, until finally – he trying to balance his emotional responses to her demands – she would undermine his self-confidence and leave him with no defences.

I couldn't put this to Oliver. He would have dismissed it as fanciful.

'Do you understand now why we need to find some truth in it all?' I asked, as I started the car.

'I don't think you do, yourself, Phil, but I suppose we'd better give it a try.'

From then onwards, while I searched for the route to our destination, which I could actually see but not reach, he was silent.

Then he said, his voice normal, 'Try the second lane on the right, Phil.'

I did so, and abruptly it was the lane I recognised. But I was involved with a sudden concern for my engine. In the background, it seemed to be making a tinkling sound, a jangling dissonance.

But then, in the approach lane, I caught a glimpse of the obvious source. An ice-cream van was manoeuvring carefully ahead of us, with its jangly tune blasting away on full volume. 'Rudolph the Red-nosed Reindeer' – in June! Where, in that naked expanse of countryside, did he expect to sell even one ice lolly?

Soon I discovered where, as the van turned into the entrance drive to Collington House. I assumed that indeed I was going crazy, as we then passed two men pushing a baked-potato wagon, and then I had difficulty overtaking a farm tractor towing a trailer, which seemed to be loaded with poles and rolls of near-white sailcloth. Even before we reached the belt of trees, cars, bikes, a horse-drawn cart with no horse, and a small twenty-seater coach were all parked, well over. When we reached the shade, three men with ladders were stringing coloured lanterns through the trees. Two more were walking off, uncoiling a large spool of wire. And somewhere an engine spluttered into life; their power generator under test, I guessed.

'What on earth's going on?' I asked, leaning forward, drifting the car along slowly as children ran madly in and out of the trees, screaming and laughing. Now Oliver was laughing too, having suffered an abrupt jolt back to his childhood.

'What is it?' I insisted.

'Oh Phil – it's just that the word's got around. Clare's home! It's a welcome-home party ... and they're obviously going to combine it with their annual fête. It hasn't been the same, held on the village playing field. Oh no. For years – for ever – or in any event ever since Mad Harry built this place, the annual fête's been held in June in the Collington grounds. They've missed it ... missed Clare. Couldn't wait. The word's about ... Clare's back. There'll be people here from six or seven different villages. And the rivalry! Tug-of-war contests, knobbly-knees contests, wellie whanging...'

'What on earth's that?'

'Throwing a rubber wellington boot.'

'How ignorant I am.'

'You'll see it all. It's a pity you don't make your own jam.'

'I never have.'

'Best pot of jam, best bottle of home-made wine, baby contest ... you'll see the lot. And poor Clare'll have to judge them all. It would terrify me. And there'll be tombola stalls and bingo tents, and a huge marquee full of people eating and drinking, and rides on the horses for the kids, and skeet-shooting in the lower meadow, and boating in the moonlight, if we get a moon. I'm afraid I can't row, with this arm ...'

'Can I back the car out?' It hadn't sounded too attractive to me.

He looked over his shoulder. 'Not a chance. You might as well park it right here.'

We were still under the trees. It would be dark along here, later, and I felt that the general expectation was that the festivities would keep going well into the night. While I'd been thinking this, my car had become encircled with sundry vehicles, from pushbikes to tractors. We were positively and truly caught.

'Will the car be all right if I leave it here?'

'Of course. You're not in a city now. Relax, Phil. You'll enjoy yourself.'

That I doubted. I locked up the car, and we stood there. It was around three o'clock, and I felt exhausted already.

'What's skeet-shooting?' I asked.

'The same as grouse or pheasant shooting, except that they fire at clay discs instead of live birds.'

'With shot-guns?'

'Yes. They bring their own, of course.'

I began to feel a little better about it. My background had never included any protracted acquaintance with shot-guns, and it seemed to me that I ought to know more.

'Well – let's not just stand here,' I said.

63

'I was waiting for you,' he explained. 'For a minute, you weren't with us.'

'Yes. Sorry. I was thinking. Let's go and see what's happening.'

We were no more than fifty yards from the point where the trees ceased and gave way to the final circular sweep round the maze at the front of the house. Packed around that circle, jostling for a glimpse of the proceedings and already in a heady state of excitement not far from inebriation, seemed to be the entire contents of at least half a dozen villages. Children sat astride their fathers' shoulders, dogs chased each other frantically about and around legs, larger children were perched on hefty branches in the trees, and the clamour shimmered the heat haze.

A man, up in front, was shouting something. He was standing on a box. Clare was sitting even higher, lifted on to the shoulders of two other men, not comfortably because one was taller than the other, and was giving a very good impersonation of somebody loving every second. The shouter wasn't receiving much encouragement. From his first few words, it was clear that he wanted to make a speech, or whatever it was, and the comments hurled at him indicated that nobody was interested in his speeches. Clare was back, wasn't she! She was home! Wasn't that what it was all about?

This, so it seemed, was the opinion of the large man on my opposite side to Oliver. I had a brief impression of a smelly hacking jacket with leather reinforcements, a waterproof cap with a large peak, and a remarkably jutting jaw. He put two hands to his mouth, forming a huge megaphone, and shouted, 'Shurrup, Jamey. It ain't the time for speeches. Three cheers for Clare Collings! Hip, hip...'

I didn't join in the roar of hooray. Collings, I was thinking. In their minds she wasn't Steadman. Harris Steadman had been erased, removed, expunged. And the three cheers rang out heartily, as Clare blushed, laughed, kissed her hands and waved, and fell from the supporting shoulders into other hands ever ready to catch her. In that second I caught a glimpse of her expression. This was not exactly to her liking; she was not in any way in control of the situation.

Everybody wanted to touch her, as though she carried a special charm around with her. They wanted to hug and kiss her and cheer her, and this they all attempted to do, in one way or another, because it all became a seething mass in which she, being quite small, seemed to vanish. Only the swirl-centre indicated her position at any one time. I detected that she was trying to make her way to the front door, to escape in that way.

'Edge round to the side, Oliver,' I said. 'Get to the front door.'

Though he still didn't have the full use of his right arm, and it still gave him a certain amount of pain, he could nevertheless use his bulk and weight, by leading with his left shoulder. I kept very close to him, slightly disconcerted by the surge and noise of the crowd.

We edged round and through, and back round the other side of the maze. Oliver went to the door, and I found I was quite correct in my supposition in regard to Clare's arrival. She must have been waylaid before she reached her porch, and now, if she were able to slide free of them, her retreat would be quick and simple. And Oliver had the keys.

He unlocked the burglar alarm, then the door, and held it ajar. We waited. She edged her way free of reaching hands and thrown kisses, fumbled behind her for the door, encountered my hand and an open space, slid through it, and in a second I had the door secured.

She stood panting before us, dishevelled, her hair flying, her eyes shining and manic, her face flushed, and her arms whirling around as though still fending off reaching hands, which had wanted only to touch, and gain something from the contact.

'Oh ... they're wonderful! Aren't they simply marvellous? I'll have to sit down. Have to ... I'm going to ...'

Then she did, break down in tears with her hands over her face and fingers digging into the flesh, huge eyes staring at me above drawn-down lower eyelids, the tears welling. But no sobs. The tears streamed and her lips made bubbling sounds against her palms.

Eventually she moved them enough to be able to speak, leaning her back against the wall in the entrance lobby.

'I'll have to sit down.'

But there was no chair. Slowly, her legs gave way, until she was sitting on the floor with her back against the wall. In such a position had her husband, Harris, died.

I stared down at her, convinced that she was over-reacting, and said, 'Didn't you expect it, Clare?'

'No, no.' The hands came away from her face now, and she hunted frantically for a handkerchief in the shoulder bag on to which she had somehow managed to cling. She found a tissue and dabbed at her eyes with it.

'I must look terrible.'

'Oh no . . .' began Oliver.

'Of course you do,' I said encouragingly. 'Pushed and shoved and pawed at . . . anybody would. You'll need a shower and a change. But there'll be no hot water, and I suppose your clothes – '

'I'm not a helpless, poor creature, Philipa Lowe. Is that right: Philipa Lowe? Yes. I've had time to plan things. I knew more than a month ago that I was coming out. Help me up, Oliver, please.'

'Yes, yes, of course. Here . . .' He could offer only one hand, but he made the most of it, so that when she was on her feet she was somehow clasped in his good left arm. It seemed to be taking a long while for the strength to return to her legs. Meanwhile, her tongue not fatigued, she went on:

'I wrote to people, and they came in to tidy up and get some food in and put the fridge on, have the electricity switched on . . . oh, you know all the things that have to be arranged.'

'Yes. It's complicated,' I agreed, not mentioning that nobody had done any dusting. 'How did they manage to get in?'

'Oh . . .' She flicked a hand dismissively. 'I told that estate agent person to let them have the keys. The various people. She got *that* right, anyway, and it's about all she *has* got right. Stupid creature. I wrote to her six weeks ago to take the place off the market. Didn't I tell you that? But she didn't do it. Let's go and look at the kitchen. I want to check that *something's* been done right. Come along.'

Now she had all her strength back, and the emotion no longer affected her. She was entirely practical, leading the way with rapid steps – she hadn't a long stride.

'Here,' she said suddenly, halting and diving her hand into the shoulder bag, retrieving a crumpled sheet of paper. 'Is that what she gave you – that pitifully inadequate person?'

I took a copy of the prospectus from her. She at once walked away, and I had to stand a moment to scan it. Then I rushed to catch up.

'Yes . . . it's the same,' I said, and Oliver removed his supportive hand from her elbow.

'Then you ought to know what's wrong with it.'

'I can't say I do.'

'This is the kitchen,' she informed us, flinging open a door.

While it might have been too small for the Café Royal, it would nevertheless have been adequate for a medium-sized restaurant; it now looked empty without half a dozen chefs managing their appointed stations. She peered into two large refrigerators and two larger freezers, and seemed satisfied. She looked up.

'They got the price wrong,' she informed me casually.

'In what way?' I might have guessed that something had to be wrong.

'You can imagine ... People would see the place and say they're happy with it – then find the price is quoted wrong. That's a let-down. Of *course* it would be. So ... no sales.'

'What's wrong with the price?' I was a little annoyed that she was stringing it along. 'Did you want it in Deutschmarks, or something?'

'They missed a nought off the end.'

Oh, what a difference a nought can make! A nil, a zero, a nothing. But add it at the end, and it multiplies everything by ten.

'What', I said, 'an unfortunate mistake.' I failed to sound casual. And Oliver said, 'Unfortunate for a lot of disappointed people, Clare.' Then he spoiled it. 'But it does mean you've got a home to return to.'

'Home!' she cried, turning in a circle and flinging out an arm. 'This place – on my own! That's no home, and you know it, Oliver. A woman needs a man ... and I lost mine.'

Lost ... as though he'd died of an illness, or been mislaid.

Then, her mood changing in a flash as the thoughts darted through her mind, barely pausing to make an impression, she went on, 'You'll stay with me for a while ... of course. Just a little while.'

'No, no,' I whispered, not sure whether or not the idea suited me.

'I'm afraid I've had only the one guestroom prepared.'

'We really need two,' I ventured.

'Then *that's* all right.' She seemed pleased that we needed two. 'It does solve the problem. Oliver can come in with me. Can't you, Ollie?'

I could have kicked myself. This was part of the running battle I'd been pursuing with Oliver, refusing him my favours (as I thought of them) until I had persuaded him into marriage. But it was becoming more and more difficult, and sharing a room – a bed – would have put an intolerable strain on me. In such a situation, I had to admit to myself, the favours would become his. I most definitely needed a solid wall between us. To Clare, this would have been incomprehensible, but she hadn't hesitated. She had snapped briskly at the opportunity. I waited for Oliver's response.

5

I watched as his eyes glazed, as his nose turned grey and his lower lip protruded, quivering, as though rehearsing various combinations that might see him through it. Yet he was barely a couple of seconds before answering. It was a magnificent performance, though his voice emerged dead and unemotional.

'It's usual for a man and wife to share the same room,' he said.

It was not a lie, but simply a misleading statement of fact. Her eyes flicked to my left hand, which I obligingly raised to touch my lips. I was still wearing the wedding ring from my first marriage.

'In that case ...' She shrugged. I could almost see her mind working on the different surnames.

And there had been just a suggestion in Oliver's statement that implied a disagreement between us, leaving it open for me still to protest. Bless him! So I laughed lightly, murmured something about his arm, and said, 'It's as you wish, Oliver.' And his eyes lit up hopefully. Then I turned back to Clare. 'But shouldn't you be outside, meeting your guests, judging the babies and the jams, and throwing the odd wellie?'

She grimaced. 'I suppose.'

'You must be good at that,' I said.

'At what?'

'Wellie whanging, as they call it. Anybody who can throw shot-guns back into the gunroom from the lawn ... heavens, Clare, you'd run rings round the local blacksmith.'

'Are you trying to be funny?' she demanded, danger in her voice and flashing in her eyes. These were directed at my throat, though perhaps because she was shorter.

'Of course not, Clare,' I assured her. 'I'm filled with admiration. When Oliver told me all about it – '

'He did?'

'Oh yes. The whole story. And I couldn't help myself getting a mental impression. I thought you would be a great athletic bundle of muscle.'

'And I turned out to be a little squirt?' Was she laughing at herself? 'I'll show you that room. I don't suppose you'll like it, but it's somewhere to lay your head.'

She then led us back through the house, and to a door next to the gunroom. As Oliver had explained, the house was really a bungalow. This window, too, overlooked the terrace, the last ten feet of it, but it didn't open out like a door on to the terrace, being an ordinary window, and one whose catch, when I tried it, wouldn't open.

'Here. Let me,' said Clare. 'It's years since this room was used, and my father had special, tricky catches put on the windows.'

I didn't manage to spot the trick, but she opened the window easily enough.

'There,' she said, and then, 'Somebody's cut the lawn. Well . . . fancy that. How good of them.'

Only a combined burst of energy could have brought all this about, and it had arisen the moment the news broke that Clare was coming home. The lawn smelt gloriously green and lush, and on it a group of people were playing croquet, doing it in a casual and placid manner (in so far as croquet can be placid) that suggested the game had barely been interrupted during the past five summers. It was as though they had never existed, those years, the continuity unmarred. This was a subtle compliment to Clare. I wondered whether she realised it, and glanced at her. Her lower lip was between her teeth, her eyes bright.

'The bed's been changed,' she muttered. 'You'll find it all fresh and clean. I'll have to get out there, I suppose.'

Then abruptly she was gone, and Oliver was at my shoulder.

'Lovely view,' he said.

'You were very quick and clever, you know. Very.' And he had verged on claiming me as his wife.

'Not really. In any event – we could be back at Penley inside an hour. If we want to be. If you think . . .' He glanced cautiously at the bed.

'Then we've got plenty of time to decide about it, haven't we!'

I turned, and for the first time really looked at the bed. It seemed narrow and uncomfortable.

'I wouldn't want to sleep in that, anyway,' I told him. 'Let's go and sample the fun, Oliver.'

We simply went through the gunroom next door, and out by

way of the french windows. It was necessary to skirt the lawn, so as not to disrupt the croquet. An elderly man was playing against a delicate old lady with a wicked swing, and balls were getting lost amongst the rhododendrons. These, having been left to their own devices, had been glorying in their freedom, and were a severe barrier when it came to pushing through. The old gentleman called out, 'There's a gap in the corner.'

'Thank you. Come on, Oliver.'

'I'll never get through that lot.'

But he followed me, though if I'm ever faced by the possibility of making a wrong choice you can bet I'll make it. The gap I chose was narrow. It wasn't the one that anybody would reasonably be expected to take, the real entrance being further along, and on emerging once more into the sunlight I trod on a hand. Or rather, I trod on two intertwined hands.

It was a glorious location for stretching out in the sun, sheltered from behind by massed shrubbery and with the slope running gently away to the meadow below, the grass close to the hedge being lush and inviting. Given the choice, and with that bed in mind, I would have gone for the grass for the night.

'Oh ... I do beg ... I'm so sorry,' I apologised, all flustered, as the hands were snatched apart and two faces stared up at me – inverted.

His face I didn't need to recognise, because I was at once aware of the smelly hacking jacket with the leather inserts, the water-proof cap now lying in the grass, and that aggressively thrusting jaw. He was one of Clare's champions. I didn't recognise the woman. Stepping through between them, I turned. She was obviously amused by my embarrassment, though shaking her head to dismiss it as she sat up. Her hair flowed like water, a very light cascade of blonde. Her face was long, with a sharp chin, sharp straight nose, and a wide mouth with a full lower lip. She might have been a little younger than myself; I shall all too soon see forty. I couldn't help admiring her blouse, which I felt to be hand-made, and which was in a delicate flowered cotton. She was wearing tailored slacks rather than jeans, and had kicked off her white trainers.

There was no suggestion of embarrassment on their part. After all, they were in full view, there, of the whole landscape, so that nothing serious could have been proceeding. They seemed amused, rather.

'We've met,' the man declared. 'Wasn't it you who rescued Clare from the crush?'

'With the aid of my friend.' I gestured towards the end of the hedge.

'It wasn't', he observed, 'a welcome to her liking. Not what she would have planned herself.'

At that point Oliver walked round from the gap he'd at last located. The man I'd been talking to sat up with more attention. 'And I know you too,' he declared, scrambling to his feet.

Oliver paused, his head cocked. 'I believe we've met.'

'You're a copper, aren't you?'

'Was. I'm retired now.'

A hand was thrust out. 'Glenn Thomas,' he introduced himself briskly. 'You could've made a charge out of it, but you didn't. I've not forgotten.'

Oliver grinned, stared at the hand, and offered his own. He still wasn't too free with the arm that had been damaged. 'It was very close to criminal assault, the way I recall it.'

They shook hands. The woman, now sitting up attentively, was introduced as Josie Knight. We nodded to each other, and Oliver beamed. He introduced me to them. 'Philipa Lowe,' he said. 'We came here to look at the house. Philipa's idea, that was. But it's no longer on the market, we gather. And now ...' He shrugged. 'Now we're stuck here, because there's no way of getting the car out.'

'Then you might as well sit down for a minute,' said Glenn. 'You can get a good view from here.'

I sat beside him, Oliver lowering himself beside Josie. Glenn leaned over towards me, and spoke quietly.

'No longer on the market, you said. Huh? I don't reckon it ever was, between you and me. We all knew she'd never let it go. Typical of Clare, that was, putting it on the market. One of her damned stupid gestures. You never know where you are with her, I can tell you that. Maybe it amused her, advertising it then refusing all the offers she might get. You'll have met her, of course.'

'Oh yes. We've met her.' I tried to be non-committal.

'Then you'll have got the general idea,' he assured me. 'It was only a gesture or a joke, or ... well, anything. I think she's crazy, but everybody loves her. Am I right, Josie?'

She craned her head forward and peered past him. 'Not crazy,' she said thoughtfully. 'You just need to get to know her.'

'Umm!' said Glenn. Then he seemed to think he'd said enough about Clare, as he changed the subject abruptly. 'You get a grand view from up here. That's my property, over there, beyond that far hedge.' He leaned forward, the better to consider it.

There was, indeed, a fine open view of the scene before us. It was in the form of a lush and green saucer below us, with the lake way over in the base of it. Down the slopes the fête was constructing itself, with the assistance of men running about and working like beavers. On the lower slope, where it was probably more level, a marquee was nearly fully raised. Stalls had been erected, lightly protected by awnings from the piercing sun, and a steam tractor, apparently there just to be stared at with nostalgia, was getting up steam. Children were dashing about wildly as preparations were going ahead for the races later, by which time they would have exhausted their excess of energy. Some had found that they could toboggan down the steeper slopes on metal trays.

'You certainly get all the action up here,' Oliver approved.

'Not', said Glenn, 'when people step on your hands.'

He said this gloomily, but there was a light glowing in his wide brown eyes as he glanced at me. I'd noticed that his chestnut hair was showing a bald patch. The migrants seemed to have resprouted as eyebrows, which were very bushy.

'What was I saying?' he asked amicably.

'About Clare,' I told him. 'Everybody knows her ...' I was determined to get him back on to my central interest.

'Oh yes. Yes.' He levered himself on to one elbow, so that he could gesture with a free hand. The gesture embraced the pasture, now seething with Clare's friends, who must have come from the far corners of the county. 'They all know she's strange,' he said. 'She makes fun of everybody and everything, mainly herself, but she's never hurt a soul. Herself, perhaps. Nobody else.'

'Her husband,' I suggested, probing gently, merely encouraging him.

'Not Harris. Not even that bastard Harris. Not on purpose, anyway.'

'So she said. Didn't she say that, Oliver?'

'Eh? What? Oh yes ... she pleaded not guilty in court. I was there.'

'All right,' Glenn agreed. 'But she didn't *hurt* him. Just killed him. Put him out of his misery. But that jury had to decide it was murder.'

'Now, Glenn ...' Josie warned him gently.

'Well – he deserved it, didn't he?' He looked at us, as though challenging us to dispute it. 'So she pleaded not guilty! All right.

Good for her. She's a fighter. But all the same, I bet she filled that courtroom with lies, ankle-deep. She's always been grand at that, throwing her distortions all over the place. For a bit of fun, perhaps, or to protect somebody somehow, maybe just to keep her eye in, sort of. She lies – oh yes. But offends ... never.'

Clare, it seemed, most certainly had a champion. I glanced at Josie, who had every excuse for being jealous of Glenn's enthusiasm, but she seemed undisturbed. Glenn could praise Clare, but she wouldn't be able to prise him from Josie. And Josie knew that. But now she tugged at his wrist. 'You're giving people the wrong impression,' she told him. 'Behave, Glenn, you big idiot. Clare can stand on her own two feet.'

'That she can,' he agreed.

It occurred to me that these two people were being very generous with their information, and to strangers. Perhaps they had the wrong impression of us, seeing us as bitterly disappointed victims of Clare's whims and eccentricities. They could even be under the impression that they were excusing her for having misled us over the house. Did everybody so treasure their Clare in this district, that they should surround her with a veil of excuses?

Josie was leaning forward, obviously intending to speak to me once she had my attention. I smiled at her encouragingly. 'And generous after Harris died,' she said, adding to Glenn's glowing testimony. 'She came to my help ... the company's ... but so very discreetly. It was sort of one of those quirky things she was always doing. The money came from Glenn, here, so I knew she'd asked him to arrange it. Clare's like that. Isn't she, Glenn?'

He caught my eye. An eyelid briefly drooped. His chin moved, but he said nothing.

'But of course,' I said. 'Clare mentioned you. Josie Knight, who makes lampshades. Aren't you a cousin or something?' I wasn't sure whether or not this information had come from Clare, but it didn't matter.

'Not a cousin,' said Josie. 'Certainly not. Just an old schoolfriend. I had no claim on her at all – if that's what you're talking about. Not one. It was Harris who was my partner. Or rather, he originally put a bit of money into the company, and owned five shares. You can't form a limited company on your own, you know. Shades Of Knight Ltd, I call it. But Harris ... oh hell, who wants to talk about that lout – '

'Bastard,' Glenn stated.

73

'Correct,' Josie agreed. 'Why am I telling you all this?' she asked me, pleasantly enough.

Because she wanted to make it quite clear that Harris had got all that was coming to him. I didn't say that. What I did say was, 'Because I'm a good listener, perhaps. And because you're wondering whether we might be two detectives, hired to prove Clare's innocence. Well, we're not. But all the same, I'm sure she didn't kill Harris, and I'd like to discover who did.'

Josie made a choking sound, as though suppressing a laugh. 'Whatever gave you that idea?'

'What she failed to say when she had the chance – what she did say when she didn't need to.'

'Oh ... it's riddles now,' said Glenn, laughing lightly. 'But why ... what's it to you – who did what and who didn't?'

'I'm intrigued.'

'Oh, that's great!' he said, 'Intrigued! What's the point in disturbing sleeping dogs?' Abruptly, he was angry and aggressive. He wouldn't want an outsider casting a cloud on this fine and celebratory day.

I realised that I would have to justify our interference in their lives, if I was going to get anywhere.

'Because they *are* only sleeping,' I said. 'And dogs who wake from nightmares might bite.'

Oliver laughed. I could have killed him. He was being no help at all.

'And?' asked Josie, smiling still in an encouraging way.

I shrugged. 'And it so happens that Clare and I are both in love with the same man.' She, at least, would understand that.

'Now Phil ...' put in Oliver. He clearly didn't.

'And Clare believes it was he who shot Harris,' I added quietly. They'd been free with their information, so I thought they deserved a hand-out of their own.

There was a silence. I knew that this information, this justification, would spread through the throng below like a forest fire, insidiously and in whispers, not a single one of which would be drowned by the shrieks and shots and the amplified music, and the bursts of applause when somebody won. Or lost.

For a moment I thought that it was I who'd lost. It had been a gamble, revealing this, but if everybody thought my investigations were on Clare's behalf, or justifiably on my own, then I might get some co-operation. Especially from the women. They would understand.

After a long silence, Josie whispered, 'You can't mean that.'

'I'm afraid I do. She as good as told me, in her peculiar way.'

'Then she was lying.' Glenn's voice was flat and dismissive. 'I warned you what she's like. It doesn't have to mean – '

I cut in sharply. 'Then she was lying about a previous lie. How many inversions have I got to consider? And I don't intend to try. I'd rather have the plain, flat truth.'

Glenn said gruffly, 'I'd better get down there and supervise the wellie whanging.' The interplay had been lost on him.

Josie did not protest, nor did she make any move to go along with him. He hesitated, hands on hips, looking around as though assessing his own domain – and yet it wasn't his.

'Look down there,' he said abruptly. 'All joy and happiness. But I could take you to twenty people, men and women, who'd have killed Harris Steadman, and enjoyed it. They'd have drawn a lottery for the honour. Winner gets him. And you talk about finding the truth! Don't take the trouble. You're wasting your time. They'd all confess to it, and then where'd you be?'

'Relieved, perhaps,' I answered quietly.

He glanced down at me. His jaw looked like a thrusting rock, but he couldn't prevent a tiny smile softening the line of his lips.

'But don't ask me,' he went on. It was an instruction. 'I'm not going to confess. Coming, Josie?'

'I'll watch from here, Glenn. I'm sure you'll win.'

He nodded, and strode away down the slope. It was a farmer's stride.

Josie sat with her hands clasped round her knees, resting her chin on them and smiling placidly in the direction of Glenn's striding figure.

'He always wins,' she said fondly. 'You can depend on it. Depend on *him*. God, how I love that man,' she said softly.

Oliver seemed to have distanced himself from us, and was standing with his eyes on the scenery. We could talk quietly and intimately to each other, Josie and I.

'Then why aren't you two married?' I asked.

'He's never put it into words. Just takes it for granted, waiting for me to say yes.'

'So the obvious thing to do, in such circumstances, is to tell him the date that suits you best.'

'Any date would suit me best.' Then she lifted her head and turned to face me. 'But we'd gain nothing. We practically live in each other's laps as it is. And we've got our own businesses to run. What would we gain?'

But Oliver had been listening. 'My attitude completely,' he put in, quite unnecessarily, I thought.

'I've got my lampshade company,' Josie went on, throwing Oliver a tiny smile. 'And he's got his farm. Both solvent – and if they weren't we'd help each other out. Glenn gave me money when Harris cheated me out of it. He'd worked out a complicated ...' Then she shrugged herself to silence.

'But,' I said, 'you just said it came from Clare. Glenn just handed it on.'

'Perhaps some of it did,' she said dismissively. 'But I know Glenn added some from his own pocket, perhaps all of it. He's never said ... but you can understand why I love him. He does these things, quietly and in the background. And that sod, Harris ... oh, what's the point in talking about it now?'

'None at all,' I assured her. 'What about the children though?' I asked.

'What children?'

This I was slipping in for Oliver's benefit, seeing that he was eavesdropping. He hadn't mentally explored our relationship in detail, and I wasn't too old. But I would be, if he went on stalling.

'The children you might have ... wouldn't they be better brought up in a safe and solid home – by two parents?'

She put her head down, resting her forehead now on her knees, and spoke quietly.

'Pardon?' I asked.

'There couldn't be any children,' she said softly.

'Oh...'

It was one of those conversation stoppers. There's nothing you can say to follow it that will not be embarrassing.

Then she lifted her head and stared at the distant, flowing landscape not seeing a square inch of it. 'And some day,' she said, 'Glenn is going to realise he wants a family – and then he's going to have to look elsewhere – and I might as well be dead.'

Beyond her, Oliver caught my eye. He made a small gesture with his head, indicating he would rather be elsewhere. I shook my head. We couldn't walk away from her now. Silently, we waited until she tossed back her head, her hand to her hair. Now she properly focused on the distance.

'There they go,' she said, pointing.

76

Very tiny, way below us, a rubber wellington boot flew through the air.

'I understand', I said, 'that you run the business – but do you design your lampshades yourself?'

'Oh yes.'

'How on earth do you work out the panel shapes? I've always wondered.'

'Oh, it's quite easy.' Josie was relaxing now. 'You start with the frame ...' And she went on to explain with enthusiasm.

'Do you do Tiffany?' I asked.

'Oh yes. All sorts of variations. We're into fluorescent patterns and LEDs and fibre-optics. It's a booming market.'

'I'm very pleased to hear it.'

'I'll have to ask you to excuse me,' she said. 'He likes me to be there when he wins. Men are such children, really.'

She got to her feet with lithe grace, straightening to a slim five foot ten. Her hair floated in the slight breeze, her blouse flapped. No doubt the same material appeared on some of her lampshades.

'Perhaps we'll meet again,' she murmured.

She was a woman who needed a confidante, preferably a stranger. Already, she'd confided more to me than she would have done to a local friend.

Then she nodded, and strode away down the slope. I watched her go, to become a small moving doll, before I turned to Oliver.

'Do *you* want children, Oliver?'

He looked startled. 'Well ... I suppose.'

'Little Ollies running around?'

'I'd never be able to handle them, with my dicky arm,' he suggested hopefully.

'Nonsense. Nine months from now your arm will be a hundred per cent.'

'From now?'

'A figure of speech, Oliver. I wonder how far he could throw a shot-gun.'

'What?'

'Just a thought. This wonder-man, Glenn Thomas ... I wonder if he could throw a shot-gun as far as Harris Steadman obviously could.'

He got to his feet. 'Now what're you thinking?'

I put out a hand. He took it with his left and hauled me up. I was suddenly aware of the clack of mallet against ball behind us, and cries of triumph.

'One shot-gun is missing, Oliver,' I explained. 'You must've realised that we can't just dismiss it. There was one extra shot, too. So it could be important. Obviously, the police – '

'That includes me, Phil. Remember? I was here, that night.'

'You were the very first here.'

I was flapping at my slacks, though at this top edge of the field the grass had grown lush and thick, right up to the nodding overhang of the rhododendrons, so there'd been no dust.

'I was in on the search, Phil, if that's what you mean. Once Clare had come out with the basic story, the super – he was there by that time – got us to collecting all the guns from the lawn. That was absolutely necessary, because poor Clare was close to hysteria, almost fighting to get out there and collect 'em up herself. And damn it, she'd have been capable of it, though she was close to a nervous and physical collapse. So the super gave her a solemn promise he'd have all the guns collected from the lawn. As he'd have done, anyway. They were part of the evidence.'

'So you searched?'

'A whole squad of us. We'd got a bit more light laid on by that time ... and I heard that another team came on when it was daylight, and they searched too. So we can't have missed one. All this, you understand, was routine, not simply to satisfy Clare that we'd got all her guns safe inside. Just tidy procedure. And we did get 'em all, Phil. After all, the grass wasn't long. They couldn't very well hide in it.'

'I did wonder about the grass,' I said softly, really to myself. Oliver seemed eager to get moving, to head down the slope and into all the excitement of beautiful babies and slightly mouldy jams. I didn't feel the same about it. The fête was a distraction, as far as I was concerned.

'Phil?' He tilted his head at me.

'The point is, Oliver ... you didn't get them all, and you can't get round that. One's missing. So where did it get to?'

'Let somebody else worry about that,' he said, somewhat impatiently, 'and let's go and see what's going on. I wonder if I could throw a wellie with my left arm.'

'I wouldn't let it worry you, Oliver. You'd be up against the best wellie whangers in the county. And there *is* a gun missing, and I *am* worried about it.'

He sighed, lifted his shoulders, leaned down and plucked a stalk of grass, chewed it, spat it out in disgust, and said, 'We got all the guns that were gettable, Phil. I promise you. The furthest Harris had thrown any of them was no more than three-quarters of the way across the lawn. What in heaven's name did you expect? It wasn't hammer throwing, you know. He wouldn't have had the room to whirl 'em round and round. And he couldn't have whirled 'em vertically. Ask yourself. He'd have hit the ceiling. All he'd have been able to do was ... well, throw 'em. Just throw. What're you thinking?'

'Perhaps I'd better ask Glenn Thomas.'

'He couldn't tell you different. And I was there.' He hesitated, ran his hand up the back of his neck, glanced furtively at the activity down at the bottom of the slope, cocked his head at me, and said, 'Why're you staring at me like that, Phil?'

'What you said. You were there. But you weren't there when they were actually being thrown, and you said, yourself – remember? – that people can do remarkable things when they're under emotional stress. And aren't we assuming, perhaps wrongly, that Harris was one of those completely unfeeling people who're never under any emotional stress? Perhaps he *could* have done it. Perhaps Glenn would know what Harris was like...'

'What're you getting at, Phil?' He was now sounding impatient. 'Sometimes you're – '

'I don't know,' I cut in. 'But somehow a gun went missing. If it could've been thrown far enough – I'm only saying if – well, look at the slope. Look at the kids sliding down on their trays. And on *that* night it would've been soaked. A flying gun could slide down, right down there. Even into the lake. Perhaps.'

But there's a limit to Oliver's patience. He made an angry gesture and turned away.

'Oh, stop talking nonsense, Phil. Sometimes you take things too far. I'm going down there. Are you coming?'

And he didn't wait to find out, but strode off in one of his huffs. It wasn't that he was impatient with me, it was because I'd disappointed him. As he had me.

I didn't look round to follow his progress, but stared miserably at the hedge. Oliver had failed to discuss it with me, and thus help me clear it in my own mind. And he'd completely missed the point I'd been trying to make.

If someone we knew nothing about at the moment had been the other side of that hedge, on the lawn, or had been crossing it, on that special night in September six years ago, then he or she might have picked up a gun, which would have been lying there asking to be picked up, loaded it, and ... and ... done what? He could not possibly have subsequently shot Harris with it. Clare had said she'd closed the front door after her when she'd run round to the front.

But it would explain Clare's mysterious third shot, though why, if someone *had* picked up a stray gun and taken it away, would that person have troubled to fire it? At nothing? Certainly it couldn't have been at Harris, because he would have been inaccessible at that time.

That idea simply led to a dead end. So what was I thinking? Or rather – what thought was niggling at me, demanding to be brought out into the light? *That* was where I needed Oliver's help. And he wasn't there.

And even here, I realised in disgust, my eyes focusing again, there were people who managed to leave their litter behind them.

Hidden in the long grass, a little way beneath the overhang of the rhododendron and behind where Josie had been sitting, I could just detect a hard, brown shape that suggested a discarded beer bottle.

Except that it wasn't, when I parted the grass sufficiently to be able to see it.

Then I was on my feet, with my hands cupped to my mouth.

'Oliver! Oliver! Come back...'

He paused, turned, stared.

'Quick, quick!' Though there was no hurry.

Then, catching the tone of my voice, even though shouted, he came hurrying. Not running, not up that slope, but he was striding fast.

'What is it? What?'

I knelt down and parted the grass. He knelt beside me.

It was a flat piece of wood, walnut or mahogany perhaps, about eight inches by five, nailed to a stake or the like that had been hammered into the ground. Into its surface, indelibly, had been burned – probably with the end of a red-hot poker – the inscription:

HARRISON
B/D 5 SEPT
1986

'What could it mean?' I asked. 'Was that the date?'

'When it happened, yes.'

I bit my lip. 'Perhaps the poker slipped.'

We got to our feet, but not before I'd rearranged the grass to cover it again.

'What d'you mean – slipped?'

'Perhaps it was intended to read: D-stroke-D. Then it could've meant: Harrison, date of death, 5 September 1986.'

'But his name was Harris.'

'Short for Harrison,' I suggested.

'There's no Christian name of Harrison.'

'There's an American film star, Harrison Ford.'

He was throwing objections at me, stimulating my imagination. It was something Oliver loved doing.

'This was before Harrison Ford's time.' He reached out and touched my cheek. 'Oh Phil,' he said softly. 'Don't reach too far. It's that romantic streak of yours. You're imagining some woman, planting that...'

'He's supposed to have had several women. Wasn't it you who said that?'

But I was taking it too far for him, and his mind wasn't fully on it. 'So what if he had?' he demanded, his patience very thin indeed, beaten thin, like gold, till it was nearly transparent. 'It's you, imagining somebody so potty over him that she'd plant a memorial to him...'

'Where he died.' I found I could agree with that proposition. I had recently been talking to a woman who would be devastated if Glenn Thomas met a sudden death.

'Then it should've been nailed to the wall in the gunroom,' he said facetiously. 'That's where he died.'

'You don't *care*!' I cried. 'And – potty! Where did you get that from?' I had to get back at him in some way. Suddenly, it was all going wrong between us.

'Potty is a grand old slang word meaning: feeble-minded.'

'Oh, I see. So the sort of love and devotion necessary to bring about that kind of gesture has to be in the mind of some feeble-minded female? If that's your opinion of love, it strikes me, Oliver, then it's not for me.'

'Now ... Phil...'

'Love! You don't know a thing about it. All you want is to get me into bed. If *that's* your love, you can keep it. Yes, keep it to yourself, because it'd mean it's yourself you love, and ... and...'

But he was walking away, and couldn't see that he had me weeping.

For once, our to-and-fro method of dredging for logic and reason had broken down. I had been too persistent.

'Oliver!' I shouted. 'Wait for me.' And I ran, stumbling after him, because, I suppose, I was potty.

6

Five summers had been lost. They had no doubt held their annual fêtes, but these had been paltry things, unsatisfactory when compared with the expansive freedom that Collington House and its successive owners had been able to offer. Clare had to do nothing now but be there, walking amongst them, but she was like a flame darting through tinder. Look around, and where there was a flash of activity she would be at its centre. So many women wanted to kiss her cheek; so many men wanted to lay their arms across her shoulders, and hopefully kiss her on the lips. And she carried it along with a sublime air of dignity, gaiety and perfect poise.

I made no attempt to approach her. We ... Oliver and I ... were the strangers here, accepted, but not of her congregation.

Oliver and I had said no word of reconciliation. Words were not necessary. I'd simply linked my arm in his, and he'd smiled down at me and bent to kiss my lips. Then we walked on together quietly content, and watched from the sidelines.

We were there when she judged the babies. There had to be rules, I supposed, perhaps being born since the previous fête. This year's crop. But if anything was required to put a person off starting a family, this was it. They were a uniformly drab and depressing collection. I watched as Clare performed. She picked each one from the doting mother's arms, and kissed and hugged it with apparent joy and admiration, sublimely unaware of the dangerous path she was treading. There were seventeen. Whatever she did (and there was nothing at all to recommend any single one) she was going to be hated, if only temporarily, by sixteen mothers. Even Clare's popularity couldn't possibly override this inevitability, I thought. I wondered whether she herself, at that early age, had looked so unattractive.

Yet she made her choice, and managed to convey the difficulty she'd encountered in choosing one beautiful baby from the most wonderful collection she had ever seen. Then, strangely, she was applauded, and everybody knew how correct she had been.

It takes quite a personality to do that, I realised. But I had already decided that Clare was somebody out of the ordinary.

'I'll be over by the wellies,' said Oliver with yearning, and he slunk off. Coward.

I watched, now alone, as Clare judged the jams, as she judged the fruit cakes, the home-made wines, the flower arrangements, and so on. She fascinated me. It was quite a while before I understood exactly what she was doing. Each of the original seventeen baby-displayers in some way won a first prize for something. Or someone in their family did. That was very clever of Clare. I couldn't help clapping my hands as she awarded the seventeenth, for a crocheted doily.

A man's voice beside me said, 'She does that every time. Everybody sees through it, and nobody would have it otherwise.'

I turned. He was a slightly built but tall man, somewhat formally dressed for such an event as this, even wearing a neat tie to his crisp white shirt, and he was eyeing me with grey, twinkling eyes that indicated he knew who I was.

'You're Philipa Lowe, I believe,' he went on. 'It's got around. I thought I'd have a word with you.'

'I'm flattered.'

I was also suspicious. There was a suggestion that his intention was to give me a warning, if only a one-word warning.

'And you are?' I asked politely.

'Ralph Purslowe. A local resident, you could say.'

'Pleased to meet you.'

We formally shook hands. There was, I thought, a mocking glint in his eyes, but, I was pleased to note, a degree of admiration and interest.

'And why', I asked, 'could I say that you're a local resident? Is it that I'm permitted to say it? I'm intrigued. Say on, Mr Ralph Purslowe.'

'Inspector,' he corrected me. 'Of police, not drains or buses.'

'You're off duty?'

'In so far as I ever am.'

That had to mean that he was in the CID.

'And you're wondering what I'm doing here?' I asked, smiling up at him in what I hoped he'd take as a friendly manner. 'And worrying that I might disturb the innocent enjoyment of all these splendid people?'

'Not at all.'

'You ought to have a word with my friend, Oliver Simpson. You'll find him watching the wellies being thrown. Whanged, they call it.'

'I've done that. We know each other – sergeants together. And he isn't watching, he's chucking with the best.' He nodded solemnly.

I laughed. 'Left-handed?'

'What's the matter with his right arm?'

'Oh . . . that. He tried to take a shot-gun off somebody.'

He clicked his tongue. 'Typical. He always was a bit of a fool.'

'Isn't he!' I agreed.

'But he's doing quite well with his left, I thought.'

I nodded. Oliver would. We began to stroll around. He was known, apparently, to most of the people swarming past us. I cocked my head at him.

'Let's not pad around it discreetly,' I suggested. 'There's nothing social about this little interview, as I'm sure you're aware of the reason I came here in the first place, and you know, or you've guessed, why I'm still here.'

He walked me a few more paces silently, deftly warding off a rush of children, screamingly intent on getting from A to B in the shortest possible time and for no apparent reason.

'You're still here, I'd guess,' he decided, 'because you've got your car blocked off, and you're not concerned too much about that because you reckon you might as well use the time exploring some grand idea of your own.'

'What grand idea?'

'I'd suggest you're trying to find evidence that Clare didn't kill her husband. No – let me finish, if you will. No harm in that, you would say. But . . . why trouble? Nobody cares around here, in fact they're all on Clare's side, and it's the people around here who matter to Clare. Harris Steadman was universally disliked – hated, even. So who might gain, even if you succeeded in proving her innocence?'

I answered briskly. 'If I could prove it, she might finish up with a tidy sum in damages.'

'Would that matter to her? She's loaded.'

'Vindication . . .'

'Quite frankly, I think she's proud of her reputation. Basks in it. The woman who shot Harris Steadman. She's even envied . . . so many people would've pounced on the chance to do it. You know how it is, these days ... anti-authority. They're on her side. It's as though she sacrificed herself for the good of the whole community.'

I gave a tiny bark of a laugh. I couldn't hold it back.

'Oh yes,' he went on placidly. 'You can laugh, but it's where her popularity lies. You're wasting your time, Philipa Lowe. That's what I'm trying to get across to you. You're up against a blank wall. You might as well go home and forget it.'

We paused for a few moments of silence, in which I was supposed to be considering his advice. The sports events were in full flow, the really young ones at this stage. They were falling over in the three-legged race, and little girls were concentrating with bulging eyes in the egg and spoon race.

'You told me you know Oliver?' I asked at last.

'Oh yes. We worked together for several years.'

'Friends?'

I noticed that he was smiling at me knowingly, already aware of what I intended to say.

'Good friends, yes.'

'So you ought to be aware that he was taken off the Harris Steadman case because of – '

He held up a hand to stop me. 'Because of a certain amount of intimacy with Clare?' He smiled at my expression. 'But if you know that, I'm surprised you aren't anxious to get him away from the vicinity.'

'I'm not worried on that score.'

'No.'

I studied his bland expression. Had there been just a hint of a question mark after that monosyllable?

'That's over,' I said, lifting my chin.

'Good. I'm pleased to hear it. As long as Clare thinks so.'

'It is not a matter – '

'It *is* a matter of what Clare thinks about it,' he interrupted me firmly. 'If she doesn't want it to be over, it might not be over. She need only raise one eyebrow ....'

'You're being damned insulting.'

'Not intentionally. Sorry. I meant – Oliver – knowing him. Oh hell ... why did we get on to this?'

'You. You brought it up.'

'So I did. Sorry.'

'Shall we move on? Or shall you move on, and me in another direction?'

86

He took my arm, possibly to prevent this. 'Oh no. I'm not going to lose you now.'

'You're already assuming', I accused him angrily, 'that he'll drop me and return to her – and then I'll be in the open market for you to practise your charm on, and maybe – '

He cut me off with a laugh of pure joy and, I felt, even some admiration.

'By heavens, Miss Philipa Lowe, I can see you'll give Clare a good fight for it. I'm a married man with two children. My wife wouldn't like me to ...' He shrugged.

'Then don't you see, you stupid man ...' I cried, perhaps too loud because several people stopped and stared. 'Don't you see ...' I shook my arm, but he held on. 'I've got the best reason in the world for wanting to find Harris's murderer.'

'No. I don't see that.'

'You wouldn't. Then let me tell you. Clare, I'm convinced, didn't do it. Whoever *did* do it, therefore, did it with Clare's gun, and left it where she'd dropped it. Deliberately did that. Do you believe she would think highly of such a man – or woman? No ... she'll do her best to destroy that creature, when she gets a chance. And the one she thinks did that – the only one who could have done it, unless I can find another explanation – is Oliver Simpson, over there and making a fool of himself by throwing wellies in the air. And you say she's only got to raise an eyebrow! D'you think I'm going to stand around and watch it happen? Am I going to let her take him from me – then sit back and wait for the press notices of his death? Oh no. Not on your life, Inspector Ralph Purslowe. I can't relax until I can at least prove he didn't do it. *Prove* it. By producing who did, if I have to.'

And the inspector gazed up at the sky and whistled softly to himself.

Oliver was, indeed, over there and throwing wellies with his left arm. There had to be a technique to it, I decided. Theory indicated an angle of forty-five degrees to the longest throw, though air resistance had to be taken into account ... and why the devil was I thinking of such things when the subject under discussion was his life?

And Clare was also over there and watching, and clapping, calling out encouragement whenever Oliver matched a throw from Glenn Thomas. That left arm was developing muscle, having to ease the load from his right.

'Come *on*, Oliver!' she cried, and she ran to him and kissed him on the cheek when he beat Glenn's previous throw by a foot. A foot, I thought hysterically, in a wellie!

'You see,' said Purslowe quietly.

I could've slapped him across the face, if it hadn't been for his smile.

He turned me and walked me away from there before I could add my own congratulatory kiss to Oliver's other cheek, I thought in order to spare me the embarrassment of not being first with the kisses.

'And you think she could kiss a man she might intend to kill?' he asked.

'Yes. Any woman could. That woman, certainly.'

'You've got your teeth into this, haven't you?' he asked, though not expecting a reply. 'Now it's a crusade, to save his life, to rescue him from the wicked – '

'Don't make fun of it, please.'

'Sorry. I was being facetious. Would you like me to save you a lot of trouble? I can take you around and introduce you to the various people who would've loved the chance to kill Harris Steadman. That would save you having to dig it all out yourself. I'd tell you their individual motivations: the ones whose wives he'd seduced, or daughters he'd got into trouble, or the ones he'd cheated over money, the ones he'd shopped to us over paltry misdemeanours – oh yes, he was an informer. We reckoned he was trying to build up goodie-points, so that we'd slide over his own questionable activities. Or maybe you'd like to meet the ones he'd ruined with snide rumours – and simply because they'd offended him. Or . . . women. The ones he cast off – oh yes, I know it's equality time. They'd claim they'd done the casting. But if so, he'd given them ample cause. The man whose son he crippled with his dangerous driving, and we could never prove it. The man he blinded in one eye with half a bottle in a pub fight. The one – '

'All right. All right,' I cut in. 'That'll do. But can you show me one person amongst that lot who didn't like Clare – enough to plant the shooting on her?'

'Now *that* would be difficult, to find anybody who doesn't like her.'

He looked at me for a long while, waiting for a reply, and I had to say something.

'Perhaps somebody who's seen through her.'

He shook his head, perhaps in mild approval. 'And you've known her for how long? An hour – two hours? You're very quick,

Miss Lowe. Clare lives an act – all her own scripting. I bet she'd have difficulty, herself, sorting out the real Clare from amongst it all. But nobody takes her too seriously.'

'Not enough to – '

'To harm her, no.' He smiled. 'So you'd have difficulty in finding one person with sufficient motive for both – a strong enough motive.'

'A fallacy!' I said sharply. 'What seems paltry to one person can be vastly important to another. And surely you could find me one person who doesn't like Clare.'

He nodded. Now his expression indicated that he was at least taking me seriously. 'Oh yes,' he said. 'There're people who don't like her – jealousy, perhaps. She has her own special way with men – and why not, with her own husband gadding about...'

'All right. You've made your point.'

'But if you'd care to have lists of both suspects – those who hated Harris and those who didn't like Clare – and match them together ... you might get a few names that way. Or we could feed the names into a computer, and see what that throws up...'

'You've made your point. A surfeit of suspects.'

'You'll have to face the problem some time.'

I was, by that time, unable to decide what we had seen of the fête and what we had not. It had become a confusing kaleidoscope of movement, in which I no longer had an interest. I wanted only to get away from this persistent creature, time to collect my thoughts.

'But of course,' said the persuasive voice in my ear, 'you could approach it from the opposite direction. Look carefully at your intentions, and it doesn't have to include the production of another murderer.'

'Then what?'

'Clare's not your basic concern. It's Oliver's positive innocence you're really after, and you'd do best to concentrate on that. Proving Clare's innocence wouldn't help Oliver, and might do just the opposite. So ... I'd advise you to try to find some fact or detail that makes it absolutely impossible for Oliver to have done it. Then nobody's going to worry that you might come up with a fresh and possibly embarrassing murderer.'

I was so involved with my thoughts that I hadn't noticed we had entered the refreshments marquee. He left me standing while he fetched me a terribly strong cup of tea and six lumps of sugar – playing safe. He sat me down at a trestle table. He leaned forward, a can of beer in one fist.

'But the trouble with that,' he said, as though there'd been no break, 'is the fact that Oliver's innocence in this matter would be difficult to prove.'

'You think so?' I was distant with him.

'Yes. The motive's there, you see. He would wish to free her from that monster she was married to. The weapon was there, her gun left on the terrace, and he was the first on the scene. And the opportunity: she'd left the front door open for him. She heard a shot when he could have been in the house, and he said he hadn't heard it. And only Oliver could have fitted all these points.'

I'd used all six lumps of sugar, feeling I was in need of energy. 'So you'd suggest?' I asked softly. 'My next move?'

'To take him away from here. And soon.'

'No.'

'No? Then let me tell you ... why d'you think he was taken off the case?'

'His involvement with Clare.'

'Amorous involvement? No. Not because of a question of possible bias. It was because the chief super suspected *him*. From the very beginning.'

'The beginning ...' I wasn't seeing him clearly.

'He didn't think that Clare would've been capable of shooting her husband, him sitting against that wall and incapable of movement, shooting him callously...'

'He couldn't have known her. She is,' I assured him. 'But he thought that Oliver would've been quite capable of it?'

'Apparently.'

'But you didn't?'

'No.'

'Then why didn't you tell him, that stupid chief super?'

'He didn't ask.'

'And you didn't offer...'

'It wasn't my place.'

'Damn your place!'

'Shall we go and look at the stalls?' Abruptly, he dismissed the subject.

I got to my feet. 'You can – but not with me.'

'Madame Acarti, the gypsy fortune teller, is with us. You could ask her about your future prospects. It'll cost you fifty pence.'

'Madame Acarti! I bet she's a pretty little WPC you've planted...'

'Sergeant, actually.'

He was not to be shaken. I couldn't shame him into anything. He was hard, a professional. He did it by the book. I walked away as he got to his feet, but he was at my shoulder before I emerged into the blinding sunlight. He steered me free of the crowd, slowly up towards the house.

'It's logical,' he said. 'She knows most of the sins committed in this area – and everybody knows her. So she can safely predict their fortunes – unless they behave. Call it a gentle, private warning.'

'Like a witch doctor,' I said in disgust.

'Or a priest,' he suggested gently.

'The gypsy's warning!' I paused and stared at him. 'And they *pay* for it?'

'Oh yes. It's a bit like paying a tiny fine in order to avoid a larger one. And it all goes to charity.' He grinned disarmingly as I stopped and stared him in the face. 'And unofficially she can reveal that we know rather more of what's going on than they thought.'

So he didn't work exactly to the book.

'Perhaps I ought to consult her after all.'

'It might be a good idea.'

'I know what she'd say. I'm a star-crossed lover who ought to take my man away. Before it's too late.'

He shrugged. 'I haven't her vision. She communes with the spirits, and they speak to her.'

I laughed. 'The spirits she communes with – I bet she couldn't talk back afterwards.'

For several moments he stared at me blankly. I had the idea he was suppressing a smile, because he intended to say something I should take seriously. Then he nodded, and said, 'All the same, I'd advise you to visit her.'

'Perhaps I'll do that.'

He strolled away without another word. I watched until he'd disappeared in the crowd around the hand-wrestling table. His choice of the word 'visit' instead of 'consult' had been, I was sure, intentional.

Then I saw Oliver approaching, bouncing up the slope buoyantly, his red face shining with sweat and a magnificent grin, and walking with one hand behind him. He stood in front of me, legs spread, and produced what he'd been hiding. It was a battered old rubber wellington boot.

'Look what I've won!'

'You came first?'

'Third.'

'Oh! What was the second prize?'

'The other one. It's in better condition.'

'And the first?'

'A whole pair.'

'And who won that?'

'Glenn Thomas. You might have guessed. He does it every year, they tell me.'

'Then I'll have to see our Mr Thomas later,' I told him. 'We'll weigh it first, then we'll ask him, and if he's willing to give it a try...'

'What on earth are you talking about, Phil? You've been out in the sun too long.'

'We still haven't discovered what happened to that missing shot-gun. I want to try a little test. We haven't got a shot-gun, so we'll put gravel or stones in your wellie, hold them in place with a bundle of newspaper or something, and get it to eight or nine pounds ... *then* we'll have something to experiment with. How clever of you to win it. You must have known how useful it would be.'

He clutched his trophy to his chest. 'You're not having this.'

Sometimes he can be irritating, either on purpose or because he doesn't realise. He was staring at me now with a fierce possessiveness.

'What d'you want to do with it?' I demanded. 'Spray it with gold paint and stand it on your mantelpiece?'

'You're not going to throw my wellie around.'

At that point I realised he was ribbing me. 'Idiot!' I said. 'But you do see what I'm getting at?'

He held out his left hand, palm upwards, his wellie standing on it. No doubt he was considering its effectiveness on his mantel. 'I've been to consult Madame Acarti,' he told me, squinting at the boot.

'A fake.'

'Oh yes. It's Sergeant Alice Carter. She warned me to beware of a woman with ginger hair.'

'It's not ginger. It's copper.'

'Spun gold, and I'd still have to beware. Now I'm beginning to see what she meant.'

I was feeling impatient with him. 'But you *do* see what I'm trying to prove, or demonstrate, or whatever it is?'

'Not really, Phil. Perhaps you'd explain.' But he wasn't taking me very seriously.

I had to admit it was tit-for-tat. Men do make such a fuss about their physical triumphs, and they expect them to be applauded. I had very nearly brushed his aside when it really had been an achievement, as he'd had to use his left arm when he's basically right-handed. And he'd probably never before whanged a wellie.

'But of course,' I said, 'we don't need to call on Glenn Thomas. If you can't do it, nobody could.'

He looked blank.

'Don't you see what I'm getting at?' I asked, and he plainly didn't. 'There's a gun missing. You maintain that the lawn was searched meticulously. So one got away. I simply want to find out if it would have been possible to throw a shot-gun from the french windows, and over the hedge. If so, it could have slid on down the slope and been picked up later – the next day or the day after that – by literally anybody, and kept on the principle of finders-keepers. In which case, we could forget the missing gun. It wouldn't enter into things. But if it couldn't have been thrown that far, and it wasn't on the lawn when your lot searched ... then it was deliberately taken away from there. And the point would then be – why? You *do* see that, Oliver?

He had long ago lowered the wellie, and in fact had dropped it at his feet. Now he was eyeing me with pursed lips, gently shaking his head.

'And if you reached that point, Phil?' he asked. 'If it came to the question: why? Then what? Frankly, I don't care why. *Nobody* cares. Only you, Phil. Only you.'

'Oh, but they do.' The interruption came from just behind my left shoulder. I turned. Glenn Thomas was nodding in agreement with me, Josie clinging to his arm.

But somehow he managed to project a hint of aggression, possibly a leftover from the effort of winning a physical challenge. He still bore the air of bouncy complacency that one associated with a winner. His jaw was thrust at me, his smile robbing it of any suggestion of displeasure.

I raised my eyebrows at him, not sure what he meant. He moved round to face me, now standing at Oliver's left shoulder.

Josie was left standing beside me, apparently in my support. Glenn was no longer wearing the jacket he'd had on when we first met him. Now it was jeans and a shirt open to the waist, displaying quantities of sweat-glistening hair.

93

'Everybody cares,' he assured me. 'Look around you. How many people can you count? One hundred, two hundred? Three? It doesn't matter. But ask any one of them, over the age of fourteen, ask 'em if they want you here, sticking your nose in their affairs. Oh, you'd get your answer, Miss Philipa Lowe. It's over. Done with. Clare's served her term, for doing the whole district a favour. It's over and done with.'

I could have argued with this. She'd earned remission. It wasn't quite the same. But I nodded. Let him say it, I thought. What he said could matter. I nodded for him to go on.

'He's right, you know,' said Josie at my elbow.

And Glenn went on, 'You and your proving this and proving that ... I've heard. The rumour's around – there's a gun missing from the collection. So somebody liberated a top-class shot-gun. Bully for him. You want to find out who? Is that it? Hah! Fat chance of that.'

'I'd like to know how,' I said quietly. 'Not necessarily who.'

He jerked a hand angrily. 'What's it matter how?'

'The obvious way would be if Harris managed to throw it over the hedge. The simplest. But I don't reckon that would be possible.'

'Of course it's possible. Don't you say, Oliver, old sport? Course it's possible.' He gripped Oliver's left arm, shaking it.

Oliver looked down at the hand. 'I couldn't do it, I'm certain of that.'

'Sure you could.'

'Not now you've mangled my biceps, I couldn't.'

It could not have been paining him. One eyelid flicked at me.

'Then I will!' Glenn shouted. 'Damned if I won't.'

'And the first prize, this time,' I offered him, 'will be worth having. If you can throw an eight-pound wellie from the french windows and over the hedge, I'll concede. It'll indicate where the gun got to – into somebody's cupboard. And that'll be it. The answer to the problem. And I'll leave ... if I can get my car out.'

'Hah!' He gripped his hands together, fingers linked, and flexed his chest. Stomach muscles disturbed his hairy tangle. 'We'll lift your car out for you, me an' my mates.'

'You're on,' I said.

'And I'll carry *you*,' Oliver said, reaching out and touching my cheek with the tip of his fingers.

The surprising thing was that Oliver was very serious about it. Did he envisage carrying me, kicking and screaming?

We watched as Glenn strode away down the slope, hunting for

94

his mates, Josie moving a few yards after him, then standing and staring at his back.

The afternoon was wearing on, the sun lowering, but the activities were still proceeding briskly, the throngs not lessening. Now they'd set up long tables, and crates of beer were being loaded on to them. Free beer, probably. Send the bill to me, Clare had most likely said.

'There're fireworks later,' said Oliver reflectively. 'Should be spectacular, viewed from the slope.'

'I doubt we'll be here then.'

'I've got an idea we shall,' he said quietly.

'And what did you mean ... you'd carry me?' I demanded. 'I've still got my own two feet.'

'I told you. I've consulted Madame Acarti.'

'Rubbish! Ginger hair, indeed!'

'She told me that the lady of the ginger hair, if she was in any way precious to me, should be taken away from here, if I had to carry her screaming and kicking.'

'What did you say to that?'

'I said you'd scream right enough – and kick.'

'No!' I nearly stamped a foot. 'The first bit. If I was precious to you ... even if it *is* copper and not ginger.'

'Oh ... I said yes, you were.'

'Were what, damn you?'

'Precious.'

'You don't make it sound convincing,' I said suspiciously, perhaps wistfully.

He didn't seem to notice my tone, but was staring way out into the distance.

'And she also said that if I didn't – that's carry you out kicking and screaming – I might find myself carrying you out limp, and getting colder and colder every second.'

'Now wait a minute ...' I pulled at his sleeve.

He took no notice. 'Ah ... here he comes now, and with his support team. Let's start filling my wellie with stones. Got any newspaper?'

I was gripping his arm. His bad one. If there was any pain, he ignored it.

7

I had to bear in mind that Madame Acarti hadn't made that statement, Sergeant Alice Carter had. And female police officers don't get promoted unless they've got a fair quota of intelligence. Ralph Purslowe had suggested that I should consult her. Visit, was the word he'd used. The implication was subtle. To consult suggested that I would be seeking advice; to visit suggested she had advice she wished to pass on. And if she knew of something that might render me limp and rapidly becoming cooler, then it would be a good idea, I thought, to learn what she had in mind. I wasn't taking this very seriously, though.

But now there was no time to spare. A group of men had separated themselves from the pulsating masses, and they were advancing on me up the slope. They maintained a purposeful and somewhat disconcerting silence, as though it might be me, and not a wellie, that they'd be hurling around.

Amongst them I saw a man with only one eye. Another man had a youngster in his teens clinging to his arm, limping with a foot twisted inwards, his head at a strange angle. These were two of my suspects, if Inspector Purslowe were to be believed. And Josie was there with them.

Oliver was no longer at my side. Doubtless he'd gone round to the front and was collecting gravel. No word was spoken as the cortège reached me. It might have been that I was not there, was no more than an irritating noise in the background.

It was perhaps as a gesture of solidarity with her own sex that Josie moved to my shoulder. To me it seemed that the hint was there – that I needed support. I glanced sideways at her.

'You don't approve?'

She pouted. 'It all seems very silly to me.'

'But you must see', I said, 'that it could be important to find out *how* a shot-gun could have just disappeared.'

'You're putting a blight on the whole day. Do you realise that, Philipa Lowe?'

'It's not intended that way. Oh, Josie! I'm really sorry, getting Glenn involved like this.'

'Don't worry. He wants to do it. If it'll persuade you to leave us in peace, he'd throw the damned wellie over the steeple.'

A certain amount of emotion was involved now. It irritated her, too. But it was necessary that I should be silenced, and if a far-flung wellie would do that, then they would whang it well, and Josie would cheer them on.

There was no need for me to offer help or suggestion. They knew the way through the gap in the corner of the hedge. They knew where the french windows were situated; they were now facing them. And the croquet players had decamped. It was apparently open house, because the windows were already flung wide in welcome. They streamed into the gunroom. They said nothing until Oliver appeared.

There was, fortunately, no sign of Clare.

Oliver held his wellington boot beneath his left arm, his hand under the sole as though it was now heavier. He nodded to his friends. They nodded back. A third prize entitled him to recognition. It in no way entitled him to intimacy.

'We'll have to get the weight right,' he said, I thought with a note of apology in his voice. 'Or it'll mean nothing.'

'Kitchen scales,' suggested Josie softly, and Glenn darted a glance, possibly disapproving, in her direction.

We all trooped into the kitchen. I was trying to be quiet and circumspect, being the pest who'd plagued them into this. Josie touched by elbow and whispered, 'It's just a game to them.'

I nodded.

Glenn found a set of kitchen scales. There was then a discussion as to what weight to aim for. Ten pounds was considered unlikely. Nine was perhaps still on the heavy side. Seven wouldn't have been a fair trial, as it would be a light weight for anything but a single-barrelled gun. We knew, now, that the missing gun was a Darne with a sliding breech, but although it was known that it was double-barrelled, nobody knew how heavy it had been. So in the end they settled for eight pounds. What I'd said in the first place. Four bags of sugar, roughly, before they started packing it in kilos. All right ... just over three and a half bags. I tried it, when they'd got the gravel packed in tightly with paper kitchen towels. Six feet, I might have thrown it.

Then we went back to the gunroom, to find that Clare was waiting for us, studying the dirty footprints and the trails of grass on the polished oak parquet floor, her eyes following their line out into the hall.

'Would someone be kind enough', she said, in a dangerously calm voice, 'to tell me what the hell's going on?'

With the exception only of Oliver, who decided to consider the view from the windows, they concertedly turned and stared at me. To my surprise, Josie chose to stand at my shoulder. I saw Glenn frown at her. She lifted her shoulders fractionally.

'We're about to conduct an experiment,' I explained.

'What damned experiment?' Clare's fingers were playing invisible keys on the top of the table. Rat-a-tap-tap...

'There's a gun missing from your collection,' I reminded her. 'If it had landed on the lawn, the police would have collected it up. They didn't. So I thought we'd see how far it *could* have been thrown, using a weighted wellington boot, because if it could've gone right over the rhododendrons, some casual passer-by might have picked it up and taken it away. That would explain it – '

'Wait!' she cried. 'Wait, wait, wait, damn you!' She drew in a deep breath. 'What the hell does it matter now?'

There were murmurs of agreement from the group.

'You heard a third shot, Clare.'

She stared at me blankly.

'You *said* you heard a third shot,' I went on, trying to maintain a steady voice. 'If that's not true, then we can forget all this, and our fine and manly team can get down to the beer table. If it wasn't true ... But you said it was.'

'I heard it.'

Her face was set. Her eyes were huge, slightly moist with an emotion I couldn't rationalise, and her lips were thin and pale. She was tired. I could tell that by the slump of her shoulders.

'Then if you *did* hear it ...' I ignored the dangerous glint in those eyes. 'And there's a gun missing, then the assumption has to be, considering that the forensic people didn't find a fired gun in the ones they had – other than the one you fired – then ...' I took a deep breath, surprised she hadn't interrupted. 'Then that missing gun has to be the one that fired the third shot. I just thought ...'

I stopped there, deliberately to allow her to say her piece, for her to bring out a string of protests. But all she did was shake her head, and her whole body seemed to become limp. She was exhausted through and through. It had been a long day for her – and there was still plenty left.

'Oh ... do what you like,' she said sharply, then she turned away.

That she turned so that she faced Oliver might have been pure chance. But he didn't take his eyes from me, and the abrupt and momentary glance of sheer panic she addressed to him was wasted.

'All right,' I said, turning to the waiting and silent men. Very nearly I clapped my hands for attention. In Clare's presence, in the presence of her displeasure, they were like a bunch of cowed children.

'Let's get started.' I tried for a voice that would boost them, but managed no more than a weak plea. 'Who's going first?' They shuffled their feet and glanced from under lowered eyebrows at each other, but no one offered.

'I'll go first,' said Oliver, rescuing me manfully.

'All right.' I raised my voice, now more confident. 'It doesn't matter who goes when, or how many times. The idea is to throw it over the hedge and into the field. All right. Understood?'

'Yeah. Sure. Right enough.' Their muttered responses had all the inspired enthusiasm of a soaked postman.

'And I'll bring it back for the next throw,' I offered, my own optimism misplaced.

So we did it. Clare now sat – how long since she'd taken the weight off her feet? – on one of the upright and uncomfortable chairs. Throughout, she offered no cries of encouragement. Her face was pale and set. I went across the terrace, down the steps, and way over the lawn, keeping to one side at first. Oliver threw it, making a great show of working up to the climax. I collected it up and trotted back, up the steps, across the terrace, and returned it. The throw had been ten yards short of the hedge. The others, once started, took their turns. Each one must have realised that he was trying to prove that Clare was not a liar. To do this, the boot needed to clear the hedge, or so they simplified it.

They had varying styles. The fact that they had to throw clear of the open windows somewhat limited them. But they tried. By heavens, how they tried! Faces flaming red, pouring with perspiration until they could barely grip the wellie, they launched their whole beings into it. And not one throw landed further than six yards short of the hedge. Oliver threw only twice. I felt that his concern was for Clare, who, towards the end, drooped pallidly over the table.

At first, as I said, I dutifully returned it to the gunroom, then it became too much effort to carry it further than the edge of the terrace, until eventually I could barely make it to the terrace, and then was hard pressed to lift it on to the surface.

At this point, Josie, no doubt feeling sorry for me, quietly took over. She seemed stronger than me, even had breath to spare in those moments between the arguments as to whose throw it was next.

'A pity Harris isn't here,' she said vaguely.

'Why's that?'

'He could throw further than any of them.'

For a moment I feared that this would invalidate the experiment. 'Throw it over the bushes?' I asked.

'Oh no. Not that much better.'

'If he *was* here, we could ask him,' I pointed out.

'Ask him what?'

'If he threw one of the guns over the bushes. That would explain it, you see.'

She stared at me. 'Harris couldn't have said . . .'

I sighed. My little pleasantries so often die a death. 'Everybody calls him Harris,' I said quietly. 'Was it short for Harrison?'

This too didn't go over well. She stared at me, her expression blank.

'What?'

'His name. Harris. Short for Harrison . . .'

'Of *course* not!' She was very vehement about it.

'Look out. They're starting again. I'll take over, if you like.'

But there were only half a dozen more throws. The point had been well and truly made.

'That's enough,' said Oliver, to my infinite relief. He said it in a firmly authoritative voice, one that I hadn't heard before. I crawled up the steps and tried not to stagger across the terrace.

The men stood around uncomfortably, wiping the backs of their hairy hands across their dry mouths, until Glenn said, 'Clare,' and nodded, and the others followed him out with grunts of, 'Miz Clare . . .' Josie went with them.

And they disappeared rapidly in the direction of the beer.

'So what does *that* prove?' demanded Clare, with a flash of anger. 'Ridiculous display . . . Oh God, I need a drink.'

I caught Oliver's eye, and nodded. Me too. Quietly, he left the room. I fetched the chair from the other end of the table and placed it firmly in front of her, then sat down and eyed her carefully. The fire had died from her eyes.

'So where does that get you?' she asked. 'And what the hell does it matter, anyway?'

'I'd have thought I'd made that clear. There's only one way ... no, two ... two ways that your gun could have gone missing. Either it was thrown, by your husband, right over the hedge, where anyone could've come across it – or it was picked up from the lawn and taken away.'

'All right, all right.'

'I wish it *was* all right,' I assured her. 'We weighted that wellie to eight pounds...'

'The Darne was nearer ten.'

I sighed. 'That only makes the test more positive. Your blasted Darne couldn't have been thrown anywhere near the hedge. So someone must have picked it up from the lawn – that would've had to be after you'd shot the hole in the window, and after you'd run round to the front. Picked it up and loaded it and fired the shot you heard as the third. More distant, you said. So it probably was the third. But what was it fired *at*? Certainly not through the hole in the glass, and at Harris. And why was it fired – and the gun taken away?'

'I don't know,' she whispered, her voice a little hoarse. 'And I'm tired of hearing about it. I want a bit of peace ... oh God, Philipa, I want to lie in my own bed and sleep, sleep...'

Then Oliver entered, with a decanter in one hand, a bottle in the other, and three glasses somehow gripped in his spare fingers.

'Brandy or sherry?' he asked brightly.

As he placed his cache on the table, she reached out a hand and rested it on his wrist. She managed a weary smile for him. 'Brandy, Ollie, please.'

I said, 'Sherry,' and Oliver followed my lead.

There was no other chair for him, so he wandered the room casually, as though considering the expert carving of the dark oak panelling. I thought that he had realised we'd reached a critical stage in this matter, and was allowing me to get on with it.

The brandy seemed to restore Clare to some of her energetic norm. Her eyes were now bright. There was more mobility in her features, and spots of colour appeared on her cheeks.

She said, her eyes now holding mine, 'I'll tell you what I want,

101

shall I.' Not a question; she intended to, anyway. 'I want you to go away from here and forget all about it. As simple as that.'

'But don't you see, Clare,' I cried, full of enthusiasm now that we had a positive result from the experiment. 'If we could find the answer to these two questions, it could well prove your innocence. Why would anyone steal a gun from you? And if it was simply stolen, why was a shot fired from it? At nothing. Probably into the air. It's all so illogical...'

'If it's so damned illogical, why can't you let it drop?'

'I'm trying to help you, Clare,' I told her patiently.

'I don't see why you've got to pester me like this!' she said forcefully. 'You and your stupid ideas. What does it matter, for Chrissake!'

I sighed. It was an uphill struggle with her. 'If something happens that's illogical in the known circumstances, then there have to be different circumstances in which it *is* logical.'

'So what?'

'So the whole picture could change, and the new one could include proof of your innocence.'

'Who asked you to prove anything?' she demanded, her chin lifting, her eyes angry. Then she glanced up at Oliver, as though anticipating agreement from him. But he stared at her blankly, and she shrugged in disgust.

'I'll have a little more, Oliver, please,' she said, hissing the final word.

He beamed at her, possibly because she hadn't called him Ollie. She missed it, sipping morosely.

'But don't you find it fascinating, Clare?' I was trying to fire her imagination. 'That someone *would* be walking across your lawn in the middle of a thunderstorm, and tripped over one of your guns. "Oh goody – look what I've found," he might say to himself. "And a Darne, too." That's always supposing it was someone who knew his guns. Would that person then put a cartridge in the breech – one that happened to be in his pocket, *and* the right size – and fire it, just to check that it worked? And so near the house, too! Why not take it far away – if all that was wanted was a shot at nothing? *That's* what's so fascinating.'

She sipped at her brandy, then she pointed it at me, one finger extended round the glass.

'It doesn't fascinate *me*.' She said this emphatically, the internal spark glowing brighter every second. 'Frankly, I don't give a tuppenny cuss. It's over and done with. I'm home. So why should I

102

trouble who did what, and why?' She darted a quick look at Oliver, as though this noble comment had been aimed at him. He was forgiven – whatever needed to be forgiven. 'It's in the past,' she went on grandly, flicking a hand in that direction. 'I don't care what happened, and nor does anybody else. Oh, thank you, Oliver. Yes, I'll have a little more.'

Her face was flushed. She raised glowing eyes to him. It was over, it was done, it was in the past. We were meant to understand that she included any possibility that Oliver could have been closely involved in it. But I couldn't bring myself to accept that such a volte-face – she was normally so determined and inflexible – could be relied on. After all, the wellie experiment had in no way affected Oliver's possible involvement.

As he poured the brandy, a very small measure, she twisted round to look at me, her lips pursed. Her glass wasn't steady.

'There'll be fireworks later,' she told me. 'Do stay for that.'

The implication was: but no longer.

'We shall probably have to, the way my car's blocked in.'

'And Phil's still got so much to see,' Oliver put in, attempting briskly to lighten the mood. 'She hasn't even consulted Madame Acarti...'

'What! She's here again?' The fire within her was growing now, brandy-fuelled. 'I warned her off, last year.' She bit her lip. 'Last time.'

'It's not the same Madame Acarti,' Oliver assured her. 'This one's more astute.'

'All-knowing,' I put in. Then, in explanation, I added, 'Ralph Purslowe told me. He said she wished to see me.'

'Then you must go, Phil,' said Oliver.

Clare was darting her eyes from one to the other of us. 'She'll see somebody she doesn't want to, if I hear any complaints.'

I was interested. 'You've had complaints in the past?'

'Have I just! The previous one, she was putting the galloping fears in them all, forecasting doom and distress right and left. I had to put a stop to that.'

'This one', I assured her, 'encourages. Offers light at the end of a shady tunnel, so long as certain things are done or not done, as the case may be. I think the general impact ought to be beneficial, in the long run.'

She gave me a twisted smile, tried to straighten it and failed, then giggled. 'Then you'll *have* to see her. Maybe she'll tell you that the thing to do is go home, and forget you ever came to this house.'

'As a warning?'

'Oh ... you mustn't say that. Even think it. You're always welcome, and you know it.' She nodded, though it didn't carry any conviction.

I waited, but she didn't amplify that remark.

'We might stay for the fireworks,' I said at last. 'If I were you, I'd have a little rest.'

'Yes, yes. I'll do that.'

'Oh ... and Clare ... I meant to ask you. However did you manage to throw those guns inside here from down on the lawn? I could never have managed it. Not throw them.'

She gave me a slanted glance of sheer animal mischief.

'Well, you know ... I didn't ... really.'

'You didn't throw them back?' I looked up in despair to Oliver's hovering face, meeting only the patient resignation of one who's been there before and knows the pitfalls. Clare's character was riddled with traps, deep holes in it only lightly covered with flimsy fabrications. She was now contemplating the glass in her fingers, looking down at the ripples in the surface as it shook. She spoke to it.

'Of course, I tried. I mean – they were mine. A fortune in precious guns. I tried, but I couldn't *throw* them. You couldn't have done it. Admit it.'

I already had. I did again. 'I couldn't have done it.'

'I had to pick them up, one in each hand, and ... sort of ... carry them, and place them on the edge of the terrace. Just place them. I remember ... I had some sort of idea that I would carry them inside, afterwards. Sort of. But Harris kept throwing them. And they were *mine*. Mine! I could barely see for the rain running down my face – or the tears. So I placed them, and Harris kept throwing the others from inside the room. *This* room. Oh – he was furious. At that time, furious. Because I wouldn't give him *one* of them, for him to sell. Not one! And he'd said one would probably do it – two at the most. But I wasn't going to. Hell, Philipa, I could've found the money without selling any of my guns. But he hated them. Hated. Because they were mine ... my precious guns. All I had left of my father – my lovely, lovely guns.'

She stopped. Her eyes seemed completely blank, but on her lips played a tiny, hesitant smile. At the memory of her father, no doubt. She had wandered away from what I had wanted to find out, but into a pathway I hadn't guessed existed. Now I had to discover where it led. Yet she was lost to us for the moment, in a distant and, it seemed, pleasurable past.

'So you placed them on the edge of the terrace,' I said quietly at last. 'And your husband went on throwing the others out.'

'And laughing at me. When he watched me crawl up the steps . . . yes, crawl, because I could barely stand by then, at that time he was laughing. Because he was only waiting . . . oh, I knew he was only waiting until I'd got them all ready to carry back in . . . and I was right, because *then* he slammed the french windows shut, and I heard the lock go over – and there he was, the other side of the glass, still laughing. But I'd found out there were cartridges in the pocket of the Barbour jacket he'd left on the hallstand. Crawling up, they'd dug in my side. So I loaded one of the guns. A gun. The first one that came to hand. As it happened, it was a twelve-bore, and the cartridges were too, so they fitted. I loaded both barrels, and . . . and . . . let him have it. One barrel. Let him have it.'

She was now cradling the glass in both hands, staring down at it, spilling her words into it.

I didn't dare to raise my eyes to Oliver. Only by concentrating on Clare could I urge her to carry on. As she didn't seem about to, I said softly, persuasively, 'This isn't quite the story you told the police, is it?'

Without looking up, she claimed, 'The one I told them was better.'

'Better?'

'Sounded better. Dramatic, sort of. Not stinkingly wet and ghastly and . . . and miserable, and a bloody stupid farce.'

I took a breath. 'You're a show-off, that's what it is. A downright exhibitionist. You'd lie your head off for a good, rounded-off story.'

At last she raised her eyes to mine. There was a child's impish-ness in the way she drew her lower lip between her teeth, and a very mature challenge in the way her eyes opened wide, staring in mock innocence.

'And I suppose it was a lie about the dyke and the Eurasian girl?' I went on, as she seemed unmoved by my provocation.

'Oh yes.' She was proud of it. 'Not entirely,' she amended. 'I shared a cell with the girl, and she *did* teach me things.'

'And you've scattered lies all over the place, in between?'

'In between what?'

'The shooting, and when you came home, Clare. Today. Lies. Now you tell us that you did aim at your husband.'

'His name was Harris. Call him Harris. And I aimed at the glass.'

'Very well – Harris. And did you aim at Harris, through the glass?'

'Harass, he should've been called. He certainly harassed me.'

'Did you aim at him through the glass?'

'Oh yes. But they told me it wasn't *that* that killed him.'

'It wasn't. No. But you thought you had?'

'Thought it – yes.'

'So you were pleased with your efforts?'

'What?'

'You aimed at him, and you thought you'd killed him. So you would be pleased. At that time, you would have been pleased.'

That drew a small amount of aggression from her. Clare was on the attack again. 'Yes, I was damned well pleased. How *dared* he try to ruin my guns?'

'But ... you said ... it was only about money. And you could've given him the money. So why all the anger and the fury and the frustration?'

'I wasn't going to give it to him for *that*.'

'For what? If I remember rightly ... Oliver, didn't you tell me it was a debt, some money he owed a man he'd been out shooting with?'

I knew the answer to this – it was just that Oliver had been silent for too long, and I wanted to draw him into this. Why was he so silent? Was it that he was encountering a Clare he hadn't met before?

'What?' he said. 'The debt. Yes.'

Clare twisted her lips sourly. 'Oh yes. A debt you might as well call it. Except that it was he who'd done the giving in the first place.'

She gave an abrupt, even disconcerting giggle, then clamped her free hand over her mouth. Above it, her eyes were huge with an emotion I couldn't analyse. Was it mischief?

'Clare?' I asked tentatively.

'But it'd grown. The interest on the investment, you could call it.'

'Riddles, Clare? Is this the time for riddles?' I had to be more patient, the more she tried to irritate me.

The hand was lowered, and abruptly she showed her teeth. Her emotions were apt to fly around all over the place. Now she was savage.

'Oh, I knew all about his women. But he'd always been ... careful ... circumspect covers it. But one ... he'd got her pregnant.

106

And he wanted me ... expected me ... *me* to pay for her abortion. How d'you like the sound of that, then? And d'you know the argument he threw at me – the persuasive logic! Oh, he was a beauty, my Harris. Something unique. He said, if I didn't, she'd have to have it on the health service, and it'd get about, but if I paid for her to go away – some private hospital far away – then nobody would know. And I wouldn't need to face the knowing eyes and the nods and sneers...'

She stopped. With her face now lowered, she was staring into the empty glass which was still in her hand, sobbing, the tears dripping into the glass.

I glanced up at Oliver. His face was set and expressionless, distaste freezing his features. Very gently, because I had to know, I asked:

'So why would they sneer?'

'Because,' she chattered, as though a chill had brushed against her, 'Harris and I didn't seem to be able to have children, and he thought they'd sneer ... in the village ... if it was shown to all and sundry that *he* could, with a different woman.'

Then, abruptly, the mood shattered, as did the glass when she hurled it at the floor. Her head came up. No chill now, because there was a glowing fury burning in her eyes.

'And if he thought I'd pay for *that* ...' she shouted. 'If he thought I was frightened of sneers, then he'd got another think coming. I'd have seen him dead, first.'

I allowed a restful few seconds to elapse before I commented on that. I took a deep breath. 'You *did* see him dead, Clare.'

She took that literally. 'I couldn't see him clearly through the window. I *thought* he was dead. That was why I phoned. But he wasn't, was he! Somebody else finished him off. And not before it was due, I can tell you that much.'

I looked at Oliver, who shook his head. I couldn't decide why. Did it mean he wanted an end to it? But so did I, and to demonstrate the fact I thrust back my chair, its feet squealing on the floor. A fit comment. I felt like screaming, myself, if only with pity, though I wasn't sure for whom.

But Clare reached out a hand to stop me. I couldn't interpret her expression, then it flowed free, and I realised she was laughing, though tearfully.

'Don't go. You've got to hear the best bit. I lied. Oh yes, I've told another lie. Suggested one, anyway. It sounded better. Made *me* sound better, I mean. Isn't that what lies are for?'

Clare, being sweetly candid, had to be living another lie, but if so she'd told it to herself. I was cautious.

'Your lies, Clare, that's what they're for,' I agreed. 'Are we to hear the truth? And will we recognise it as truth?'

We now stood facing each other.

'Harris and I didn't seem to be able to have children,' she said. 'I was sure I was normal, and that it wasn't me. So it had to be him, something wrong with him. But I hadn't told him that. I mean, you don't like to throw things like that at a person's face. Now – do you? Of course not.'

A Clare reluctant to throw anything at anybody's face I found difficult to imagine. I murmured something about tact, but she didn't seem interested.

'But you get the point,' she demanded, leaning forward in emphasis. 'You see it, surely. It meant that the child he wanted the money to destroy wasn't even his. Now – *there's* a laugh for you.'

Then she tried to embroider the point by laughing, but she was weeping at the same time, and it didn't come out properly. I could do no more than stare at her blankly, because if there was anything in what she said that was amusing, then I'd missed it.

'And no doubt you told him that,' I said tentatively.

'You can be damn sure I did. Shouted it in his face. Because there was something he didn't know. He was my second man, second husband. Harris wasn't born around here, so he didn't know. About my baby, I mean, because I'd never told him. But she died, my little girl, in a car accident. Clive – that was my first husband – he died too, in the car. But I *knew* I could have children. And that was what I told Harris. This new baby wasn't his. Oh … you should've seen his face! His face! That's what I shouted after him, right out into the hallway. And when he went into the gunroom and locked the door, I knew it was just to get away from me. From my voice. Coward. Ran away from my voice.'

There was so much emotion involved with this claim – if that was what it was – that I was sure she felt it deeply. Yet there seemed to be nothing I could say.

Clare lifted her head. Her voice was dead. 'So why the hell can't you drop it!' she demanded.

'I would've liked – '

'Forget it, and go away from here.'

It was no good telling her what I'd have liked. There was nothing now to say. How could I explain that I wanted to help her, when all she wanted was to see the back of me?

Oliver cleared his throat. 'Phil . . .' he said softly. Then he nodded towards the open, clean air.

I was aware that he had taken my arm. We negotiated the terrace steps and walked diagonally across the lawn to the gap in the rhododendrons. Then we stood and looked over the spread of activity down the slope. It had in no way decreased. In fact, the crowd seemed to have grown. The sun still poured down on them.

I found this to be surprising. It had seemed so oppressively dark in Clare's gunroom that I had expected to find the sun declining over the meadow.

Oliver paused. He said, 'The house faces west, so we're looking east from here. The ideal location for the fireworks would appear to be the other side of the lake. That'd give a darker sky, and a reflection in the water. And all those people down there will be able to gather here, on the slopes, and get a splendid, unobscured view.'

He was trying to distract my mind, to drag it into the sunlight. I knew that, but I went along with him.

'Need I know that?'

'It was just in case you thought we ought to reserve a place.'

'Quite frankly,' I said, 'I don't think we'll be here that late.'

'You'll have sorted it all out by then?'

'I'll have managed to get the car out by then. Let's see if we can find Glenn and his mates.'

He didn't say anything for a while, but walked me slowly down the slope. Then:

'You're giving it up?'

'I can't sort her lies from her truths, so I don't think she's worth helping. And I think the danger's past, anyway.'

'You're talking in riddles,' he complained. 'You're catching it from Clare.'

'You know exactly what I mean. Let's look for Glenn Thomas.'

8

We failed to find him, though I didn't get the impression that Oliver was searching with any enthusiasm, as he seemed more interested in distracting my mind by dragging me round the numerous entertainments. It was some little time before I realised that he was stalling. Now it was he who wanted to stay around a little longer.

'She was upset,' I suggested, exploring.

'Who? Oh ... you mean Clare. Yes. Well, she would be. You stuck a lot of nerve-racking memories under her nose, Phil.'

'It's a wonder you didn't want to stay behind and comfort her.'

It slid right past him. He didn't even react. 'I haven't had a chance for a good chat with Ralph Purslowe yet. Only a quick word...'

'So you're looking for him?'

'Just to keep in touch.'

'Old friends...'

We walked a little further, and he hadn't taken it up. A race new to me was in progress. Hay-rolling. It didn't seem to me to be the period of the year for hay, but somebody had produced, possibly from the back of a barn, four or five of those big rolls they bale the hay into these days. With these they were racing, two men to each bale, which seemed, on the face of it, to entail no technique at all, only strength, as the course ran uphill. But I soon realised that it did. Two men pushing ... if one pushed harder than the other it swerved, and time was lost. Likewise, if they pushed out of unison. And they had to lean forward for it, so that they could barely see over the tops of the cylinders of hay, and thus aimed incorrectly. Oh yes, technique was necessary.

'Old friends, yes,' said Oliver, after so long an interval that I'd forgotten our previous remarks. Yes, of course – Ralph Purslowe. 'I want to ask him something.'

'You do?'

There was no immediate response. Two bale-rollers had collapsed in coughing spells, the dust being a major hazard. Their bale escaped and ran out of control down the slope, scattering a few sunbathers, and finished up in the lake.

'You do?' I repeated. 'Such as what?'

'I thought we ought to know which – if any – young lady of the parish had an abortion at around the time Harris died. If she didn't have the money, it would've been in a local hospital. So ... common knowledge.'

It surprised me a little that he seemed to have completely accepted Clare's revelations, but more that he seemed now to be questioning what she'd said. In any event, pregnancies can be terminated in other ways but abortion, the most common being birth. I didn't pick him up on it.

'If it was common knowledge, you ought to know,' I pointed out.

'I was in the CID at that time. We didn't get the contact the beat coppers did.'

'No. I suppose not. Can we watch something else, Oliver? The dust's getting in my throat.'

'Of course.' He led me away, towards the lake. It was looking more extensive the closer we approached it. There were rowing boats on its surface, scudding and splashing around, and one or two lying idle.

'A boat?' I suggested.

'My arm...'

'I can row, Oliver.'

'Is there *anything* your father didn't teach you? It's a wonder he didn't send you to Oxford, and get you in one of the eights.'

I was silent. We stood on the shore and stared out over the water. On the far side of the lake, as Oliver had expected, there were people, experts, setting up the firework display.

It was the first time he had expressed any bitterness in respect of his disability; the first time he'd directed it at me. I was quite aware that the lusty competition going on in all directions must have brought this to his attention, so that my offer had done no more than thrust it to the fore.

'Is it that you hate my father, Oliver?' I asked at last, trying to sound casual, as though I was merely searching for knowledge.

'Not hate him. Of course not.' His arm tightened round my shoulders. 'I love what he made of you. It's just...' He allowed it to fade away.

111

I waited, but he did not amplify. 'Just what, damn it? I'd like to know in what way I fall short to requirements.'

'It's just that ... oh hell, why did I get into this?'

'Yes ... why? What's upsetting you, Oliver? What've I done wrong?'

'Nothing. Never anything wrong. But sometimes...'

'Sometimes?' I managed to purr it.

'Sometimes, I think, you ought to be more feminine. That's all.'

That's all! To tell a woman that she ought to be more feminine! Did he class me as a hawkish, loud-mouthed feminist...

I turned and gave him as hard a shove as I could, given the weakness of my sex. He slid down the bank, rolling into the water. And I forgave him at once.

He came up spluttering, the bale of hay nudging him, and I offered him a hand, digging in my heels because I reckoned he would do his best to pull me in beside him. And up he came, splashing soggily.

'Now look what you've done,' he complained, swinging his arms about. 'I've got no change of clothes and we're thirty miles from home. You're too blasted touchy, Phil.'

We both ignored the laughter from the near-naked sunbathers around us.

'Oh, stop fussing,' I told him. 'Get your clothes off and hang 'em in a tree. They'll be dry in no time. You can keep your Y-fronts on if you like. Look around you. Half the natives are nearly naked.' But these were teenagers, and might therefore be excused. However... 'We would be considered more peculiar clothed than undressed.'

'We?' asked Oliver, peeling off his wet clothes. He was wearing boxer shorts.

'It would look unfeminine if I remained fully clothed,' I explained. 'And you wouldn't want that.'

'True,' he said, grinning. Oliver's darker moods last a very short while.

So we lay there on the bank of the lake, me in bra and briefs, and no one would have regarded us as different from the pairs of youngsters around us. Except, I noted, that they all seemed to be tightly clasped together. For a moment I considered whether, in order to merge completely, it might be better if we, too, were tightly clasped together. Perhaps it was the reaction from pushing him into the water, but suddenly I felt a warmth for Oliver that almost demanded that we should be similarly entwined. But so far, in my quest for marriage, I had resisted what would inevitably follow if I relaxed – the sun warm on our naked flesh – and though that would add the final touch to our acceptance into the youthful exploratory club that surrounded us, I felt that the price of admission would be too much to pay. The way I was feeling, our performance, being more mature, would probably attract a round of applause from our fellow members. Severely, I forced my mind to the mundane matter of murder.

'And why', I asked, 'would you want to discover who had an abortion, when Clare's made it very clear that she doesn't want us asking around and troubling people?'

'Because I suspect that nobody did, at that time. And not simply because Harris was dead, and couldn't come up with the money. No. It's just that it didn't sound right, Phillie. Not right at all.'

I rolled over and faced him. 'You mean you're disbelieving the golden truths your ex-mistress trusted to us?'

'I wish you wouldn't call her that.'

'It's what she was.'

'It's what she wasn't. Only rarely, Phillie. Not often. Not often enough to be a mistress.'

'Can you put a positive figure on your definition – '

'Keep to the point, please,' he said severely. 'I believe Clare was lying again. Doing it very well ... and I don't think her anger was put on. She *was* angry, at that time. But ... would Harris have gone to her and asked for money for *that*? Wouldn't he have invented some other debt, or something? Clare herself mentioned that Harris was in desperate need of money. And isn't it more usual for the pregnant woman to do the approaching? Wouldn't it be more natural for *her* to go to the wife, or at least threaten to go to the wife? No, Phil. I just can't see Harris going to Clare for money, and then even suggesting it could be for another woman's pregnancy – suggesting that Clare would want it to be hidden. No ... she was reaching for some sort of pity. Or rather, for sympathy. Pity would be no good for her. Pity's empty.'

Sometimes he surprises me. 'Yes, I see what you mean. She's been coming round to the point of actually admitting she shot him.'

He looked startled. 'Did it sound like that? I can't imagine such a thing from Clare – an actual admission.'

'Then she was trying to put across the fact that she had damned good justification for shooting him.' I nodded severely.

'Does she need that?'

113

'You said it yourself – she was angling for sympathy and understanding.'

'She's got it already,' he said, waving an embracing arm. 'From everybody.'

'Not from me, and she knows it.' I rolled back, staring at the sky. 'Not perhaps enough from you, Oliver, either.'

He sounded annoyed. 'What the hell...'

I spoke very softly, picking my words with care. 'If – in spite of the fact that she did kill him – she had your sympathy and forgiveness for her deceit – '

'Drop it, Phil, please.'

'Then she could hope you would be able to persuade me to accept that she did, after all, shoot him – and I would then leave her in peace.'

'For God's sake!'

I sat up. There was a completely alien anger in his eyes.

'But you maintain that Harris would never have gone to her for money to terminate another woman's pregnancy?' I asked this casually.

Still he seemed angry. 'I can't see it.'

'Then – it seems – she's failed to obtain your full sympathy and understanding.' I grinned at him.

A vestige of his anger still remained. But, as I'd expected, my grin softened it, and he knew I'd been ribbing him. Or thought he knew. I hadn't been.

'Correct,' he said flatly. 'I wonder if my clothes are dry yet. I'm beginning to feel a bit conspicuous.'

'Are you? Why?'

'We're the only couple here not exploring the joys of sex.'

I sprang to my feet to check. Yes – his clothes were dry. Well ... dry enough. Mine, of course, had not been wet.

We dressed. It took me half the time that Oliver needed.

'And I don't agree,' I said.

'With what?'

'That Harris wouldn't have gone to Clare about another woman's pregnancy. Look at how it was, if we've got the partial truth and it wasn't *all* a string of lies. She knew she could have children, because she'd had one. She lost that child, and her husband, in the same car crash. Then she acquired another husband – Harris. Don't you think that having another child would be her first thought, when she chose him? Big and masculine. Don't you think that would be foremost in her mind? And when a child

114

didn't come along, she would blame him. She would torment him to go for tests. She would demand her right to have a child. Heavens, Oliver, have you thought of *this*? She had other men, you amongst them. Perhaps *that* was in her mind. No affection involved. No love. Sex without love! Revolting. Yet she – '

'Does this go on much longer?'

I sighed. There was a dangerous light in his eyes.

'It stops right here, Oliver. She would taunt him – Harris. She would plague him. So ... if he *did* get another woman pregnant, wouldn't he throw *that* fact in her face? Yes ... he would love going to her for money, to terminate a pregnancy she'd claimed he could never bring about. And heavens ... wouldn't that send her way over the top into a bout of uncontrollable fury – '

'You've made your point, Phil.'

'You go along with it?'

'Oh yes, yes.' He sounded impatient. 'He'd ask her for money, but not with any expectation of getting it. Not a chance. And he'd know that. But that would be the ultimate insult, to wave a pregnancy under her nose – and he'd love it. The icing on the cake, he'd see it as. Oh yes.'

But if Oliver accepted it, he certainly wasn't at all happy about it. In fact, he looked thoroughly miserable. Crimes of violence would have been routine to him. Theft, jealousy, self-protection, he would be able to accept all of those, and remain emotionally uninvolved. Crimes of sex were a different thing. We were down to the basic reasons for existence. He would hate such crimes, and this one brushed against him too intimately.

'So don't you think, Oliver,' I suggested, as he forced damp socks into damp shoes, 'that we ought to be enquiring about local abortions at around that time? As you suggested.'

'Let's see if we can find a cup of tea and something to eat.'

'Well ... don't you?'

'Why else d'you think I was looking for Ralph Purslowe? I did say that.'

'Yes, so you did.' I took his arm. 'Oliver, I wish you wouldn't do this to me.'

'Do what?'

'Lead me on. You'd worked all this out before, so why did you let us get into an argument?'

'Because, my sweet ...' He reached over to squeeze the hand I had tucked into his arm, 'I love to see your eyes go all wild when you're furious. Love it.'

'Then don't push your luck. It's that marquee over there. He got me a cup of tea. Your Inspector Purslowe did.'

'But he didn't mention abortions?'

'Not over a cup of tea, no. He was concerned with impressing on me how many people had been queuing up for a go at Harris Steadman.'

'No hints as to pregnancy?'

'Only in a general way. Harris seemed to have been very active.'

'Perhaps he hadn't got anybody specific in mind.'

We walked on. The marquee became closer. There was a queue to get in, blast it.

I have a distinct dislike for queues, almost a morbid fear. I feel that I am drawn on to a production line, one of a powerless stream of jolting bottles, inevitably to be filled at the end but with no way to withdraw. Or rather, one can always withdraw, but at the sacrifice of a number of precious places.

'A quarter of an hour,' I said, viewing the length of the queue and watching how fast they shuffled. 'Get something for me, Oliver, will you? Anything. I'll be back.'

'I get all the rotten jobs. Where are you off to?'

'Your friend Ralph said I ought to visit Madame Acarti. Now's the chance.'

'Alice Carter.' He nodded. 'Ralph's wife. She uses her maiden name in the line of business.'

'Ah yes. I'll be off, then. It'll be that tent I saw, over by the far hedge, I'd guess.'

It was somewhat isolated, and I'd not noticed anyone going near it for a long while. Business was slack.

'That's it,' Oliver said. 'The messages from the other world that DS Alice Carter would wish to discuss with the locals would be very private indeed.'

I left him. My shoes were not ideal for walking on turf, though the grass was short, as had been the lawn in front of the gunroom. It's so easy to take things for granted, I thought. You are presented with a fact, and you don't query it. But now, I considered that fact. Clare had returned to a house prepared for her: groceries in the kitchen and her showcases beautifully restored. I'd noticed that although little dusting had been done in the rest of the house, those showcases had been polished when I'd seen them, the glass fronts gleaming. Preparations for her return had been made. But she had, after all, known of her early release from prison, had known over a

116

month before. Hadn't she sent instructions to the estate agent to withdraw Collington House from the market?

And, now that I knew her better, I could see that the incorrect price quoted on the prospectus might well have been a deliberate trick of Clare's. She would make the gesture of putting the house on the market, but knowing she had in reserve a means of discouraging any interested buyers. It would've been much more fun than simply refusing any valid offer at a realistic price. It had to be another of her flights of self-dramatisation.

So she had returned, knowing that everything would be ready to receive her. Including the fête? Yes, she wouldn't have forgotten that. As soon as a positive date for her release was known, she would have arranged a date for the fête accordingly. How better to greet again, as my lady of the manor, her own beloved congregation?

Damn it, the woman's making me cynical, I thought. It was annoying to have one's emotions so easily manipulated by another person.

But I walked her treasured turf on the way to Madame Acarti's den. I was in no doubt that Glenn Thomas had brought all this about, and had probably organised the fête. He would do anything for Clare.

What are you thinking, Phil? I asked myself. Glenn had his eye on Josie Knight, if the clasped hands I'd trodden on meant anything.

It was during my indecisive wanderings that I became aware of another person's interest. Standing close to the hedge, but a hundred yards further down the gentle slope from the tent, was Glenn Thomas. I wandered slowly towards him. Now he was wearing his jacket, but standing, hands on hips, with it drawn back. His shirt was still open to the navel, his chin jutting towards the lair of Madame Acarti. He was so concentrated on his thoughts that he gave a small jerk when I spoke at his shoulder.

'Trying to make up your mind?' I asked.

He darted a brief glance at me, then continued to glower at the tent. 'I've made it. I'm going to ask her to leave.'

'She doesn't seem to be getting much custom, anyway.'

'I've passed the word around.'

'You disapprove, obviously. Don't you believe in the occult, Glenn? Don't you believe that the future might be predicted?'

Again the brief glance, no doubt to note whether I was serious. 'Occult! My left foot.'

117

'There's no need to be delicate with me, you know. And there's nothing mysterious about what goes on in that tent. It's no more than gentle hints – that all is known, and that the minor misdemeanours have been observed. And if those stop, all will be forgotten and forgiven. Quite frankly, I think it's a very good idea. Better the subtle warning than the hand on your collar.'

But he was stubborn. Glenn Thomas was a man of simple but firm loyalties. Your friend, and he was a friend for life. Briefly, I wondered whether Josie realised this. A wife was a wife, and that was it. By heaven, how relaxing it would be to have such a man at your side, inflexibly. He would kill anyone who harmed you. But wasn't that why I clung to Oliver? He, too, was such a man. Didn't he realise that this was why I wanted to marry him?

But my thoughts were wandering. I dragged them back ruthlessly. He hadn't responded to my comment.

'Have you the authority to ask her to leave?' I asked. 'It's Clare's land.'

'Yes, yes. Of course it is. But it was Clare who asked me to arrange all this. She didn't ask for a police presence, though.'

'Doing no harm, surely.'

'Doing a hell of a lot of harm, if you ask me. Paltry stuff, that's all it is. The village shop open on Sunday morning! Pah! You'd think it was Sainsbury's. And old Ted Martin driving on an expired car tax. Or Julie Fisher, hawking her ... doing favours for money. The poor dear's getting past it, and how'll she live on her pension? And young Tony Leach, riding his pushbike at night without lights. Petty, paltry, a waste of time. I can take care of all that.'

Glenn Thomas, it seemed to me, was suffering from a severe attack of lord-of-the-manor-itis. He saw himself as the focal point of the whole community. People came to him...

'People come to me,' he said, reading my mind. 'I help out, if there's trouble.'

So what did he feel about the return of Clare Steadman? Would they compete in a battle for local influence? Or would they ... surely not. But Clare would certainly be looking out for another husband. Where did Josie come in all this? And did she realise it?

'So tell her to leave,' I said, gesturing towards the tent. 'Though, mind you, you might find yourself with a whole bundle of your own minor aberrations to answer for.'

'Like hell I will!' He turned to face me. 'You're being funny,' he accused me. 'They could hunt around till their eyes dropped out, and still find nothing.'

'Nobody can say that, Mr Thomas.'

'Glenn, damn it, Glenn. Nobody calls me mister.'

So perhaps I was wrong about his pretensions. 'Glenn it is, then.'

'That's my property, over there,' he said, as though he hadn't made his point. He waved towards the hedge. 'I farm over five hundred acres. Dairy and grain crops. A good portion of the village works for me, one way or another, but nobody calls me mister. So I don't want anybody to be upset. Understand?'

'Precisely, Mr Thomas.'

He turned to face me, anger in his eyes, then he saw my demure expression, and surprisingly grinned. 'I see you do.'

'So – if you wish it – I'll pass on your message to Madame Acarti. She is not welcome.'

'I don't understand you.' He shook his head violently, and his hair flew wildly, catching the sun. 'D'you still want to consult her?'

'I'm told she may want to consult me.'

'What about?' There was immediate suspicion.

'I shan't know until I see her, shall I?'

I saw then that she had emerged from her tent. Perhaps our words had reached her, carried on the light breeze. Or at least, the indefinite sound of voices.

'She wouldn't have dared put her nose in here, if Harris had been alive,' said Glenn.

'I can understand that he wouldn't have dared to consult her himself. It'd take all day to list his misdemeanours.'

He laughed. 'It certainly would.'

'It *is* Harris, I suppose?'

'Pardon? What is?'

'His name.'

'Of course. What else?'

'An unusual Christian name,' I observed. 'I thought it had to be a shortening of Harrison.'

He didn't reply. I glanced up at him. He was gazing directly into the far distance, his jaw set.

'Am I wrong?' I asked.

'Where did you get that from?' he asked gently, with the menacing softness of a hunting cat on a feather quilt.

I managed a casual shrug, wishing I hadn't mentioned it. 'No more than a passing thought. It doesn't matter.'

'No,' he agreed. 'It doesn't matter.' Yet clearly, it did.

'So I'll go and get it over with,' I said.

'You're a persistent ...' He didn't allow himself to be specific.

'I've been told that. I'm working on it. I'll leave you now, Glenn. Don't throw her out on her neck until I've finished with her.'

He shrugged. His eyes went beyond me and he scanned the higher slopes. 'I'll go and find Josie.'

I watched him walk away, and was reluctant, now, to approach the tent. She was clearly waiting for me, looking very lonely and very bored. I walked slowly uphill towards her. She seemed to be a tall, slim woman, dark-skinned, but I couldn't detect the colour of her hair. From somewhere she had obtained a brightly coloured caftan, which most certainly didn't suit her, and had over her hair a silk scarf, blue shot through with gold thread, which was tied beneath her chin.

'I've been waiting ages for you,' she told me severely. 'Where've you been?' Almost as though she hadn't seen exactly where.

Her voice was soft and melodious, not the voice you would expect from a detective sergeant, nor yet the voice of a gypsy seer.

'Around and about,' I told her.

'Asking questions, I've no doubt.' She nodded her head in confirmation, then she extended her arm in invitation and stood aside for me to enter.

It was a pitch-roofed tent, not large, its side walls barely two feet tall. I had to slide round the ridge pole support to get inside, the light suddenly dim after the sunlight outside. It was barely possible to see that there was nothing inside but a small round table with a chair each side. I shuffled around one of the chairs, having to duck my head as it brushed against the sloping wall. I sat.

'That's my chair,' she claimed.

It didn't seem to matter; they were identical. 'Sorry ... I'll just ...'

'It signifies nothing.'

Then she took her seat opposite me. Her voice had changed. What she had said were the words of a soothsayer. Now it was all business. 'Ralphie told you I wanted to see you,' she went on. 'So why haven't you come earlier?'

'I waited until the necessity arose.' I thought I put that well, hiding my annoyance that she had expected me to come running.

She didn't react. 'Well, you're here now. Give me your hand.'

'Pardon?'

'Your hand. How can I explore your future unless I see your hand?'

I offered her my right hand, palm upwards. She took it, turned it over, and stared at the back.

'Your nails are short, Philipa,' she said quietly, close to crooning.

120

'I keep them short.'

'No use for scratching eyes out, are they?'

'I had no such intention,' I assured her.

She turned it over and stared in the general direction of my lifeline, though she couldn't possibly have seen it. Although that wouldn't matter.

'I see danger ahead, Miss Philipa Lowe. Deep danger. You have been asking too many questions. There is a chill wind blowing over my shoulders. I feel it reaching for you.'

'Have you any advice to offer, Madame Acarti?' I asked, trying to sound terrified.

'The obvious. Go home.'

'But I don't want to miss the fireworks.'

She ignored that, peering closely at my palm, then leaning back. 'You are a stubborn, stupid woman, d'you know that?' Now it was Alice Carter speaking. 'Why do you persist in this?'

'In what?'

'Pursuing this ridiculous idea that Clare Steadman could be innocent.'

I snatched back my hand. 'I know she is.'

'Know, know! Who knows, except Clare herself – and has she asked for your help? Are you qualified in any way to give it?'

'Perhaps I was born with a logical mind – and I don't see much logic in what was assumed to have happened. Or I'm stubborn. Or I like truth.'

'You won't get much of that from Clare.'

'I've discovered that. But a few details strike me as true.'

We thus batted it to and fro. Getting nowhere. Then we were silent for a few moments, until I ventured:

'Why would you warn me, unless you felt I was in danger? And that couldn't come from anybody but the real murderer of Harris Steadman.'

I could just detect the slight acknowledging smile she gave me. 'Your logic, Miss Lowe?'

'It sounds logical. Is that all you had for me, Sergeant?'

'Perhaps not.'

I waited for her to offer more, but she was silent again, no doubt considering how far she dared to go.

'You don't seem to be very busy,' I commented. 'No queue.'

'I was busy earlier. But when they realised what I was after they backed off, and the word went around.'

'Ah yes.' I could guess whose word had gone around. 'And what was the word in question?'

She seemed to avoid answering. 'They will confide in Madame Acarti what they will not to Sergeant Carter. I suppose they persuade themselves I'm not a policewoman, but a special creature who will treasure their confidences.'

'You're certainly talking like one,' I assured her. 'It's a suspension of disbelief. And what did they balk at?'

'The word must have flashed round like a forest fire.'

'But what?'

'I was trying to discover, Miss Lowe, whether there'd been any pregnancy at around that time, September 1986, one that didn't produce something in the due course of time.'

'Ah!' I said, suddenly more alert. It seemed that I was not the only one who believed there were unexplained facts involved in the death of Harris Steadman. The uncertainty still haunted other people than me ... but unofficially. Such individual thinking in the force would not be encouraged. 'And was there?'

Her voice suddenly resumed its pretentious all-knowing tone. 'All is not revealed, even to the most expert visionary. The picture is blurred.' Her voice changed again. 'Of course there were pregnancies. When are there not? Whether the fathers were the expectant husbands, it has never been revealed. But others there were, the fathers unknown. The truth, though, need not be in the pregnancies, but in their termination. The truth you seek – the truth others would so dearly love to glimpse, even only as a passing shade of truth – '

'Can't you talk ordinary English?'

'Hush. I'm practising. The life of a visionary is fraught with untruths. Sometimes the truth is negative.'

'Oh ... get on with it.' She had taken back my hand. I assumed she didn't realise. Perhaps she was in a trance. 'How many terminated pregnancies can you produce at that time?'

'Pregnancies are always being terminated. Then and now.'

'Oh?'

'By birth. My own second child was born around that time. But other ways are open for exploration.'

'For heaven's sake! So you've explored. And have you had any success? Any hint...'

She sighed. 'To Madame Acarti, no secrets were entrusted.'

'You asked?'

She inclined her head. 'But got no answers.'

'Not even negative ones?'

'Stubborn, shaken heads.'

I had Glenn to thank for this. 'Which, to you, as a policewoman, would mean that there *was* something?'

She tilted her head at me, weighing me up. 'The interesting thing', she said at last, 'is that you're also on the same tack. Obviously.'

'Shall we say I've been talking to Clare – we've been talking to her, Oliver and I. An interesting pregnancy at that time, provided that Harris was the father, would have given Clare a very strong motive.'

'She didn't need one, did she? There was his action with her guns. *That* infuriated her past breaking-point.'

'So why ...' I asked softly, leaning forward. 'Why are we discussing pregnancies?' She didn't seem inclined to reply, so I went on, 'Why, unless you believe it's relevant – which has to mean that *you* don't think Clare killed her husband?'

'Ralph's always thought that.'

'But now you seem to think in terms of pregnancies.'

'That has to be considered.'

She hadn't sounded convinced. 'But you'd rather accept it was based on money,' I suggested.

'What money?'

'You know what. Harris was in financial trouble. He'd had his fingers in the funds of the company he had shares in, Shades Of Knight Ltd. If Clare refused to let him have any, that could have sparked off their final battle.'

'That ... is ... true.' She was very cautious.

'But as against that,' I went on, 'she might well have agreed to pay up. She did pay up, afterwards, I heard.'

'And where did you hear that?' She was interested again.

'I don't remember. Oliver, I think. Or Clare herself.'

'Because it isn't true. Glenn Thomas paid it. It was he who got the company out of trouble. The rumour was that he bought Harris's shares from Clare, and as a shareholder he put in the necessary cash.'

She peered at me, her head on one side. Make something of that if you can. I was getting pressures from all directions: go home, and let the guilt lie where it had already fallen.

'So go home, Philipa Lowe,' she said in a kindly voice. 'There's nothing here for you.'

'I don't believe you,' I said firmly. 'I think you've picked up

123

something, you and your fine husband. You hope to put it together and produce another murderer . . . and promotions all round.'

'Now listen here – '

I didn't intend to. 'But now I know that there's something . . . oh, you can't expect me to drop it now.'

She seemed to make a gesture towards me. In an instant her face changed, her eyes wide and startled. She made a choking sound, like a grunt, her mouth wide open, and now she was clutching for me, reaching. I put out my free hand to catch hers, and my fingers were nearly crushed as she pitched forward, choking, then there was blood from her open mouth all over my arm, and I couldn't release my hand. The fingers of her other hand scrabbled at the table top, and I heard a screaming sound. It wasn't until I finally managed to force my hand free that I realised it was I who was screaming. I tried to stop, but it went on and on.

Then I fell over backwards as my legs became tangled with my chair. Whimpering now, I crawled on hands and knees to the opening and out into the field. Then I forced myself to my feet with one hand, the other, bloodied, being held out in front of me, as far away as possible in my disgust and revulsion.

I stood and turned, looking back, unable to restrain myself. The pitch of the tent was held inwards, like the mouth of a funnel, by the haft of a knife.

A marginal awareness registered the fact that there was a rustle through the hedge, ten feet back, and just a glimpse of something beyond it moving away. Running away.

Then I was screaming again, for help, for assistance, until I must have passed out.

9

I thought at first that I was in heaven. The hot blue sky was directly ahead of me, so reason dictated that I had to be lying on my back. And I was surrounded by roses. Their perfume was a heavy mist around me.

'Just lie still,' said a quiet voice.

A face, upside-down, but I could detect that it flourished a large moustache, was leaning closer and closer.

'She's coming round.' That was Oliver's voice. He was somewhere. I struggled to look round, but then my head swam from the movement.

'You'll be all right in a minute,' the quiet voice went on. 'You fainted.'

I was utterly ashamed. I had screamed, too, hadn't I? Screamed and fainted. I had always considered that screaming was a silly reaction to danger or shock. I had thought swooning was a Victorian fad, not fit behaviour for a modern woman. Yet I'd done both. Yes, I had. I remembered the screams, though not the fainting.

But Oliver would be pleased with me, I thought. I clung to the idea, and tried to express it, but found I couldn't.

'You're all right now,' said the calm voice. 'Try to sit up. But slowly.'

Of course I could sit up. What did he think I was, some empty-headed flibbertigibbet ...

I tried. My head swam, but I persisted, and Oliver's good arm was round my shoulders, and his face was smiling, close, warm and comforting.

'She's dead, isn't she?' I whispered.

I now perceived that I was lying on a stretcher. Had been lying, but was now sitting up, on a stretcher in what must have been Clare's rose garden. From such a low position I was able to see only

125

my immediate surroundings, but clearly, if the rest of it was anything like what I could see . . .

'Help me up, Oliver, please.'

'You've had a nasty shock.'

'Don't treat me like a delicate flower,' I said, being surrounded by flowers and my imagination not working fully at that time.

He helped me to my feet. My legs were like jelly, but I concentrated. Oliver took most of the strain. The man with the moustache was replacing various items into his black case, smiling I thought at his success. 'Thank you,' I murmured, and he smiled and nodded. 'You're not the only one today. It's the heat.' I agreed that it must be, and he went away.

Clare was standing on the path, facing me with her feet spread wide, as though she too wasn't certain of her legs, and frowning, frowning and worried – and just a little annoyed.

'They brought you up here,' said Oliver softly. 'It was the nearest . . . away from the gawping crowd.'

'She's dead, isn't she?' I repeated. It was something I had to know.

'Yes, Phil. She's dead. I'm sorry.'

I heard myself moan. 'Poor Ralph . . .'

Clare had not said a word. Now she turned round and headed back towards the house.

'Yes,' said Oliver. 'Poor Ralph. He's down there with them. Nobody's got the heart to send him away. He's just standing there. The full team's here now. You've been out of touch for nearly half an hour, Phil.'

'What! I don't believe it.'

'You heard the doctor. We were worried.'

I refused to believe it. 'But I couldn't . . .'

'You did. The heat. That and the fact that you haven't eaten since that snack we had. Oh . . . a hundred reasons.'

Bless him, he had to find reasons. No, they were excuses for me, for my having behaved like a weak female. Women don't faint, these days. Surely not.

'And Ralph's down there?'

'He's there, but not with them. The Scene Of Crime team's taken over. They can't move her till all the . . . the details have been covered. The super wants to speak to you.'

I had just remembered why I'd screamed. 'Not there!'

'No. No, my sweet. Clare wants you to come inside the house, and you can relax in the sitting-room. She'll get you a cup of tea, and sandwiches. Whatever. And there's brandy.'

'Oh yes, there's brandy.'

With his arm around me, he began to walk me slowly towards the house. I was feeling stronger now and didn't need his help, but there was no hurry to tell him that.

'The knife?' I asked.

'An ordinary kitchen knife. Nothing special about it.'

'I saw it, Oliver. Don't walk so fast.'

'We're not walking fast, Phillie. Hardly moving at all.'

I stopped.

'You're tired,' he said. 'There's a bench just along here.'

The roses marched in shaped beds on both sides of us, each bed neatly outlined by low, square-cut box hedges. It was almost painful to be blinded by the flaming colours. Whether or not Glenn Thomas had been instructed to arrange payment for it, an expert gardener must have worked stolidly for nearly six years in order to maintain this scented paradise at a peak of perfection. Whenever Clare returned, it would be there to welcome her, to relax her, to tell her she was home.

Ahead, there was an arbour, a circular space of close-clipped grass, this again surrounded by the ubiquitous box hedging. In that circle there were two benches, facing each other across it. In the centre was a basin on a pedestal, a fountain tinkling into it.

We sat. I did not admit to the relief this was.

'You said . . . Oliver, you said – this was the nearest, to bring me.'

'Yes. The boundary – the hedge boundary to the field – it leads straight up to here from the tent. You understand, they wanted you out of the crush. Out of sight. It was like a football crowd down there. And the super wanted you relaxed and quiet. What's your point, Phil?'

'I saw a shape . . . the flicker of a shape, just the other side of that hedge.'

'Yes.' He didn't sound impressed. 'It'd be the only escape route for . . . whoever it was.'

I thought about that, not being able to prevent myself from lifting my head and looking round me, as though this person might be hidden near, crouched amongst the roses.

'But there's something you don't understand, Oliver.'

'Don't worry yourself now.'

'Will you please listen! It wasn't her chair. In the tent, I took her

127

chair. She commented on it. So the chair she was – the chair *she* used – that was the customer's. The client's. Mine.'

It had seemed a colossal effort to say all that, and to be able to hold on to the thought before I lost it or confused it.

'Phil?' His tone held anxiety, no doubt for my sanity.

'I'm not imagining things. That was how it was. Just think, a previous client or visitor – they would know which of the chairs ... Oh hell, Oliver, work it out for yourself.'

Now I was developing a headache. As I stared at it, the image of the fountain swayed. For pity's sake! I wasn't going to pass out again, surely. I took in several deep breaths, and the fountain steadied. As did my brain, and I remembered. There had been blood ...

I jerked out my right arm, but somebody had cleaned it. There were spots of blood, though, on the short sleeve of my blouse. I shuddered, about to say something, but my teeth chattered.

'Are you all right?' Oliver asked anxiously.

'Yes, yes. There was blood, all over my arm.' I was cold. There seemed to be no warmth in the sun.

'Yes. We washed that away,' he said quietly.

'Thank you.'

'Your mind seemed to be rambling, miles away.'

'I'm trying to concentrate. That's all.' And what an effort it was! 'My mind's getting clearer every second. What I'm trying to get into your thick head is that the knife was intended for me. For me, and all you can do is sit there with your mouth open.'

'It is *not* open. I just can't believe ... Damn it, Phil, you've harmed nobody.'

'Perhaps I've frightened somebody. How very strange. I never thought I could really scare anybody. Me!'

'You scared me,' Oliver admitted. 'I can tell you that. When you wouldn't come round ... and you were so white.'

'Silly.'

He stared at the fountain, but his hand was resting on mine. Then, because he had to offer something, he said, 'They – he or she – could have heard what you were talking about, inside the tent.' He took his hand away, and wiped it down his face.

'Of course they could, with no more than a thickness of canvas in between.'

He turned back to me, so that he could take both hands in his, the more to impress me with his earnestness. 'But how could it have been that? Something you and Alice were discussing, I mean. Even if this person might have been interested in what was being said, I can't imagine it would be somebody who just happened to be carrying a kitchen knife around, just on the off-chance of being able to find a use for it – in the middle of a field!'

I slid my hands free and laid them in the middle of my lap, talking down to them quietly, but each word carefully chosen.

'I don't think you're being honest with me, Oliver. You think my mind's not up to it, and I'm making issues out of it that don't exist. I don't have to be comforted like that – but I thank you for the thought behind it. No – please. Let me say this. I thank you – if it's that. But you were using your big masculine know-all voice, the one you use for calming the weak and feeble females, such as you'd like me to be, pouring scorn on my silly little brain because I've had a shock and I oughtn't to be troubling my poor and inadequate female mind with serious matters, which only you great oafish louts of men can handle. And if you think...'

I raised my head and turned to face him. He was smiling his big, happy smile.

'My, Phil, but you're a grand one for recovering. Full strength again, and I'm not laughing and not condescending. I know what you're getting at.'

At this moment Clare appeared, bearing a tray. 'You'll be better out here, I think. Better than indoors – all this fresh air...'

'And your wonderful roses. Oh, thank you, Clare.'

She had placed the tray on the bench between us, Oliver sliding sideways nimbly. There was a pot of tea, protected by a cosy, a plate of sandwiches cut as triangles, ham and cheese it seemed to me, and a plate of small cakes, sugar in a bowl and a jug of milk. Whoever had arranged matters, Glenn I now knew, had catered very adequately for Clare's return.

'Peaceful here,' she said, smiling. 'You can relax. It must have been quite terrible.' The smile became a grimace of distaste.

Then she turned, and walked away briskly.

Oliver poured the tea. He now knew exactly how much sugar and milk I took. I didn't feel like eating. He offered me the plate, and suddenly I did. The sandwiches were splendid, the tea a divine experience. There's nothing like a shock for sharpening the perceptions.

We were both silent for a few restorative moments. Then Oliver said, 'I suppose, in that tent, you were discussing the terminated pregnancies around about September six years ago?'

'We were. Amongst other things.'

'But of course, and I'm sure of this, the stabbing wouldn't have been related to what was being said.' He paused. He chewed and swallowed. 'At the time of the stabbing ... what was being said at that time?'

I thought about that for a moment. The fountain tinkled.

'I don't get your point, Oliver.'

'Look at it like this – whatever information was being passed over ...'

'No information was being passed over, Oliver. No names were mentioned. She was no help at all.'

'Well then.'

'I still don't understand. Explain, Oliver, please.'

He picked up another sandwich, held it up and stared at it, and said, 'What good would it have done anybody to kill one of you, simply because some awkward or even damning evidence was being passed on? Only one of you could have been killed, so it couldn't possibly have guaranteed secrecy, because the other one of you would know what it was. In fact, now that I come to think of it, it would draw attention to what secret and what name were being discussed at that time. And who's going to arm themselves with a kitchen knife, and walk off into the field on the chance of keeping some secret or other still a secret? That's crazy.'

'That knife. Probably filched from the refreshments tent.'

'Of course. Clever Phil. Who, then, would filch a knife, as you put it, when killing one of you wouldn't help a little bit?'

I poured us both another cup of tea. 'Not *one* of us, Oliver. Me. It was intended for me. I told you about the chairs.'

'If you say so, Phil.'

'I do say so.'

'Well then ... that means, if you *were* the real target, then the intention had to be to prevent you from passing on some vital information to Alice Carter – to the police, in effect – not to prevent Alice Carter giving information to you. *Then* the preparation of taking along a knife begins to make sense, and then you can just about imagine the eavesdropping until the moment when the dreaded secret is just about to be revealed. This makes *some* sense, because I managed to get a word with Ralph after all, and he told me that Alice and he had never been satisfied that Clare killed Harris.'

'Ah!' I said, peering into the pot to see whether another cup of tea might be squeezed out of it. It might, and I did. Oliver waited.

'That point we covered,' I said. 'If I remember correctly, she as good as admitted it. And the whole rigmarole – the tent and the gypsy business – that had always been no more than an excuse for reaching for information.'

'But they – she and Ralph – never got anywhere?' Oliver asked.

'So it seemed. They're a canny lot round here, and they weren't fooled. Madame Acarti was still a policewoman, fishing for information – so she got nothing. But why', I asked, suddenly realising, 'are we talking about Alice? What *she* knew, what *she* said! Oliver, I've explained: that knife was meant for me.'

'Now Phil...'

'For me – and I don't feel very good about it. And, if you consider that the knife was brought there deliberately, it wasn't in any way related to what was being said.'

'I thought we'd agreed on that.'

'It had to be related to what wasn't said,' I said emphatically. 'In other words, to something I knew. Something obviously very important.'

'Such as what?'

'I don't know.'

'You don't know what you know?'

'Precisely.'

'But suddenly, when something clicks in that pretty little head of yours, it may come to you?'

'You're finally getting the point, Oliver. I'm a walking threat to somebody.'

'Then we'll have to make sure we stay together, Phil.'

'Hmm!'

'Don't you agree?'

'I was just thinking, Oliver, that there's still a shot-gun missing. What good would it do if we shared a barrelful of shot?'

He half laughed, then stifled it. 'You're serious, aren't you? But Phil, that's rather too fanciful. I'll bet there're dozens of shot-guns in the village, so why that specific one?'

'Symbolic, perhaps.'

'You're stretching it.' But his voice was still jocular.

'I'm considering all the possibilities, that's all. I don't want you trying to take a shot-gun from somebody – never again.'

'Then I shan't try. Phil, don't you think we ought to hunt out Glenn and his mates, and get them to lift out your car? He said they could do it. Then we'd be out of it. What's the matter?'

I was staring at him, trying to control my feelings. 'You must be crazy!'

'Now what?'

'If you think I'm going to be frightened away ... if you think I'd dream of leaving here when I know that I know something that matters ... oh no. Thank you very much, but not when the answer's so close it's almost touching me. I can feel it.'

'What you might feel could prove fatal next time, Phillie, and you know *that*.'

'But now I'll be watching out. What time's sunset?'

'Oh ... hours yet. Half-past nineish.'

'Then there's time.'

'Are you sure your mind's working all right?' He looked at me with his head tilted. 'Time for what?'

'To clear it up, so that we can relax for the fireworks.'

He looked worried. 'I don't think I'll ever understand you.'

'Enigmatic, it's called. It's linked with sex appeal.'

'Hell, you've already got more than your share. I couldn't stand any more.'

'Let's go and look for that super of yours,' I suggested.

'Better not be enigmatic with him. If it's the same one – Bristow, his name was.'

'Haven't you seen him, if you were down ... there?'

He shook his head. 'I was too involved with you to trouble about superintendents. Let's go and have a quiet sit-down in the house. Out of the sun for a while. I'll be like a lobster tomorrow.'

I'm lucky in that way. It's something to do with pigmentation. I become tanned rather than burned, and I've always wondered why people go to great lengths to achieve this. A tan doesn't go with my hair.

The rose garden proved to be at the side of the house, which explained why I hadn't observed it earlier. At first, I couldn't see any obvious way into the house, and wondered how Clare had brought the tray to us.

But there was a tailored gap in the box hedge which led directly on to the lawn, where they'd been playing croquet earlier. All the hoops had gone, and the french windows were wide open. By now, the sight of those windows open sent a chill through me. Yet the terrace was still brilliantly lit by the sun. No shadows had yet reached the lawn. Nothing sinister about it.

Then I realised that Charlie Green had kept his promise, and speedily, too. He was returning Clare's guns, even, I found out later, the one with which she had supposedly killed her husband. My mind no longer hesitated on that score. Previously, I had been sure she hadn't done so, because she hadn't seized on a possible way out for her when a second shot had been suggested. But now I *knew* it. Alice Carter had died because she wasn't me. So somebody feared what I knew, and was no doubt strung tight with nerves, wondering how long it would be before I put something I knew against something I ought to know, and had at last a sight of the truth. And that person couldn't be Clare, because she had already been tried for it, and thus had nothing to fear.

Charlie Green was being very cautious not to offend. He had a gang of men and, I had to assume, a vanful of guns out at the front. But he wasn't going to have them marching through the house and soiling Clare's parquet. He was having them carried round, and directly in through the french windows.

Clare, I could hear, was supervising. 'Not there! *This* one here. And that's a pair, not three. You can't get three in one showcase! Easy now. Careful. Don't throw them around, damn it.'

But they'd all, or nearly all, been thrown around with considerably less care, six years before.

Watching this procession across the lawn, apparently with a critical eye, was a woman I hadn't met. She was taller than me, nearly as tall as Oliver, and was, even in this weather, dressed in a smart grey two-piece and a light blue shirt, top button open. But she seemed not to feel the heat. When she turned to me her skin was dry, her face rather thin and much wrinkled round the eyes. As though she laughed often, I thought, though there was no sign of this now. Her eyes were a piercing grey, her hair dark brown with grey lurking in it, plainly cut, neat and tidy. Her bosom was almost flat, which drew attention to the clip and the bulge at her breast pocket.

She must have heard our voices approaching closer, but it was only at the last second that she turned to face us directly, to face me, rather.

'You're Philipa Lowe?' she asked. Her voice was quite deep for a woman.

'Yes. That's me. And this is – '

'I know. Hello, Oliver. How's the arm?'

'Improving all the while. You're moving up fast, Gloria. Plain Inspector, in my time.'

'It happens.'

'And ... Bristow?'

'Transferred out. I guess he was persuaded to. We all think that, anyway. I mean, he didn't make too good a job of this case, six years ago. Clare Steadman went down ... but it wasn't a strong case. Too many leading questions. Casts doubts.'

'And *you're* doubtful?' Oliver asked.

'Shall we say ... I'd hope to do better with the same facts. He never covered the question of the third shot.'

'The shot at nothing?' I asked, just to show that I knew what they were talking about.

'That one. It was never explained.'

'If there *was* an explanation.'

'Oh,' put in Oliver, 'you haven't been introduced. Detective Superintendent Gloria Vosper. And you know this is Phil.'

She looked at me blandly, but I had the impression that those grey eyes were searching around right inside my head, poaching my brain.

'I think there *was* a third shot,' she said at last. 'Always thought so. I mean – why would she invent one?'

I said nothing. Her eyes slid sideways to Oliver again.

'Do *you* know, Oliver?'

'Not really. Clare's a strange woman.'

'So I gather. And now, I discover from Inspector Green, there's a gun missing.'

So Charlie was an inspector.

'He'll never live it down,' I suggested. 'He couldn't have *lost* one?'

'Oh no. But he ought to have checked the inventory. Now we have an unexplained third shot and a missing gun. How very interesting.'

Then she compressed her lips into a straight line, and it was only from the eager twinkle in her eyes that I realised she was actually anticipating that she was going to enjoy this new murder. And I didn't think she was viewing it objectively and only as a puzzle, but rather that she so desperately wanted – had to have – the arrest of the killer of Sergeant Alice Purslowe. It was a special challenge, and arose from a personal fondness.

'Now,' she said, 'I need to talk to you, Philipa Lowe. Only one L in that, is there? Right. I knew your father, so I know that I don't have to tell you the rules and regulations. This is an informal talk, otherwise I'd have somebody with me. If I switch this thing on ...' She indicated what had to be a tape recorder in her breast pocket. 'It's only my method of taking notes. Later, it'll be on paper. Any objections?'

'Not one.'

'Very well.'

She switched it on, and in that instant everything changed. She became intensely and inflexibly professional, though nothing in her face reflected that. It was an interview, nothing more, and I had to be scavenged for facts.

'Here?' she asked.

'Why not?'

And there it was, in the middle of the lawn.

10

I was aware, as I braced myself – why was I bracing myself? – that someone was watching us. I half turned. It was Ralph Purslowe, standing quietly in a far corner of the lawn, standing like a planted rock, waiting. He would have been excluded from all aspects of the investigation, and was poised now, watching his senior officer, waiting for any indication that she might need something, anything at all, which he might be able to supply, from a match for her cigarette to sharpening her pencil – or changing the batteries in her recorder. Waiting for anything at all not official with which he might further the investigation without, in any way, intruding in it. I wondered whether she was aware of his presence.

'Now,' she said. 'Your name is Philipa Lowe? One L in the Philipa.'

'Actually it's Evengeline Philipa Lowe. My mother's name, the first one.'

'Yes. And what are you doing here? You live ... where?'

'Penley. Just outside. Hawthorne Cottage, Oliver knows.'

'And you came here – '

'To look at the place, this morning.' And heavens, all this had happened in one day!

'The morning Clare Steadman returned.' She nodded to herself. 'A coincidence?'

'Not entirely. She's been out of Benfield over a week – on licence, I believe, touring around. She phoned the estate agent and heard I'd got the keys to look around the place – so she drove home. I don't think she intended to sell it, anyway. It was all a gesture. She's like that.'

'I know.'

'You can't tell when she's lying and when she's not, or even if it's just a bit of fun or serious, or if she might even be lying to herself and really believes it – or really wants to. You know...'

'Yes, I know. But you're still here. Why didn't you just back out, when she turned up, and drive away?'

'I don't know. Yes, I do. I was intrigued by the circumstances of the murder. Harris Steadman's murder. Oliver had told me about it.'

Behind my shoulder, I heard Oliver make a little sound, but he knew better than to intrude.

'What, in particular, intrigued you?'

'The third shot. The shot at nothing, which you've mentioned.'

'Why did that, in particular, intrigue you?'

'Because it *was* at nothing.'

'You don't know that.'

'Nobody's produced anything that was shot at,' I pointed out.

'Harris Steadman was shot at – from about five feet.'

'Ah yes, but that was the second shot, the killing one.'

'Clare's second shot?' she asked, raising her eyebrows.

'I don't think so. Not Clare's. I'm certain it wasn't. What do you think?'

'I'm not here about Harris Steadman's death.'

'But both the killings are related. Harris's and Alice Carter's. Don't you think so, Superintendent?'

'No.' She smiled thinly. 'And I'm the one who's asking the questions. May I continue?'

'Certainly.'

She flicked a glance at Oliver, a glance that said: where did you find this one?

'Thank you. And why are you still intrigued?'

'Because of the set-up. This lawn here, the gunroom there, the thunderstorm, the fact that only Clare could've done it, on the face of it, when I'm certain she didn't.'

'And why are you so certain?'

'If she'd been guilty she'd have invented a second shot, and said she'd heard it, but she had to be prompted. Then she mentioned *two* other shots, instead of just that one. Why would she have done that, unless she was innocent? It didn't make sense.'

'There's no necessity for you to make sense of it,' she observed. Then she turned. 'Ralph – why don't you rustle up some tea? A big pot and four mugs.'

Like a flash he burst into action, darting for the open french windows. It seemed that all the shot-guns were now inside, but Clare hadn't yet finished with Inspector Charlie Green and his men. 'No – not like that. Oh, you fool, not the Remington with the

Winchester. And never mind the dates. I tell you, they're both 1901. Why can't you listen!' It was one continuous outpouring of anger.

'Shall we sit on the edge of the terrace?' the superintendent suggested. 'They seem to have finished running in and out.'

That was what we did. Neither Oliver nor I mentioned that we'd recently had tea. She continued.

'Though of course, I can see', as though there'd been no break, 'that you would want to make some sense of it, if only for Oliver's benefit.'

We were sitting with our legs dangling, me with the super on one side, Oliver on the other. He leaned forward. 'What was that?'

'I'm talking to Miss Lowe. Please don't interrupt. Wasn't it because the third shot might have been invented as an alibi for Oliver's benefit, as he was with her at the time?' she asked me, smiling.

'That thought crossed my mind.'

'It wouldn't please you. No. It wouldn't please you that he needed an alibi at all.'

I said nothing to that.

'Would it?'

'Sorry. Was it a question?'

'It was.'

'Well, no. It didn't please me.'

'Was that why you were so determined to look for an answer?'

'I thought we'd covered that.'

'Wasn't it the main reason?'

'I suppose you could say that.' I hesitated. 'But of course, he didn't need an alibi.'

'Didn't he? My impression was that he did. But after all, that was an alibi only for the third shot – and it could've been conjured up in Clare's active mind. It was no alibi for the second shot, the one that killed Harris.'

'Now listen here ... which crime are you supposed to be investigating?'

'I've told you that I don't answer questions. I ask them.'

I shrugged. 'Ask on, then.'

'Why did you go to see Madame Acarti?'

'I knew she was Woman Sergeant Alice Carter, and Ralph said she wanted to see me.'

'Did he say why?'

'No. You'll have asked him that, surely.'

'I did. He said he thought you might have some information for her.'

'Well – I hadn't. We talked a little, but to no good effect.'

'You milking her for information – she milking you?' She looked up. 'Ah – thank you, Ralph. Put it down there. You can be mother.'

But he *was* a father, I realised, shocked at the realisation. Two children, he had said, no doubt being minded for the day by friends, neighbours ... and he had to go home and tell them their mother was dead! I was suddenly overcome by such a flood of grief and sympathy that I couldn't answer the superintendent's question. Couldn't even remember it.

'I asked', she said severely, 'whether you and she were swapping information.'

'You could say that,' I whispered.

'*You* say it. What information were you reaching for, Miss Lowe?'

Oliver's hand touched my arm. I didn't know whether it was a warning. If it was, I ignored it.

'We were talking about women in the district who'd had a pregnancy, probably terminated, at around the time of Harris Steadman's death.'

She turned away to accept a cup of tea from Ralph. Clare, apparently, didn't have mugs. She sipped it. 'Good,' she said. 'You've remembered I don't take sugar.' Beyond her, Ralph mouthed: Milk and sugar? I nodded. Oliver nodded. They were handed over. The cups rattled in the saucers. I realised I'd have to be looking for a bathroom soon.

'What?' she asked over the rim of her cup. 'What's a pregnancy got to do with it?'

'From what Clare told me, that was what their grand row was about. He wanted money from Clare to send away a woman he'd got pregnant, to have a quiet abortion.'

'Did *she* want one – this woman?'

'I don't think her wishes were explored. I don't think he was necessarily telling the truth. I don't think Clare was necessarily telling the truth about Harris's lies. I don't know anything – not for a fact.'

'And your visit to the sergeant was useless?'

'Yes. Nothing serious was mentioned. Nothing that anybody eavesdropping could possibly think to be serious. Nothing that would have required me to be stabbed in the back.'

'You?' she asked gently.

So I told her about the switched chairs. I also said that we had discussed nothing to provoke a violent response – in order to shut my mouth. And that the fact of the knife having been taken there implied a planned attack, so it must have been provoked by some circumstance arising before I went anywhere near the tent.

She twisted her lips at that. At no time had she been pushing me or leading me. But she didn't like what I was saying.

'And do you know what circumstance could have necessitated your death?'

I realised then that I was to blame for Alice Carter's death, to blame for having taken the wrong chair, to blame for having taken the danger into Alice Carter's sphere. At that moment I found myself desperately trying to suppress a flood of hot tears. I could do no more than shake my head.

'Would you say it, please?'

'I can only guess that I've found out some information that I don't at the moment appreciate. Some passing remark. Please. Is that all for now? Or shall I say out loud, for the benefit of your blasted tape, that the subject broke down in tears?'

'Phil?' said Oliver softly, worriedly, which really provoked them.

The superintendent got to her feet. Ridiculously, I registered the fact that she'd left half her tea.

Oliver had his arm round my shoulders when she paused. I looked up, the image blurred, but she didn't wish to speak to me.

'Oliver,' she said, 'you'd better not leave her side.'

'I've got to go to the bathroom,' I choked.

'Then he'll have to stand outside, won't he?'

She left. I thought miserably that she hadn't advised me to leave the district. She had wanted me within reach. Ralph Purslowe, after a bleak grimace at Oliver, trailed miserably after her.

Then I buried my head in Oliver's shoulder and finally wildly wept. He bent close, my hair in his mouth. 'You'll feel better, Phil.' And, bless him, he added, 'I've seen big, tough men weeping.'

After a while I straightened, put my hands to my hair, though it's resilient and holds itself together well, sniffed, and said, 'I'll need to do some repair work, and I've left my bag in the car. I'll have to pop back and fetch it.'

'No,' he said. '*We'll* go and fetch it.'

We took the longer route around the house. My BMW was even more firmly blocked in, a batch of motor bikes being arranged in front of it.

'We'll never get home,' I said.

'Glenn and his mates could get it out.' He said this in a persuasive voice, almost wistfully.

'I want to see the fireworks.'

Which was true, though he knew it was no more than an excuse. But I felt we were so very near a solution, and I couldn't walk – or drive – away from it.

I fumbled for the keys in my slacks pocket, jingled them in my hand, and bent to the lock.

'Oliver.' I cleared my throat. 'Oliver, look at this.'

I was indicating the edge of the door. There were abrasions to the paintwork. I hadn't had the car long, and I'd run up no more than about a thousand miles.

'Some rotten devil's scratched my car!' I cried, furious.

'Wait.' He took the keys from my fingers, then he peered through the windows, walking round to make sure. 'Nothing disturbed, that I can see.' He crouched down on the grass and ' squinted underneath.

'Looking for bombs?' I asked, feeling hysterical.

He straightened. 'Checking for oil drips. Your brakes.'

Then he stood over me, looking down into my face. There was more than concern in his expression, an anger, a determination.

'What *is* it, Oliver?'

'Somebody's tried to get in your car. The old bit of bent wire trick, running it down the door gap. But the BMW's got a sunken lock, so it didn't work. So they went away. A rank amateur.'

'But what does it *mean*?'

He shook his head, not indicating a lack of understanding, but refusing to accept what he saw in it.

'Open the door, Phil. Your bag's still on the seat.'

'If you think it's safe.'

'I'm sure nobody got in.'

I opened the door. The lock operated as normal. Quickly, I hunted through my bag, but as far as I could see everything was there.

Oliver was still watching me thoughtfully when I closed the door and locked it.

'I was wrong, wasn't I?' He took my arm as we walked away.

'In what way?' I was completely confused.

'I thought ... once we could get away from here you'd be safe. But now I'm not sure. I believe ... it's the only thing I can see ...

I think somebody wanted to look in your bag, and the only reason for that ... well, wouldn't it be for your address?'

I stopped in mid-stride. 'You mean, they'd follow me?'

'Anybody who'd take such a risk as stabbing a person in a wide-open field in daylight, with a thousand people around ... they must be very desperate, or afraid, or completely unfeeling. If it's *that* important, then they might have in mind the necessity of following you home.'

I stood there, looking up into his face, bleak and dangerous. My voice wasn't strong. 'You mean this, don't you?'

He said nothing. We went on walking, back round the house.

'We could go home, Oliver, if that's what you want. If you think we ought to. And make sure nobody follows us.'

'Aren't you forgetting ...' Was his anger aimed at me? 'You gave your address to the superintendent. On that lawn with the french windows open, and with God alone knows how many people within hearing, the other side of that hedge.'

'Oh!' I missed a step and nearly stumbled. 'So what *do* we do?'

I had been keenly anticipating the sunset, looking forward with pleasure to the fireworks. Now a sudden dread of the darkness was like a shiver all through me, and my skin felt tight over my cheekbones.

'We try to find the truth before it gets dark.' He didn't sound optimistic. 'And you, Phil – and I can't help you with this – you'd better track back through your memory for something you've heard or seen or mentioned. Something that's frightening somebody.'

'A fat chance ...'

Then, without collusion, we were each silent as we found our way back to the lawn. We were within hearing distance of the house. I turned. The sun was sinking towards the west, behind the house. Another ... how long? ... less than an hour, and it would be sunset.

Clare was standing on the terrace. She had found time to change, and was wearing different slacks, a blouse, and a Fair Isle cardigan. Now, prompted, I felt cooler around my shoulders.

'There's a cardigan in the car, Oliver.'

'Shall we go back for it?'

'No. It doesn't matter.'

It had to be even darker under the shroud of those trees. Those pretty lights hadn't been lit.

142

We climbed the steps to the terrace. Clare, now alone, seemed pleased with herself, comfortably complacent.

'They're all back,' she said, a quiver in her voice from excitement. 'All my guns. And oh – it's so wonderful to see it again as it was. I've waited ...' She didn't tell us about the waiting.

'All but one,' I reminded her.

'I'll have to start looking round for another Darne. It will have to be exactly the same model – a sliding breech job. And they're so rare!' That they were rare seemed to boost her. The challenge of the pursuit flushed her cheeks. Or it could have been the sun, verging into the warm end of the spectrum. Nevertheless, she crossed her arms and hugged herself.

'A bathroom?' I asked.

'Oh yes. It's right opposite that room I showed you. You're staying for the fireworks, I suppose.'

'That seems likely. I expect you'll be able to watch from here.'

'Well, yes. It seems the best place.'

I paused, and turned back. 'Did you arrange all this, Clare, from your prison cell?'

'Oh yes.' She dismissed it as a trifle. 'I wrote to Glenn ... oh, he's been simply marvellous. I knew, weeks ago, the date I'd be released. So I contacted Glenn – he came to see me. Wasn't that good of him! He agreed to fix it up. He loves organising, and I gave him a free hand with the finances. I said ... I picked today. The fête, too. To fit in. I hadn't forgotten that. Hasn't it all turned out splendidly?'

'Marred only by the small matter of a murder,' I said quietly.

She clamped a hand to her mouth. 'Oh lordy-me ... and it'd completely slipped my mind. So much to do ... How silly of me! You must think me terribly unfeeling.'

Oh no, not unfeeling. She was packed full with bubbling emotion. The fact was, though, that it was all turned inwards, *her* gratification, *her* sorrows, *her* joys.

'Of course not, Clare,' I assured her. 'Your guns ... you've been so much involved, one way or another. Oh ... there was something I wanted to ask you. This morning, you told us you'd returned here, in a hurry, because you'd heard that the estate agent had handed out your keys. Now you tell me it was all planned ages ago, including the day of your return. It contradicts itself.'

'But I *did*.'

'Did what?'

'Come back this morning because I'd heard somebody had got

my keys. I'd planned it different from that – from what it's turned out to be.'

'In what way?' I was trying to sound casual, but I was determined to tie her down to something that wasn't hedged round and distorted by her inventive brain.

'Oh ...' she said, gesturing vaguely. 'You know. Not that stupid crush we ran into at the front. What I intended was ... me to drive back here, yes, but a bit later. Give them all time to get out and around the field – when everybody had arrived. You know...'

For once, she expected me to understand. Was there a hint of embarrassment? If so, it was alien to Clare's personality.

'I *don't* know, Clare.'

'You're not very bright, are you?' she asked severely, annoyed that I was pressing her. 'Walking down that slope, *that* was what I'd planned. Walking down all casual-like, pretending I was just another ordinary visitor, walking down to be lost amongst them. Then somebody seeing me, and the word going round. Like a fire in a gale. And swarming up towards me, welcoming, wanting to shake my hand, kiss my cheek. Welcoming.' She paused to take a deep breath, for the flush to fade from her cheeks.

'Clare?'

'Oh ... I didn't want that ridiculous crush. So degrading! You don't know – you can't imagine – what it's like. Shut away. Nobody who's really your friend. And in the background, waiting ... *this*'. She waved a hand majestically, embracing the whole scene. 'With this here, and me there, and all my local friends from far and wide ... waiting for me to arrive. I wanted it all, in one big slice. My home, my fields, my lake, my fête, my friends, all welcoming. Oh dear God ... and now you've got me all...'

She put both hands to her face, and I knew she was weeping. Clare was a woman with too much emotion compressed into that compact and vibrant body. She was a woman who could in no way control it. But the joys, the compassions and the distresses were her own. They did not extend beyond her compact aura.

'I'll leave you for a minute, Oliver,' I said, not looking at him.

'No, you won't. I'll be right outside the door.'

Clare looked at him fondly. 'You've got a good man there, Philipa,' she told me, as one who knew. 'Make sure you keep hold of him. Never let him go.'

Oliver said nothing. I felt his hand urgently on my elbow. We walked past her, through the gunroom – not pausing to admire the guns, also back home – and into the corridor.

'I don't know what you saw in her,' I said quietly.

He hadn't released my elbow. 'You know ... in the country of the blind.'

'One eye on your career, and the blind one for Clare?'

I left him to work that one out.

It was a guests' cloakroom, this one for the ladies. Oliver would have to find his own, or a hedge. No, not find the gents'; he was intending not to leave my side, which worked the other way round, too. A hedge it would have to be. The set-up in there was delicately correct, pale blue porcelain wash-basins, and those small individual cakes of soap, lavender perfumed, in their wrappings. One long mirror filled the facing wall, its glass tinted blue.

I had to suppose, this having been Mad Harry's creation, that the boys got the pink suite.

Josie Knight was washing her hands at one of the basins.

'Hello again,' I said. 'It's been quite a day.'

'That it has.' But she seemed repressed. 'Shocking, isn't it!'

'What?' Though I knew what she meant.

'That revolting stabbing. How *dare* they ruin the day!'

That seemed an original point of view.

'I don't imagine that would've been the intention,' I said mildly.

The hand-towels were beautifully soft, these in a darker blue, with an embroidered motif in the corners: CS.

'They could've done it somewhere else, couldn't they? Some other time. If somebody hated the woman ... oh, damn and blast it!'

'She had two children, Josie.'

'Oh dear lord!'

'And I don't think she was the intended target, anyway.'

'What d'you mean by that?' She gazed down at her soapy hands.

'I took the wrong chair. She had what should have been mine.'

Josie clamped her hands to her face. I hadn't had the impression that she'd intended to wash it. Her response was violent, but distorted.

'That's sheer bloody nonsense,' she burst out. 'Who'd want to kill you?'

'I don't know.'

'And why? Why, in heaven's name?'

Now her eyes were visible above her fingers. Perhaps she'd got soap in them; they were flooded with tears.

'I don't know.'

'Of course you know.'

I shrugged, and proceeded to wash my own face. I managed to say, 'I haven't the faintest idea.'

'You must have,' she persisted. She was drying her face, not paying attention to details. 'You'd know if somebody had got it in for you.'

'I know they have. I don't know why. Somebody I've offended deeply, something I've heard or seen, and it might suddenly mean something. Something relative to Harris's death. But I don't know what.'

I smoothed the towel gently over my cheeks. To myself, in the mirror, I looked pale and exhausted.

She was tidying herself in a desultory fashion, patting her hair into position, flexing her lips and running a finger along her eyebrows. She picked up her bag. Previously, I recalled, she had been wearing minimal make-up. She made no attempt to replace it.

'Well ...' she said. 'I'll see you again, perhaps.' Then, at the door and as though as an afterthought, she added, 'Look after yourself.'

I heard her make a small tense sound, no doubt at Oliver's presence at the door.

It didn't take me long to complete what I had to do. Like Josie, I'd never used much make-up. I did a quick job of it, suddenly longing to be at Oliver's side again. I'd paid special attention to my hands and arms. Somebody had cleaned off the blood, but I had to be certain. There were traces behind my nails. But I felt restored when I went out to Oliver.

'Josie was upset,' he said.

'Yes. I think she hadn't realised – about the murder. It was just a person who'd been killed, an incident. She hadn't realised that Alice Carter had two children. That brought it close to her.'

'Being a woman...'

'Not simply that. She'd said something earlier, about her relationship with Glenn. How long, she said, before he decided he didn't just want a wife, but a wife and children. Or words to that effect.'

He paused as we reached the gunroom door. 'Meaning – she can't have any?'

'That was how I took it.'

'Yes. Poor Josie, then.'

He reached for the door handle. I put my hand on his wrist. 'Just a second, Oliver, please.'

'What's the matter?'

'It's just – this was the door that was locked, wasn't it?'

'On the night of the storm, yes.'

'There's still the question of how she got in, Oliver. If it *was* locked.'

'There's the evidence of the smashed table – bits all over the floor, where you're standing. That seems to indicate it was locked. If you look closely, you'll even be able to see the dents she put in the surface.'

'I'm sure I would. But *was* it locked? I mean – we're getting to know Clare and her truths and untruths.'

'She said it was locked.'

'So how could she have got in?'

'She claimed she hadn't got in.'

'If she was lying, and it was unlocked . . .'

'She said it was locked,' he repeated stubbornly. 'She was so confident it was still locked when she got back in the house that she didn't even trouble to try it. So she said.'

'Yet it was unlocked when *you* tried it.'

'That's true.' He looked at me with a slight smile. It might have been me hammering at an oak door.

'Put it another way, then, Oliver. How did your lot maintain she got in?'

'I thought I'd told you this. The super reckoned that Harris must have unlocked it himself, when he realised he was seriously hurt.'

'I just can't accept that. He'd be in shock. Wouldn't know *what* he was doing. I can visualise him staggering back and slumping against the wall. But managing to unlock a door, no. Unlocking it during the gun-throwing session? But he didn't have time – and Clare would've seen him do it, surely.'

'But Phillie, sweetheart, it was unlocked when we got here.'

'Then perhaps it never was locked. Don't forget, that's Clare's story, and you know how much credence you've got to put on that. In any event, somebody must have got in, because he *was* shot. So . . .'

I shrugged in dismissal, and left it at that.

'So why not ask her?' he suggested, grinning.

I had no objection to that. The only difficulty involved would be to tie her down to the truth. Small chance of that, I thought, unless we had the time to pull out a few nails. Toes first, or fingers?

I was still making a decision when Oliver opened the door, and we walked in.

Clare was closing the french windows. She turned on hearing us.

'Ah – there you are. I thought we ought to have a talk.'

11

'I thought so, too,' I said.

I left it there, indicating that I was waiting for her to take the lead. There was something about her, an aura, that led me to hesitate. In some way I couldn't tie down she was different. In this room – her special room – surrounded by her lovely, lovely guns, she had acquired more confidence, as though their potential for violence offered something to her, a resilience. She was now, and at last, her own person, restored to her rightful place.

'I think I must ask you to leave,' she said flatly.

'I can't do that. My car's blocked in. And anyway, you suggested we should stay for the fireworks.'

'I can change my mind, can't I!'

'The car's still blocked in.'

'A snap of the fingers . . .' She illustrated, throwing it at the air. 'And I could produce a gang of men who could lift it out.'

'And if I refuse?'

It wasn't that I was feeling stubborn, just that I wanted to understand this sudden change in attitude.

'Another snap. You're forgetting that there are gangs of police all over the place.'

'But not to do your bidding, Clare. Try it, and I think you'll discover that's so.'

Oliver made a supporting noise.

'You're trespassing,' she declared.

'You've asked me to leave – so I suppose I am. I think that's the law.' But nevertheless, I managed to sound confident. 'All right, sue me for trespass. It'd be difficult, seeing you've thrown the whole place open to the public. But you could try it – though you'd have to produce some damage I've done, to back it up.'

'Damage!' she cried, allowing herself a theatrical fling of her arms. 'Hasn't it been nothing but damage, ever since you've arrived here?'

'I wouldn't say that.'

'Another murder! Isn't that damage?'

A killing on the day she left the house, under arrest, another on the day she returned! I thought she had a viable reason for being upset. The only trouble with that argument was that she was not upset. Angry, imperious, distraught, yes. But not upset.

Oliver spoke at last. He'd been leaving it to me, nervous of taking sides. 'It was aimed at Phil, Clare, that murder. There was a mistake.'

I watched as her eyes became blank. It was a new proposition, and she had to think it through. At last ... 'I can't believe that.' She said it with a toss of her head.

Oliver produced his soothing, no-nonsense voice. 'The police seem satisfied that the knife was intended for Philipa, Clare. Not for the sergeant.'

'All the same ... that's as good a reason as any for her to leave, then.' She nodded to herself at this rationalisation.

'So that if I'm to be murdered, you'd prefer it to be elsewhere?' I asked.

'Naturally.'

'But if I was killed anywhere else,' I said patiently, 'it would still come back here, Clare. Because the necessity for it is here. So wouldn't it be better for me to stay here until I've got at the truth?'

'You?' She dismissed that possibility.

I pressed on, ignoring her interruption of scorn. 'Then I'll be safe, and you'd be able to sigh with relief.'

'You're playing with words, Philipa Lowe,' she claimed. 'Using them for your own ends.'

I tried to smile at her, but it came out more like a grin. 'Then I'd expect your understanding, Clare. Isn't that what you're always doing?'

'That's a lie!'

'No, it's not. You've been doing it from the moment we first met. Right up to and including now. Making an impression.'

'That is not so.'

'You as good as told me, yourself. Isn't that what lies are for, Clare – for yourself and your damned childish ego that demands that everybody should think you're marvellous? The bee's knees, as my father used to say. The whole façade's empty and false. You lie and you lie, in order to hide any truth you might find distasteful or unflattering. Or frightening. You don't need much of an excuse: you lie, if only to keep in practice. From the moment we first met – '

'Will you be silent!' she shouted. The walls rang with it; the cabinets quivered; the guns stiffened at the shock.

I was silent, smiling at her now, waiting. Oliver cleared his throat. I prayed he was not about to intrude. There was just a chance – a slim chance – that I might have trapped her into the truth, for once. I'd been reaching for the correct mood.

She moistened her lips. 'All right!' Her head jerked up in challenge. 'Tell me one lie I've told. Prove it was a lie ... but you can't. I bet you can't.'

For a second she'd slipped back to her childhood, and taken me with her.

'Bet what?' I challenged. 'A glarnie and five oncers?'

'What?'

'Didn't you play marbles, Clare?'

'There was nobody I could play marbles with,' she said in a flat voice, and a small tragedy peeped out at me. Had her craving for attention been born then?

'I'm sorry. I shouldn't have said ...' I jerked my hand, angry with myself. 'Your lies, Clare ... wasn't it all a lie, what you told the police about Harris's death?'

She perched herself on the edge of the table. Another of her multiple personae was taking charge: the casual Clare, the relaxed Clare, too bored to trouble with lies.

'Not much of it,' she said, her mind searching back. 'It's as I told it. We had the row, he locked me out of this room, and he threw my guns out on to the lawn. All truth – or as close as they deserved.'

'But not the truth, that you actually threw the guns back?'

'I told *you* the truth about that – it cancels it out.' She was almost laughing at me.

'But only because I'd tried it with that damned wellie.'

'Yes – that's so,' she conceded. 'But it *was* the truth.'

All right, so accept that I'd got her round to some element of truth. But she was still allowing herself the luxury of an evasion or two. I let that go.

'And the row with Harris?' I asked. 'Was *that* the truth, as you told it earlier?'

'Oh yes.'

'That you virtually shouted it in his face – that he was sterile?'

She grimaced. 'If you want to get down to brass tacks – words to that effect.'

'And true that he told you he wanted the money to procure an abortion?'

151

'He knew that would hurt me.'

'And true that you followed him into the hall and shouted at him...'

'I didn't say that.'

'Didn't you? I seem to remember that you did. But you were so furious and distraught that you *would* have done that. It was, I could claim, a lie by omission.'

She gave me a tiny smile – one that got away before she could trap it, when she really wanted to sound angry. 'It's not good enough to earn you a glarnie and two oncers, whatever those are.'

'Conceded,' I said. 'But how... and you realise I'm trying to get a true picture here, Clare... how, if you followed him all the way to the door of this room, did you give him the chance of getting in here and shutting you out?'

I was taking it step by step. Only in that way, indicating that I intended to pick her up on every detail, could I expect to extract anything acceptable.

'D'you think I hadn't got that in mind?' she demanded. 'Hadn't he said something about my guns might as well be like him, shut out in the cold? Oh no, I wasn't going to let him get in here, with me locked out.'

This was new to me, and the way she was nodding to herself in self-congratulation indicated it was a truth she could claim with some pride.

'But he *did* get in here,' I said.

'Yes. But you see – I knew the key was on the outside of the door, and the door locked, because I'd left it like that. So I intended to reach past him and grab the key. Intended. But it wasn't there. Not any more, it wasn't. And before I knew what he was up to he'd opened the door, slid in, slammed the door in my face, and I heard the lock being turned over.'

I was watching her with fascination, this new Clare, this truthful Clare. An expression almost of shame was distorting her face. Shame at telling the truth, or shame at allowing herself to admit it? I couldn't be sure. All I knew was that it *was* the truth – or very close to it.

'So you then proceeded to smash a small table against the door?'

Minimally, she shrugged. 'I had to smash something.'

I knew the feeling. She was standing there now, having slid off the table, her eyes fixed on me, her chin raised in an attitude of challenge, and I found I couldn't take it on further. Abruptly, my mind had gone chasing away, trying to capture a thought, an idea, that I knew was important. For several moments, it eluded me – then I had it. It was necessary to examine it...

'Phil?' said Oliver.

'Oh ... yes ... sorry.'

But I had never given concentrated thought to this so-called locked door. I had simply not accepted it. Clearly, the jury had been of the same mind, as the door hadn't been locked when the police arrived, and it was really too much to have expected Harris himself to have unlocked it. Not before he started throwing the guns, not during the throwing, not after the shot through the glass. So the jury had accepted that it had not been locked at all, and I'd followed suit.

But now ... This was a new, circumstantial and graphic description that Clare had produced. It had the clear ring of truth. The door had been locked on the inside. The proposition called for an entirely fresh appraisal.

'Phil?' said Oliver again. He was no doubt worrying about the state of my mind.

'Sorry. Just a thought.' I returned my attention to Clare. 'But don't you see, Clare, that if it *was* locked – this door here – with the key inside – '

'I'm telling you that it was.' She nodded. An item of truth had been hurled at me, and she was pleased with the reaction. With a nod, she now hitched herself back on the edge of the table.

'Then *nobody* could have got in here and shot him,' I told her. 'Not in by way of the french windows, because they were jammed, and not through the door because it was locked.'

'Somebody did shoot him, though.' She nodded emphatically. There was almost a childish glee that she'd found something – and a truth, into the bargain – that had thrown me.

'But the police claimed that *you* managed to do it.'

'Tcha!'

'And was the door still locked when you came back into the house, from round the front?'

'How do I know? I didn't even try it, just assumed it still was.'

I paused. Then I went on, 'Did you tell the police what you've just told me – that little detail about following him to the door with the intention of grabbing the key?'

She shrugged elaborately. 'What would've been the point?'

'The point was ...' I found I was shouting, and moderated my voice. 'The point is that it indicates you were telling the truth about it.'

'Of *course* I was telling the truth.'

I didn't comment on that. She so annoyed me that I felt like slapping her in the face and walking out of there. I had to content myself with a sigh.

'But Clare ... don't you see ... if the door was locked *then*, and was unlocked when the police arrived, that could've happened in only one way. You have to think in terms of where the key was – inside. In other words, it would've had to be opened from the inside, and as Harris was in no condition to have done it, then there must have been somebody else in that room with him. And it was that person who unlocked the door.'

Oliver gave a long sigh of relief. He saw this as a major breakthrough. Clare completely ruined the impact, though.

'Don't you think I realised that? Oh – you *are* slow, Philipa.'

'Realised it ...' I glanced at Oliver. His face was expressionless. 'And realising that, you shouted at him through the door that he was a sterile bastard, and he could go and tell that to his pregnant bitch?'

'Words', she said, 'to that effect. If you want the full truth, it'd take me quite a while to remember every precious word I threw at him.'

'Knowing somebody was in there ... here? What good could that have done?'

'Good! I wanted to do bad. It'd flash around the district – Harris Steadman couldn't get a mouse pregnant. Shame him ... that was what I wanted.'

You just couldn't tell, with Clare. Either she was very clever, or very stupid. Harris had already been basking in exactly the opposite reputation.

'So tell me', I ventured, testing her story, 'how you knew Harris had somebody in here with him.'

She smiled at me in a most condescending manner. 'But my dear, you don't know him. He *never* came home and then straight into here, to leave his gun. And he never went into the kitchen to leave his coat where it could drip. Oh no. Not Harris. And it was obvious that he *had* come in here – straight in here when he got home – because the key was on the inside of the lock. This side. And I knew I'd left it on the outside. So it was common sense. Slovenly, he was. He would always dump his jacket and his gun on the hallstand – leave it for me to tidy up after him. For me to clean and oil his gun.'

'You did *that*? Clean his gun...'

'He knew I couldn't let a gun hang around, all wet and fouled.'

'All right.' I was hurrying on, now, as I clearly had her in a truthful mood. Every word had struck home. 'All right, so they were there on the hallstand...'

'So I knew,' she said, nodding, a tiny complacent smile on her lips. 'I knew the moment I saw the key had been changed from outside the door to inside. That he'd brought somebody back with him. And that he didn't want us to meet. The Barbour jacket and the gun on the hallstand – they only confirmed it. And there they were, when I ran out the front.'

'Bloody hell!' I heard Oliver whisper. I trod back on his toe, to warn him not to interrupt.

Then I tried to pretend that all this was of only a casual interest. 'But you didn't tell the police that?'

She shrugged. 'It was irrelevant. Can't you just imagine it! He owed somebody money. He'd say, "Come back with me – I'll get it out of Clare. And if she won't cash up, you can take a gun or two." So they'd go straight to the gunroom, here, quietly, Harris and this Tom, Dick or Harry or whatever, and Harris would say, "Don't make a sound." Then he'd go in to me – but he already knew I wasn't going to be signing a cheque for him. I'd told him. The last one *was* the last. So he just had to make a scene. He was like that – had to work himself into a fury, as a kind of self-justification. Does that make sense?'

'It makes sense. But Clare, the police ought to have been told.'

'Of *course* not! That friend of his didn't come into it. He'd have been off and away across the lawn ... with my Darne in his grubby hands. Like a flash. *Now* I know it. Then, I didn't, because I didn't know at that time that a gun was missing. What chance'd I got to check on the guns – that night? Oh, Philipa, talk sense.'

I glanced round at Oliver, who stood stolidly at my shoulder. He raised his eyebrows. I shook my head, more to clear it than to keep him quiet. Then I returned my attention to Clare.

'So it wasn't a complete surprise to find your collection was a gun short?'

She hesitated a fraction. 'No. If I'm telling the truth, I suppose I might as well tell the lot. I only guessed it, till I went to see the guns. Why d'you think I was so anxious to get it done?'

'But you'd had time. You'd been out more than a week. That doesn't sound to me like being anxious.'

'Oh, don't keep pouncing on every word I say, Philipa. I kept putting it off because I didn't want to face it alone. I could've been wrong ... all the time ... wrong about assuming he had a friend in here, who'd taken a gun away. I – sort of – couldn't face the disappointment, if I'd been wrong.' She explained this simply, like a child caught in a disdemeanour. 'But you turned up here, you and Oliver, and Oliver knew his way around there, where they'd got my guns. I've always been so sure Harris had given one away. Certain. But if he hadn't ... Anyway, as you know, it turned out all right. I just wish it hadn't been the Darne.'

She seemed restless even now, having to put it into words, not being certain of her own reactions at that time. She was more insecure than I'd suspected, still not having recaptured her proper place in life.

'I could've killed him,' she said reflectively.

'Who? Charlie Green?'

'Harris. If he'd been around now, I could've killed him.'

'So *that* was the third shot – your Darne.' I hadn't really accepted that third shot.

'Must have been.'

'You *did* genuinely hear a third shot?'

'I told you that. I did.'

'But possibly you were in your lying mood at the time.' I looked round at Oliver again, and spoke to him quietly. 'Is that how you see it, Oliver? This person, he hung around outside for a while, possibly to watch the fun. Then, when it seemed to be over, he fired a single shot. That would've been intended as a signal to Harris that he'd got clear away.'

'Clear away?'

'The police arriving on the scene. *You* turned up, Oliver.'

'Ah yes. But ... watched the fun? Watched the throwing and the shot at the glass?'

'Possibly. But he wouldn't realise exactly what'd happened. Yes. I can see that. And he'd say nothing, because he'd discover later that there'd been a murder here.'

'You can bet he'd keep his head down,' he agreed.

I turned back to Clare. 'But don't you realise', I asked her, 'that if you'd said all this to the police they'd have had a thorough go at Harris's shooting friends, and if they'd traced one who'd just acquired a new gun there'd have been *some* evidence to back up your story.'

She slid down from the table and took up a stance she intended to be seen as dignified, though it rested on her insecurely.

'For every question,' she said coolly, 'I answered with the truth.

156

And how could this person, who must have been off and away the moment Harris opened the french windows, have seen *anything* of the actual murder? Talk sense, please, if you're going to talk at all. *That* came after it was all over, the throwing and the scrambling and the shutting of the french windows again.'

'And also, of course, you'd have to bear in mind that this mystery person might have noticed you taking your shot-gun round to the front with you – and then you'd have had no leg to stand on at all. So you said nothing. It was probably for the best.'

But she was unshakeable. She shook her head, even managing a wry smile. 'He'd have seen I didn't.'

'Then he'd have been useful to you as a witness.' Was she stupid, or something?

'No, he wouldn't. They couldn't have tied him down. D'you think he'd ever have admitted to having the Darne? And I can tell you they're so rare he couldn't have claimed it as his own. Not him. He'd act dumb and innocent. It would've been theft, after all.'

So it had been. It had robbed Clare of one sliding-breech Darne and five, nearly six, years of her life.

I felt weak and empty, and lost. There seemed to be no way in which I could understand this woman, who appeared to be able to wriggle through a maze of self-contradictions and evasions in order to reach a situation satisfactory to herself – to her under-standing of herself. I sighed.

'But don't you see, Clare, you've now just about admitted that you, yourself, callously killed Harris, because there's only you left who could possibly have done it.'

'If you say so.' She shrugged elaborately. 'It doesn't matter now, so I don't see why you can't drop it. Drop it and go away.' This last was said in a sharp and bitter voice.

'But it does matter. Oh ... you're so damned thick! You're down in the Big Book as the murderer of Harris Steadman. Yes, I know you're out on licence. But only on licence. There're inconvenient and difficult things involved. Reporting regularly – you'll prob-ably not be able to hold a passport ... Oh, I don't know it all. But you're not *free*, Clare. Your conviction still stands. There has to be an answer to it all. Give me time, and I'll find it for you.'

She was staring at me with contempt. 'As though all that matters.'

'To you, to the whole community, it matters. Especially to the real murderer, it matters. You *have* to be shown positively as innocent.'

'No, I don't. I'd lose my standing in the community. Oh no – no thanks.' This she said with fierce possessiveness.

I wanted to grab her shoulders and shake her till her teeth rattled. For long moments we stared at each other, she with a smile of superiority glowing all over her face, and me with heaven knows what.

'To hell with you then!' I burst out.

The shortest route out of her house – out of that gunroom – was by way of the french windows. I walked over to them, my legs stiff, and flung open the right-hand one. Then I was out on the terrace.

Oliver was at my side. He said, 'We'll have to hand this information over to Superintendent Vosper, Phil.'

'What information? Clare would either deny she said it, or wrap it all up in pretty words and obscure it.'

I stood there, hugging myself, my arms crossed. The sun was going down, and it felt distinctly cooler. Here, we were in the shade.

'Do we have to care?' he asked softly.

'Yes, of course we do.'

I led him away from Clare's hearing, to the far end of the terrace. 'You're forgetting something, aren't you, Oliver!'

'Am I? What?'

'The visitor . . . it all explains where the Darne went to, and puts it neatly out of the way as far as we're concerned. And it explains the locked door that wasn't locked, and how that came about. Possibly. But Oliver – remember? *You* were on the possible suspect list.'

'You're talking nonsense.'

'No! I have it from Ralph Purslowe, and I suspect that you were dropped off the suspect list *only* because of the gunroom door being possibly locked. Now we know it wasn't locked, and we know who could have unlocked it – except that we'd never be able to place a name to him. But it puts you right slap bang in the middle . . .'

'This is ridiculous. As though they'd take that up, after all this time.'

'But Clare might. Clare *would*. If it amuses her.'

He stared at me fixedly for a moment, then he gave a small, choked laugh. 'Nonsense!' he said flatly.

'It is *not* nonsense.' I nearly stamped a foot. 'To her it's logical and sensible, and she's a dangerous woman.'

'*Now* what're you saying? Really . . . Phillie!'

'If Clare suspects . . . if she actually allows herself to believe you

158

killed Harris, that would mean you deliberately planted the murder on her. How many times do I have to hammer it into your head...'

He considered me gravely for a few moments, his eyes empty of any emotion. 'Let's go and see if we can get your car out, Phil.'

'What d'you mean? We can't just run...'

'If I'm in such danger, we'd better go running, and fast.' He tilted his head at me.

'Don't you take that attitude with me.'

'It's all been too much for you, Phil.'

'Damn you, Oliver, don't be so bloody insulting.'

'Now we've got some anonymous person who's supposed to have unlocked that door. But not to get out of there. Oh no. For the specific purpose of involving me – according to you. And he must've done that in a fully lit room with the windows wide open and Clare able to see the back of the room – and she wouldn't have noticed this stranger? The whole thing's just stupid.'

'Will you please ... stop!'

'And on top of that,' he went on, at full steam like that tractor down in the field, 'firing a farewell shot from out in the night somewhere. To tell Harris he'd got clean away? Choff!'

It is difficult to put into one word the full dismissive contempt that Oliver managed to convey. It was like a slap in the face.

'Sometimes', I said heavily, though feeling I would prefer to shout it, 'you can be very stupid, Oliver. Don't you realise ... we're both now in danger.'

His smile was sympathetic. 'You'd make a lousy wife, I'll tell you that. I can see where my danger really lies.'

I turned away from him. 'I'm not sure I want to marry you,' I said coldly. 'What use'll you be if they give you a life sentence?'

'Phil!' He tried to put his arm round my shoulders.

I shrugged him off. For a few moments he was silent. I didn't dare to turn in order to observe his attitude.

Then he said, 'You stay here. I'm going to look for Glenn Thomas.'

'I'm supposed to stay with you, though what protection I'd get from a murderer, I don't know.'

He ought to have understood me by that time. One correct word and we'd have been laughing together.

'You'll have to come with me and risk it.' He'd hit the correct note. I put my fingers on his arm.

'What d'you want him for?'

159

'To get his team together and get your car tree.'

'No.'

'I'm taking you away from here, Phil.' Now he was taking exactly the wrong attitude. 'The whole thing's upset you.'

I'd been poised on a sharp edge, and about to step back. His condescension pushed me that fraction too far.

'Upset! Upset! Who's upset? Somebody tries to kill me, but do I care? Of course not. Nonchalant, that's me. Cool in the face of danger. I *see* the murder, face to face, but does it shake me? Oh, not a bit. Philipa presses on. And I'm asked to run away from it – when the only peace of mind I'll get is when I can get a grip on the truth. Oh ... I'm not upset. Not a bit. Not even when you start giving me orders.'

'Phillie!' He tried, this time, to take my arm.

'No!' I shook him off. 'You want Glenn, I'll get him for you. And *you* can damn well drive yourself home. Here ... here's the keys.'

I threw them at him, and they hit him in the chest. Then I began to run, starting with one great leap down to the lawn, and then heading off, stumbling because I could barely see through the tears, aiming for the gap in the hedge that I'd used before. He couldn't follow me through there, that was my thought. Too narrow.

'Phillie!' he bellowed, and he was not too far behind.

Taking no other protection against the stiff branches of the rhododendrons, I raised my arms across my face, and plunged through, tripped over, and went flying forward on the grass the other side, sliding until I dug in my toes and fingers.

I lay there, panting and wailing in sheer infuriated frustration.

I was then aware that Oliver, having gone through the larger gap in the corner, was bending over me. 'Now look what you've done,' he said, not really the comforting words I would have welcomed.

'It's my ankle,' I said miserably. 'I tripped over something. Oh hell – it hurts.'

'Let me see. Which is it?'

'The right.'

My anger had melted away. He needed only to touch me gently, and all other emotions were swamped – as he well knew – by a warm flow of contentment. I rolled over on to my back. He carefully removed my shoe, which was half off anyway, and his strong fingers gently caressed my ankle.

'It's not broken,' he said confidently.

'How d'you know?'

'You'd have been yelling at me by now, if it had been. Can you sit up?'

I could sit up. With the sun going down behind the house, and in the heavy shade of the hedge, I could barely see his face.

'I tripped over something,' I told him.

'You told me that.'

'It'd be that silly little plaque thing. Oh, I do hope I haven't broken it. Have a look, Oliver, please.'

'Now you're worrying about a wretched piece of wood,' he grumbled.

'It must have meant something special to somebody,' I explained. 'Can you see, Oliver? Do look, please.'

'I'm trying. More by touch than anything else. Yes – I've found the stump, but I can't see the plaque. You must've kicked it off.'

'Oh ... I've broken it!'

'There's a torch in the car...'

'Don't you dare leave me.'

He made a sound that could've been a laugh. 'You were running away, a minute or so ago.'

'I'm not doing much running at this moment.'

He knelt beside me. 'How is it now?'

'A bit better, thanks.'

'All right if I leave you for a minute?'

'Yes. Where're you going?'

'I want to see if Clare's got a torch. There ought to be one in the gunroom. Shan't be a tick.'

'I think I might be able to stand. Help me up, Oliver, and we'll both go.'

'If you can walk, we shan't need the torch.'

'Of course not! But we'll still need it, Oliver, if only to fasten the plaque back in place.'

He said no more about it, but helped me to my feet. I tried to spare him much of my weight. I could stand. I could move a little.

'I'll wait,' I decided. 'I'll sit here and wait, while you go and try to borrow a torch.'

He hesitated. Then he said, 'All right. I'll hurry.'

As he turned away, I lowered myself gently to the ground again. I looked out over the field, which was now sparkling with scattered lights. The steam tractor had been there for a purpose, then, and must have had a generator. The lights spread themselves, like a fairground, but more dispersed. The darkening sky above the lake was reflected, strangely a shade lighter, in the metallic surface. There was movement down there, restless and unceasing movement, as though the surface of the field shivered and undulated. It was the movement of people.

It was some little while before I realised they were mostly drifting in my direction. But of course, they were experienced in these matters. There was to be a fireworks display, and here, on this facing slope, was the best place from which to watch it all. I had reserved myself a grandstand seat.

Then I was aware that a shadow was moving slowly towards me along the line of the hedge. I couldn't suppress a small flutter of the heart. But then a voice reassured me.

'Hello there.' It was Glenn's voice. His night vision must have been better than mine. I supposed it was to do with being a farmer. 'You've bagged the best spot, I see. Josie and I always used to sit here.'

'I could move, if you like.'

'There's plenty of room.'

'Isn't Josie with you?'

'On her way,' he said. 'Sure to be.'

'This is your particular spot, is it?' I asked.

'For previous fêtes here – yes. But it's been a long while.' He lowered himself to the grass beside me.

'Perhaps Josie's forgotten the place – the exact spot.'

'Oh no,' he said easily. 'Sentiment, you see.'

I didn't see. Did he mean that something special had happened here? Had he seduced her during a previous fireworks display? Couldn't they produce their own fireworks? I found myself giggling at the thought.

'Pardon?' he said.

'It's nothing,' I said. 'But if it's a special place . . .' I waited for him to say something, but he was silent.

'The fact is, I literally stumbled on it,' I explained. 'Didn't exactly choose it. Came running like a daft thing through the gap, and tripped over something. I seem to have hurt my ankle.'

'Lots of things to trip over,' he said, after a moment of silence.

'Oliver's gone to try to borrow a torch,' I explained. 'Then we'll see. I think I must have twisted something. My ankle . . .'

'Not broken, anyway,' he reassured me. 'You'd be in terrible pain.'

His voice was toneless, even at the mention of my terrible pain. But I felt he was having to concentrate to maintain it.

162

'Not my ankle ... but I seem to have broken something.'

'And why were you running?' he asked, changing the subject too abruptly.

'I was going to look for you, as a matter of fact.'

'I'm flattered. What for?'

'You said you and your friends could get my car out.'

'You're leaving us?'

'No. Oliver was. We'd had a bit of a row. It was why I was running, and I tripped myself up.'

'So *you* weren't leaving us?'

'I was. I changed my mind.'

'Decided to see the show first?' It was said casually, too casually.

'Not that. Things I've been told – it rather alters the situation. It now appears that one of Clare's guns was stolen. It explains the mysterious third shot. Do you know about the third shot?'

He was silent for a moment. I felt he was merely trying to give the impression he was taking me seriously. Then he said, 'But we've heard all that.'

'Not quite, I don't think. I mean ... stolen from the gunroom. Directly from it.'

There was a long pause. He cleared his throat. 'That's your reason for staying?'

I wished the light wasn't failing so quickly, as I couldn't detect his expression. Below me the shadows were sliding down the slope, and the undulating movement of people was being absorbed by them. The hum of their voices drifted up to me.

'No,' I said. 'That's not the reason. We'll have to repair the little plaque, you see, before we go.'

'Plaque?' he asked.

'I think I've knocked it off its stump. A kind of memorial, I think it was. Perhaps a dog or cat was buried here. Funny name for an animal, if that's the case. Harrison. I don't know, though. Son of Harris? Perhaps a dog that Harris loved. It could've been one of Clare's funny jokes. Don't you think? She'd hate even an animal he was fond of.'

Then Oliver flicked a torch at me, blinding me because I automatically turned to face it.

'Oh ...' he said. 'Hello, Glenn. You here, eh?'

Then he knelt beside me. Glenn said nothing. 'She thinks she broke something,' Oliver explained. 'Ah ... there it is. The stump it was nailed to, anyway. You went and broke the plaque off, Phil. Here it is, hiding in the grass. We'll have to nail it back. Strange inscription, though. Have you seen this, Glenn? Harrison, it reads. Date of death 5 September 1986. We'll easily fix it back in place, though.'

'Don't trouble,' Glenn said gruffly. 'Here ... let me have it. I'll do it tomorrow – in the daylight.'

'It's not date of death,' I said, with my obsession for accuracy. 'Not D-stroke-D. It's B-stroke-D.'

That I'd said it with such confidence, when I couldn't even see it, was a dead giveaway. In the background somebody choked back a scream. Oliver flicked the torch sideways, then it was knocked out of his hand as somebody fell across him and collapsed at my side.

The torch rolled towards me. I scrambled for it, just managed to close my hand over it, and swung it round.

It was Josie who had fainted beside me.

Then, over and beyond the water, the darkening sky was lit up as the set-piece burst into flame, into spluttering fire in which its own smoke writhed. A cheer rose up, mounting as the set-piece settled in and ceased to flutter, and became, clearly:

WELCOME HOME CLARE

And the cheering now became frenetic, as Josie moved, moaned, and opened her eyes.

'Welcome home,' she whispered.

12

I was aware, in the back-light thrown by the set-piece, that we were now closely surrounded by people. In fact, they were tightly packed, though around our little group they had allowed a reasonable space. Instinct, almost animal in its precision, had told them that a small but significant scene was being acted out. They must certainly have observed that Josie had fainted.

Now, beside me, she was trying to sit up. I put an arm around her shoulders, and handed the torch to Oliver.

'Silly of me,' she whispered.

'Two of us now,' I said. 'It's the heat.' Though it was now considerably cooler. 'Or was it the plaque?' I suggested gently.

There was no answer. Oliver now had the plaque in his hand. For a second he flashed the light on it, then he put the torch down on the ground, leaving it to slant its rays through the grass.

'You can have it if you want it,' I said, speaking to Glenn.

He made no move to take it. I was aware that around us we were attracting attention and drawing it from the excitement of the set-piece.

Oliver put his hand on the torch, and allowed the edge of the light to brush against Glenn, who was frowning at the muttering and fluttering in the immediate area. He made a dismissive gesture with one hand, and the surrounding shadows melted away, shuffled sideways, and left a space around us. But they had not moved far.

It was clear that in the period of Clare's absence Glenn had gradually taken over her role. The villagers now had become used to looking to him in their troubles and difficulties. I wondered how she would feel about that, and whether she had already detected it. But their influence did not overlap emotionally. Glenn had their respect, but it was Clare they loved. She embodied the casual, dismissive flick of the hand at outside authority; Glenn *was* authority, in a suppressed and undemonstrative way. In the years during which she'd been away he had not mastered, and probably had not attempted to master, the theatrical and wildly unprincipled attitude she presented to life. He would not have wanted to. But whereas he might now be prepared to retire quietly into the background of her impulsive display, and smile quietly to himself at her mastery of the technique, she would demand the full measure of her former popularity. Whereas he could live without public approbation, she would wither and fade if the spotlight wavered from her.

Now, a gesture from Glenn had won us space and a certain amount of seclusion, but we couldn't move elsewhere. Josie, though I was unable to see her face except in the brief back-glow of rockets and streamers, was still clearly distressed. We sat there, and we talked.

Way down beyond the lake, the display flung itself frenetically at the sky, the whole thing repeated, muted, in the surface of the lake. A shout of approval arose from all round us. The image was distorted, too, as the hot fragments fell hissing into the water. I could clearly see the small fountains of steam that rose, caught in the same reds, blues and golds.

I took the torch from beneath Oliver's hand and turned it on the plaque, where it lay face upwards on the grass.

'I suppose the date is correct?' I asked softly.

It was to Josie I said this, she being close to my side. In fact, she had a hand on my shoulder, seeking support ... or imploring for silence. But the time for silence had passed. Josie almost breathed the answer in my ear.

'It was that night, yes.'

'The terrible night of the thunderstorm?'

'*That* night. Yes.'

Glenn said softly, 'You don't have to answer, Josie love. She's got no right to ask questions. No legal right.'

'Legal?' I asked. 'Then you know we're discussing legality and illegality?'

'Say what you want to.' But there was no anger in his voice, resignation rather, but all the same a stubbornness. He wasn't going to allow one fact to escape without being questioned.

'Yes,' I agreed. 'I can say what I want to. I can ask questions, but I can't demand any answers. But perhaps I'd better explain. We had a bit of a set-to, Oliver and I, with Clare. A few minutes ago, that was. Well ... not a set-to exactly, but she did give us a few more details about the gunroom door. You know it was supposed to

166

have been locked against her? Which was why she had to run round through the house to get to the lawn, in the raging storm. The trouble was, you see, that it was unlocked when the police got here, and it's quite unacceptable that Harris could have unlocked it – would have unlocked it, even if he'd been capable of it.'

'Can't you let me watch the fireworks?' she complained.

'Watch them of course. I'll just say things, and you can listen, surely.'

I felt her shoulder shrug against me. 'Might as well.'

'Well ... what was I saying? Oh yes. Quite unacceptable that Harris should have unlocked that door, even if he'd been capable of it. So the question's always been – who did? And Clare's now told us that she was certain Harris had someone else in the gun-room at that time. Somebody he'd brought home with him.'

I paused. There was no response or comment. Rockets hissed their way up into the sky to a chorus of ahs. Josie's breath was uneven, shuddering, at my ear.

'Had you got any inkling, Glenn,' I asked him, 'that this could've been the case? At the time, I mean. Any idea then?'

He had been grunting to himself as I'd laid this out. Now he said curtly, 'You know the answer to that. I suppose you realise you're spoiling everything.'

I had to suppose he meant the display. 'I'm not at all certain I know the answer to it, no. You see, Clare's explanation neatly fits in with the shot-gun that went missing – the Darne, she calls it. If Harris gave it to this person he'd brought home – as a kind of payment for a debt – then that person would surely have been off and away the moment the french windows were thrown open. You *do* see that?'

I had addressed this to both of them. There was no reply.

'Josie? You can see that, surely.' I was deliberately trying to involve her in this. But I was having to concentrate, as my ankle was very sore.

'I see what you mean,' she said softly. For a moment her face glowed green as the sky was filled with a huge, growing tree of light.

'It also explains in some way the third shot that Clare said she heard, it seems to me.'

'And it seems to *me*,' said Glenn, who'd obviously been listening carefully, 'that you've got the full story. So ... how about giving it a rest?'

'I'd like to,' I assured him. 'But we haven't got the full story.

We've toyed with the idea, Oliver and I, but it's still not right. I mean, now we have a positive presence in that room – somebody who could have unlocked that door. Who must have done. But on its own it still doesn't explain anything, really. I mean ... why would it be unlocked? It couldn't have been a matter of unlocking the door to find a way out, because Harris had opened the french windows, which was a clear escape route once that person got into the darkness round the edges of the lawn – or got past this hedge.'

'Does this go on for ever?' asked Glenn, his patience rapidly melting away.

'I'm trying to explain it the best I can. And I want to do it now, so that I can go home. Because I'm tired, Glenn. Tired. All right?'

'Have it your own way.'

'I will then. I'll finish it. A clear escape route, I said, once they'd got beyond this hedge. So why the unlocking of the door? And why the third shot? A parting gesture? Possible, but it would advertise a presence, still close to the house, when the instinct would be to gallop down this slope and into the far distance, and as quietly as possible, not blasting off a shot at nothing.'

I was laying it out as clearly and precisely as I could, though the effort to concentrate was bringing on a severe headache. I ached at both ends now, my ankle and my head, and in the middle was a more elusive agony, at what, I realised, I was bringing about. This last distress I was going to have difficulty casting off.

Oliver stirred uneasily. I touched his arm – no, let me say it. He reached across and squeezed my hand.

I knew what was worrying him. I was saying this in the middle of probably the whole population of the surrounding villages, and if the word went round – as it undoubtedly would – that I was airing secrets they preferred to remain secret, then we might have difficulty getting away from there. But it had to be taken out and looked at, and seen whole. Had to.

'So we're left', I said, my voice now not too steady, 'with a door that was locked, and later wasn't. The only person who could've done that was Harris's visitor. And the only necessity for it is if that person missed the opportunity to get away by the route through the french windows, and was therefore stuck there, no doubt keeping out of Clare's sight, from outside on the lawn. And that person had to witness the terrible scene of the hurled guns and the screams and the lightning, and it went on ... and on ...'

As though in comment or emphasis, one of the fireworks over the lake screamed like a terrified banshee.

168

There was no comment made. I was no longer asking questions but stating facts, as the scene gained clarity in my mind. And I felt that I was no longer competing against the spectacular violence of the fireworks, but that it was a background emphasis to what I was saying.

'And there had to come a point,' I went on, my vision seeming to clear as the reflected light played in ghostly multi-coloured display on the faces in front of me, 'a point where there could be no way out by way of the french windows, because Clare had jammed them with her single shot. One cartridge from the gun she had picked up. Poor Clare – imagine her – lost in a despair and a fury that she couldn't in any way control. And that was the shot with which she disabled Harris, though his wounds at that time were mainly from slivers of broken glass. That was the first shot of the three, that terrible night.'

I stopped, feeling exhausted, my mouth dry, and myself thoroughly miserable. Nobody said a word, though I caught a sigh, the hint of a gentle moan, from the shadows that had retreated at Glenn's gesture. But clearly they had not moved far enough. They could still hear. They wanted to hear, and I wanted them to listen.

'I've got to assume', I went on at last, during a lull in the display, 'that Harris staggered back against the wall, stunned and bleeding ... but alive. From that moment onwards, there would have been no way out of that room except the door.' I lifted my shoulders and allowed them to fall wearily.

'So that was how the door came to be unlocked. But first ... first there was something else that had to be done. Something that now seemed of the greatest importance. I don't know the circumstances that made it necessary, but the provocation must have been very strong.' I waited for a comment there, but there was no sound. Not even an indrawn breath. This was something that affected, even involved, the whole community. The truth. And now I had a vision of it. They waited.

'Harris had to be removed,' I said, trying to force strength into my voice. 'Or put down might be a better way of describing it. Like a savage dog. And there he was, no longer able to sneer and bully, and the thought of this creature possibly remaining alive would have been insupportable. And there were guns lying around, all over the floor, and cartridges available. It would take only seconds to load a barrel, load and fire, and put him out of his misery. Put the whole district out of misery.' I took a breath. 'And that was the second shot, heard by Clare as she was sitting in the room opposite, phoning the police.'

Glenn spoke up in a small, cold voice. 'Is there much more of this? You're upsetting Josie.'

'I don't want to upset anybody,' I assured him. 'I'm trying to get a firm grip on the truth, and I don't like what I see of it. There's something else...'

'Must we?' Oliver cleared his throat. 'Isn't that enough?'

'Oh... don't I wish it was. But you see, Oliver, it seems so clear to me that the visitor couldn't have been a man, as Clare assumed. It had to be a woman.'

There was a rustling, a muttering, in the background, immediately drowned by a series of violent explosions and flares of colour over the lake. I waited. Paused. There was silence. 'May I go on?'

Oliver cleared his throat. Nobody tried to shout me down. Although the night was again exploding in colour and whines and howls, strangely the silence surrounding us seemed to form a vacuum, the fireworks only a background that lent the real-life picture more colour and reality.

'Imagine how it would've been,' I therefore went on. 'Harris took his visitor into the gunroom, to wait there while he tackled Clare about money. But why the gunroom? And why – and this is what Clare told me a few minutes ago – why had he already switched the key to the inside of the door, if he hadn't planned to lock Clare out? So ... *why* the gunroom? There were countless other rooms – there's a bedroom Clare showed us. The first thought is that he'd intended – promised – to hand over one, two ... however many guns I wouldn't know ... to cover the debt. But if that had been the intention, well, he'd been refused money, so why didn't he do just that? No. Instead, he had to start, at once, on his gun-throwing act. Why? To vent his anger? Yet his anger had been aroused, by Clare, after he'd chosen the gunroom to shelter his visitor. No. I believe he'd already planned the gun-throwing episode. During the trip home, he'd planned it, knowing the probable outcome of any interview with Clare, and intending to make a grand display of terrifying brutality. It was just luck that he had a thunderstorm to add a violent background. Doesn't that sound as though he had a woman he intended to terrify? Would a man be equally impressed?'

I paused. Nothing was said. I felt I wasn't putting it over very well. I took another breath. 'And in any event, it must surely have been a woman, because a man wouldn't have let it go on – would

170

have intervened. If only verbally. But nothing was heard or seen of this visitor by Clare.'

Rockets burst high in the night, a silver-white and blue eruption.

'And I believe Clare knew that,' I said quietly, 'because the taunts and the fury that she threw at Harris were phrased around a pregnancy he had told her was the basis of his money troubles. He'd wanted the money, he told her, to terminate a pregnancy. It was another hint that he had a woman in there with him, that specific pregnant one.'

Glenn cut in flatly. 'I think we've heard enough of this.'

'No,' I said. 'If I leave it now, there'll be no end to the speculation. I'm sorry about it – but you're entitled to hear it, then you can say or do what you like about it. All right?' I watched as he lowered his head, as his hand closed fiercely on Josie's. I went on.

'I expect everybody in the district knew about Harris's debts, but these were mainly loans from his mates. Men. There's only one woman to whom he could've been indebted, the one he might have been able to cheat – his business partner. And wasn't that you, Josie?'

She didn't reply, but she knew now what I intended. I felt her hand on my knee, gently squeezing. 'Finish it,' she said quietly.

'Very well,' I said. I'd finish it, though I hated the thought. 'But I'll have to do a bit of guessing, so stop me if I go wrong. All right? Well ... after that shot, which was the one that killed Harris, it became necessary to get out of the house, and that required that the door to Clare's sitting-room had to be passed. But Clare was inside there, by that time. She could be heard on the phone, shouting that she'd killed her husband. Well, perhaps she really believed that, and perhaps she deserved the credit for it. There was no time to think about that, though. So it was out through the corridors and to the front door. Missing Oliver by seconds, I wouldn't be surprised. And still carrying the shot-gun...'

'Yes,' Josie whispered. 'I saw Oliver arriving. His car. I hid in the maze.'

They were the first words in confirmation of my theory that I'd heard. Glenn said something incoherent, though he must have known it was too late to intervene.

'And you ran round to the back?' I asked Josie.

'Yes.' She hesitated. 'After Oliver had been round there, and come hurrying back. Yes, I went round, but not exactly ran.'

'Why round the back?' I asked. 'Why not along the drive?' I thought about that for a moment, then I got it. 'Of course ... Harris

171

wasn't the only hated object around here. There was Clare. Clare with her horrid self-promoted superiority. Clare with her calm assumption of devotion and approbation. But Clare, too, with her secret, snide viciousness. Am I right? It's there, behind the façade.'

'All too right,' said Glenn heavily.

'And you would need to go round the back,' I suggested gently to Josie, 'because Glenn was the one you had to go to now. And straight across the fields was the shortest way.'

She smiled. I caught that in the back-glow, as the fireworks headed towards their climax, a frenzied arc of multi-coloured streamers.

'So,' I suggested, 'if Clare thought she'd shot Harris, that could be arranged. It would have to look as though she really had, in that room, the way it *was* done. It needed just that one small touch of detail. Only one cartridge had been fired from Clare's gun. It had to appear that she'd fired two – at separate times. That was the third shot, a shot at nothing, at the sky, from Clare's gun, which was then left where she'd dropped it, as though she'd let it fall from the inside through the hole in the window. Then the other weapon, the one that had really killed him, was taken away. And that was the missing Darne that she's been making such a fuss about.'

There was silence. Now the sky was abruptly dark, a sudden darkness which was in some way more effective than the display. The final soft whisper of the last hot detritus hissing into the water was like a great sigh.

And following it was a resounding roar of applause and appreciation. Then, in the silence, Oliver said quietly, 'Can I have the torch for a second?'

I pushed it towards him. I didn't know what he meant.

'I've been sitting on something,' he explained. 'For ages. It's been agony, but I didn't dare move a muscle. It would've distracted you, Phil.'

I felt that this was an attempt to lighten the mood, which was like a heavy pall around us. In the immediate vicinity, nobody was moving, nobody was getting to their feet, about to leave.

Oliver levered himself round and aimed the torch. 'Yes,' he said. 'It's what I guessed. It's the stump that plaque was nailed to. It felt like the stump. Agony, it's been. It's a funny sort of stump, though. Wide but not deep, and the top edge seems to be curved inwards. You know what it looks like to me – it's the butt of a gun.'

172

He said this with no air of surprise at the discovery. He had noted it previously, and he'd had time for thought.

'The Darne,' I whispered.

I was aware that there was still no sign of departure from the group immediately around us. Glenn, too, became aware of this. He turned his head. The light from the torch caught a profile that was extremely stern and angry.

But his voice was quiet. 'It's all right,' he said reassuringly.

Then they at last moved – but not very far. A few yards only, possibly still not out of hearing. It seemed a very quiet night, now. To the left, far down the slope, there was still activity around the floodlit tent where Alice Purslowe had died.

'Countryfolk,' said Glenn, 'as you'd call us, have to have good eyesight and good hearing. You need to be able to hear the lambs caught in a snowdrift, or locate your cattle in the dark. They heard, you know. They heard every word. They heard, and they'll remember.'

'I did realise that,' I told him.

'And d'you think you can take your story from here? Don't you imagine they'd stop you? Somehow.' It was a gentle, implied threat.

'It's not a story,' I told him. 'It's the truth. The only truth.'

'The police are still working down there,' he went on. 'You'd need to do no more than walk down the slope, and tell your story all over again.'

'That wasn't my intention. In any event – we haven't heard it all, have we, Glenn?'

'And when the rest's been said?'

'Then you can get my car out of the crush, if it's still necessary, and we'll go home.'

Beside me, Josie muttered in protest. Oliver, I saw, the torch still switched on and beneath his hand, was crouched in a tense posture, like a protective wild animal about to fly to intercept any approaching danger.

'And we'll go home, Oliver,' I repeated, addressing this to him now, trying to relax him.

'And tell the police there,' said Glenn flatly.

'No. Oh no. Let the guilt lie where it is now, with the real guilty party.'

'I'm not so sure – '

'Hush now,' said Josie. 'Don't be foolish, Glenn. Trust Philipa. I'm sure we can.'

There was a mutter around us in the shadows. It didn't sound like a dangerous one to me.

I hesitated a moment, then I suggested, 'The plaque? Can you tell us about that?'

Josie nodded, bit her lip, glanced at Glenn, then stared down at the grass, down at the plaque, which was lying there. Her voice was low, but now the air was crystal clear, only the acrid smell of explosives gently drifting towards us. It was becoming cold. Josie shivered.

'We could go somewhere else,' I suggested.

'No,' she said, but giving it no emphasis. 'Here. It's more real, here.'

We waited, while she collected her thoughts, while she worked out the best way to purge it from her memory.

Then she began.

13

'It was a Friday,' she reminded me. 'Wages day for us. I'd got a little girl – she's still with me, but not so little now ... anyway, she was good with the books, the day-to-day work and the wages. Margery, her name is. But I had a qualified accountant to prepare the company statements for the Inland Revenue. Everything was in order. Or I thought it was, fool that I am. But that morning, when I went to the bank to cash a cheque for the wages, that morning, they told me we were out of funds. Out of funds! Well ... I mean. You feel such a fool. I was never so ashamed in my life. Anyway ... we got round it. I went in to see the manager, and we arranged an overdraft. It's different, you know, with a company. A different thing to being a person. He said I ought to have a word with my accountant, and I said I'd do that. Back to Margery, who was wondering where I'd been. Cautious – you know – not wanting to ask but she could see I was upset. But I did get an appointment with my accountant. For that afternoon. So I had to wait till then, and me worried half out of my mind. I suppose it's the way you're brought up, but I've always hated being in debt. You know. I've never known time go so slow. Slowly. And I couldn't concentrate on what I was doing. I'll swear that everybody must have thought I was going crazy.'

She stopped. Nobody said anything. I noticed that a small amount of light filtered through the hedge behind me. Clare still had the gunroom lights on. Presumably she was still admiring her guns. Then Josie went on.

'I went to see the accountant. Nice man called ... oh lord, I've forgotten his name ... it doesn't matter. He listened, and told me he'd been worried, the last two years, about our accounts. Two years. Me, I could never understand the figures he turned out. But, I mean, you trust people like that ... don't you ... otherwise there's no point. So long as the books balanced. Oh, they balanced all right ... but only with a thumb on one pan. You get what I mean. And that thumb was something to do with certain entries. So he'd been worried ... oh, I've said that. I'm so confused.'

'It's all right,' I said. 'No hurry.'

'Yes ... well ... it came down to the fact that Harris'd been cheating me. Cheating the company, I suppose. For nigh on five years. Not slipping in cheques for himself. Oh ... nothing like that. He couldn't have. It was me that drew the cheques. But it wasn't just the odd few pounds. He was our traveller, on the sales side. You expect a bit of kind of rigging. A bit. But we were short of nigh on ... well, something in the thousands. And there I'd been, dead sure we were doing all right. I mean to say – our stuff was selling, and our designs were being copied. That's supposed to be a good sign. Fancy that. Makes you think. Anyway ... there'd never been much in the way of profits, not what I'd expected, anyway. Did I say that? Stop me if ...'

'You're doing fine,' I murmured.

'Yes. Well, you can guess. I'd got to see him. Harris. See him and put it to him. So I had to hang around the office after everybody had left, waiting for him. Waiting to hear an explanation. Praying there'd *be* an explanation, because Harris wasn't the sort of man you could reason with. Oh no. His temper was always quick and violent. And then he came. A bit drunk. I'd've expected that, 'cause he was late. He was *supposed* to report in on Fridays. But d'you know ... you'd hardly believe it ... but he'd been out shooting, keeping me waiting. Shooting, and me there, waiting! And by that time I was feeling really terrible.'

Glenn said, 'No need to go into that, Josie.'

'Oh, but it is. It's part of it. And Philipa knows that, I can tell. *Do* let me tell it as I want to, Glenn, please.' She returned her attention to me. 'Feeling terrible, as I said. I suppose it was all the tension that day, and it'd upset things. And I couldn't relax, you know, couldn't sit a minute. By the time he *did* come, I was in quite a bit of pain.'

'Yes,' I said. Oliver was silent. I guessed what was coming, and wished I hadn't got to hear it.

'I gave it to him,' said Josie. 'Face to face. As well as I could, anyway. But he was a big man. You've met 'em. Overpowering. It's difficult to throw accusations in such a person's face. And I think he'd been drinking. On his breath. You could smell it. He just waved his hand, just dismissing everything, you know how they are. And he sneered. Hadn't I ever heard of the perks of the job, he asked me. Oh yes. Perks. Of course I had, but that was the cheaper hotels the travellers went to, and they gave out fake bills. It's all right. I knew about that. *We* weren't losing. I'd have expected to pay for good hotel rates. Well ... he was angry, blustering, as though I'd got no right to question anything he did. The louse. You'd have thought it was my fault ... and I got a full list of the women he'd got lined up in the different areas, and his free nights with them. You'd never believe! No expenses there – but he claimed all the same. He as good as boasted they paid *him*. Can you imagine it! But quite simply – and he shouted this in my face – he'd imagined a large part of his claims. And me – oh, I'd never thought of querying anything. You don't do you? Then there were the other things. You can be sure he told me the lot, once he got going. Sweeteners, he'd claimed, for sales pushed in our direction, and all fakes, fakes.'

She was becoming more and more upset, as she locked herself into the memory. Glenn put a hand round her shoulders. 'You don't need to go on.' But she eased herself free. 'Yes, I do. I *want* to say it. I've been holding it back ... Leave me alone, Glenn, please. Let me say it.'

Glenn grimaced at me, and frowned: You see what you've started?

'It got to the point', she said, 'of him shouting at me and demanding how much it was. How much I thought it was. Even then, a sneer, as though most of it could never be proved, and I told him a figure ... more a guess than anything ... and he got all aggressive, walking round waving his arms, and shouting that I'd be lucky. I'd be lucky. But I was terribly frightened, and all the time the pain was getting worse. I just had to cut it short, so I told him, in the morning I was going to take it to the police. Because it was theft, after all. I suppose. Not just theft from me ... theft from the company.'

Oliver grunted. I had to suppose he was agreeing.

'And then?' I asked.

'He wanted to know how much. I've told you that. Yes. And I had to say ... oh, I didn't know, more a guess than anything ... oh, I'm getting all flustered. I'm sorry. Anyway – the way I put it – I said I'd ask my accountant to go all through it. I could see his face getting redder. But I said it, and he shouted at me. Name a figure. Name a figure! So I said ten thousand. For now, I told myself. It'd do for now. He laughed his head off. You'll be lucky, he said, sort of challenging, so I replied with the first thing that came into my head. I told him I'd see Clare in the morning ... oh, and that did it!

177

Waving arms and swearing, and in the end he bellowed in my face: ''Right. So all right. We'll go and see Clare.'' But I didn't intend *then*. I was feeling absolutely awful. Wanted to get home to my place – I've got a bit of a flat. And call the doctor. But Harris – he had to do his great big bullying act. Grabbed me by the wrist and literally dragged me out. I didn't even have time to lock the door or put the lights off. He just shoved me into his car, and drove off like a mad thing.'

There was a silence, one of those solid and compact silences, with not an indrawn breath to break it. When Glenn cleared his throat, my nerves jumped. 'I should've killed him the first time,' he said gently.

'Then we came up here,' went on Josie, settled in now, keeping it going in a flat voice. 'I was in great pain by that time, wasn't even sure what was going on, only that I wanted it to end. We went in. Front door. Down the corridor – and him saying make a sound and I'll throttle you. To the gunroom. He unlocked it and shoved me inside, and he put the key on the inside and just said wait there. And be quiet. Which I did. It was what I wanted. Had to have. Quiet, and a sit down. Only two chairs in there, though, and those hard and horrid. But I sat in a corner. Only ... I could hear them. Every word. Shouting. Nothing but shouting, that night, and I was tired of it. Tired. And d'you know what he told her! He as good as said he'd got a tart in trouble in the village and she wanted an abortion. And you can imagine ... *that* really got Clare going. She screaming at him that he was sterile and she didn't believe him, and him shouting at her that he'd show her how sterile. I was ... petrified. And it was *me* they were shouting about. It was me they made into a filthy tramp. My flesh was crawling. I felt dirty ... unclean. Then he came back in.'

'You don't have to go on,' I told her. 'It's enough.'

Without any further information, I could have completed it for her. But no – as it happened. I would have been wrong.

'No,' she said. 'You wanted it – you hear it all. He came back in. Locked the door, then went to the gun cases and opened one, and took a gun out that he used to smash the glass in the others. Then he got to throwing the guns on the table, and he went over and opened the french windows. I thought this was for me to leave. I wanted to get out of there. Oh ... how I wanted that! But I wasn't sure I could stand. Nothing was very clear any more – all kind of a blur. He'd said something I hadn't really taken seriously – about me taking a gun or two, to cover what he owed. Ridiculous! And then it began, the throwing out and the throwing back and the noise and the lightning, and if I'd screamed out in pain neither of them would've noticed. And in the end – the shut french windows and Clare's shot at the glass. I nearly passed out, I can tell you that. Harris cried out something and staggered back against the wall. I remember staring at him ... all kind of empty, just looked at him, and I can remember a thought going through my mind – well, that's the end of that bastard. He was bleeding. I heard Clare drop the gun outside. Everything seemed to be happening slowly, so that I could take it in, I suppose. Then Clare went away.'

She was silent. I didn't want to hear any more of it. I could guess the rest. Josie sat with her head hanging, living it again.

Glenn said, 'I can tell the rest. Let me tell the rest.'

'Why not,' I said. He'd hardly had a chance to put in a word.

Glenn nodded, and went on, 'Clare went away. Josie knew she had to get out of there. Get to a doctor, and quickly.'

'So why didn't she call out to Clare?'

'She didn't want to say a word to Clare. Anyway, Clare had left the lawn, and was obviously going round to the front. Josie had to wait until she heard the sitting-room door shut. Clare tried the gunroom door first, but it was still locked. But Josie knew it wasn't finished. She stared at Harris, and she told me it was as though it'd all been laid out for her. She stared at him and she hated him. Hated. How he'd treated her, how he'd used her – and she hated Clare for what *she'd* said. Because, in all that shouting at each other in the hall, Clare had used Josie's name. How she knew Josie was pregnant, I can't say. But she linked it up and used her name. And the foul language she'd used ... describing! I'm not going to go into that.'

'Please,' I agreed, 'no.'

'And there was Harris, and there were the guns, and Josie knew where the cartridges were kept. She could still think. Just about. Hardly stand on her feet, but she could think.' He glanced at her with shy fondness. 'There was Harris, and Josie had a loaded gun in her hands – she didn't remember loading it, she told me. And she knew he didn't deserve to live, and though he looked dead already, she thought she'd better take no chances. So she shot him. And *then* she had to leave, and on the way out along the corridor she heard the voice of Clare, shouting on the phone that she'd shot her husband – and so, Josie decided, that was how it would be. By that time she knew she had to get to me. Over the fields. A long way, but I was the nearest.'

'You were the only one I wanted to go to, Glenn,' she whispered. 'Thank you.'

I could just detect his smile at her, but I didn't think she was looking.

'Go on,' I said.

'There's not much more. There was Josie, and the route she had in mind very nearly took her past the french windows, and she wanted to make a bit of trouble for Clare, and it was so easy to make it look as though Clare had actually killed him, and with the gun she'd already fired. All it took was to pick up Clare's gun, fire the one cartridge at the sky, and drop it back on the terrace. But that'd been about the last thing Josie was capable of doing. She still had the Darne in her hands. She got this far.'

There was a silence. It seemed to go on and on. In the end I managed to say, 'You mean it was *here*? Here she miscarried?'

'Yes,' mumbled Josie.

'Oh God!'

The silence again descended on us. The shadows around us might just as well have been rocks, as there was not a whisper, not a suddenly indrawn breath. Silence, was their motto.

In the end, Glenn cleared his throat, and finished it off.

'She got to the farm. Left the gun lying here...'

'Oliver!' I whispered tensely. 'The police missed it.'

'We were only collecting 'em up,' he explained plaintively, in self-defence. 'Not counting. It never occurred to us to look this side of the hedge.'

I nodded. 'Sorry, Glenn,' I said. 'Go on.'

'She got to the farm. God knows how. She can't remember. The dogs warned me, and I went out with a torch, and there she was. I thought she was dead. Picked her up. Got her inside. Tried to clean her up, and phoned a doctor.'

'Who didn't connect it up? Didn't report it?'

'He's my doctor. Josie's too.' He seemed to feel that answered it. I rather felt that it did.

'And the gun?' I asked.

'I went back. The next day, after the police had left, and taken Clare with them. The rain had cleared things – and the foxes. I suppose. I dug a deep hole, and buried the gun. Here, where it had happened, leaving a couple of inches or so sticking out. For the plaque, you see,' he explained.

'No. I don't see,' I had to admit.

'My sense of justice,' he said, giving me, as far as I could tell, a twisted smile. 'There ought to be some sort of a memorial, I thought. So that was it. Harrison. Born and died on 5 September 1986.'

'Son of Harris?' I asked, unable to believe this.

'We don't know, of course. It might have been a daughter. But you can't say Harrisdaughter, can you?'

It was said in a tone of reason and common sense that I had difficulty rationalising. 'But ... *his* son?'

'Well, it was – wasn't it!'

14

Josie flashed him a quick, reprimanding glance, at his impetuosity, no doubt, but had to agree.

'Yes – it was Harris.'

'You mean . . . rape?'

'Oh no, not at all. Well . . . sort of, I suppose. We'd had a row, Glenn and I, you see. The usual thing. He expected me to marry him and pack in the lampshade business. Well – I couldn't do that. Could I? I mean, it's my life. I enjoy it. Anyway . . . that's not the point. We'd had this row, and the obvious place to go, after that, was to the workshop. I always found it relaxing, and this was late evening, so there'd be nobody there. And along came Harris. Full of beer and acting like a randy bull terrier. And me, angry with Glenn – I sort of thought: to hell with him then. Yes, it was sort of rape. I changed my mind, but by then it was too late. On the floor, it was, all covered with cut-offs of material . . . but the child would've been Harris's. And Glenn, he's been sort of marvellous.' She reached a hand towards him, but I was between. 'Silly idiot – he still wants to marry me, though they said at the hospital I wouldn't be able to have children. Not any more. But Glenn still says . . .'

'Oh for God's sake!' he broke in. 'Do we have to have this? We can adopt, can't we?'

I cleared my throat. Oliver and I might not have been there, as, I realised, the villagers who'd been around us were no longer there.

Glenn and Josie were now both silent. I had an idea that it was time we too left. They had matters to discuss.

But it wasn't quite finished. 'You said', I reminded him, 'that you should have killed him the first time. Is that connected . . .'

'Yes.' He rubbed his chin. 'When Josie told me about the rape, I looked out for him, and caught him coming out of the pub. Two nights later, this was. *Then*, I nearly killed him. Like a fool, I let 'em haul me off. Let him . . .' He nodded towards Oliver. 'Haul me off.'

There was a short silence. I wondered how much it would have changed things if nobody had interfered.

'D'you think you could get it out?' I asked.

There were blank stares. Even Oliver didn't seem to understand.

'The gun,' I explained. 'Get that out, and burn the plaque, and there'll be nothing left to commemorate that terrible night. Then we can all forget it ever happened.'

'Forget...' Glenn didn't accept that he ever would, that *they* ever would.

'The final bit of the evidence would be gone,' I said. 'And really, you know, I'd very much like to return the gun to Clare. Before we leave. So – can you get it out, Glenn?'

He was now mentally with me. 'Oh, I don't know. It goes down quite a bit. I could go and get a spade, I suppose.'

'No. Now. Can't you kick it loose, or something?'

Oliver got to his feet in order to expose the problem. Only three inches of the butt protruded. He backed into the narrow gap in the hedge, and held the torchlight on it. Then he tried kicking it, kicking it hard, his heel to the butt. Glenn got the idea. He went over and stood facing Oliver, two big men with weight and muscle behind them. And they kicked – alternating. Thump, thump. The earth was hard, but it moved, a little at a time, forming a growing gap. I could feel the thumps through the ground.

'It'll never come up like this,' said Oliver. 'We're only loosening the top bit.'

Glenn stood over it and studied it closely. 'I don't know,' he said. 'There's enough to get a grip, and the taper helps.'

He tried this, crouching down to it, both hands reaching into the gap the kicking had made. Then he gripped hard, and the pull was in his legs, those leg muscles hardened by years of farmwork. And slowly, reluctantly, the gun moved. He shook it, tried again. I saw sweat drip from his chin, and suddenly, easily it seemed, Clare's precious Darne came up from its grave, and, panting, Glenn laid it on the grass.

And what a poor, sad thing it was! Now completely encrusted with a scabbing of rust, which would have bitten deeply into the steel beneath, it kept only a vague shape of a gun. The butt, that part of it which had been below ground level, was cracked and distorted. A wad of earth filled the trigger guard, and as I stared at it a worm wriggled free of it. And at the shoulder end of the butt the heads of two nails stood proud of the wood by half an inch, cracks running down its length from them. The silver engraving had weathered the best, but that was lifting and curling, and was black.

'I'll take it,' I said, holding out my right hand. I very nearly dropped it, as it was heavier than I'd expected. 'We'll say goodnight, then,' I said to them.

'We'll be hearing from you?' Josie asked tentatively.

'What about?'

'Whether you've decided to go to the police ... after all.'

'Oh no. No, I'll have no such news. Call it our secret, shall we? But I'd hope to hear from you.'

She glanced at Glenn. He shrugged. 'From us?' he asked.

'We'd dearly love to be asked to the wedding,' I told him.

Glenn laughed. 'We'll let you know.'

'But I haven't agreed ...' burst out Josie.

He put his arm round her waist and turned her away. 'Everybody'll be there. Literally everybody ...' he was telling her.

And still arguing, they moved away into the darkness. I felt he was going to get his own way at last. After all, Harris was now well and truly dead and forgotten.

Oliver cleared his throat. 'So let's go home.'

'I've got to hand over this gun.'

'Then throw it in from the lawn. The windows are still open.'

'No,' I said. 'We've got to treat it with due reverence, and take it in.'

So we went round to the correct gap, and through to the lawn. The lights in the gunroom were still on, and, as Oliver had said, the french windows were flung wide. We walked up on to the terrace and to the windows. There we paused.

Clare was standing in the middle of the room, slowly turning as her eyes swept around her array of guns. Everybody had gone home, except us, of which fact she was obviously now aware, and she was robbed of the glow of their presence. All she had at this time was the collection, her lovely, lovely guns.

Then she saw us. There was no nervous start of surprise. 'Oh ... hello,' she said. 'I thought everybody had left.'

'We're the last. Look what I've brought you, Clare.' I dropped the Darne on the table with a clatter. The vibration jerked another worm free, this time from the barrel. 'It's your Darne, I think.'

The blood ran from her cheeks, then flooded back again. A hand hovered and was withdrawn. She suddenly sobbed. 'Oh, my poor Darne,' she whispered. 'Oh, the poor thing.'

Then at last she laid a hand on it, ran it down the length of the knobbled barrel, and caressed the butt. Then she removed it quickly with a tiny yelp of pain. She sucked her finger.

'There're nails stuck in it,' she whimpered.

'Yes.'

'Where did you find it?' Her tone was almost accusatory, as though we had been hiding it from her.

'Just say we dug it up from somewhere,' I suggested. 'Now you've got the lot, Clare. Doesn't that make you happy? You'll really enjoy yourself, cleaning it up, but don't be disappointed if it ends up all pitted and rough. Never mind – you can tell people it was in the Napoleonic wars. It'll look very businesslike, all battered and spent.'

'What're you talking about?' she demanded sharply. 'Everybody else has gone – so why haven't you?'

'We're waiting for the chance to get my car out.'

Oliver was walking round the room, apparently unconscious of a certain abrasiveness that had entered our conversation. 'They certainly make a grand show, Clare,' he said.

'You've seen them before,' she reminded him curtly.

'So I have. But it was a long while ago. I never really took much notice.'

That anybody could not really take much notice of her guns appalled Clare. 'You're a fool,' she told him.

'Have been, perhaps.'

'Oughtn't you to be leaving?' she asked me tartly. 'The rest have gone, ages ago. There'll be no trouble getting out.'

'In a minute,' I assured her. 'I couldn't leave before I'd come and told you that I've managed to prove your innocence.'

'What!'

'Your innocence in respect of the death of Harris.'

'I think you must be mad.' She turned a shoulder to me, saw that Oliver was eyeing her without any smallest gleam of approbation, and jerked her head back.

'Not mad at all,' I said. 'I've only recently been talking to the real culprit. A clear admission was made.'

She lifted her head, her eyes now a burnt umber colour. 'Why can't you keep your nose out of my affairs?'

'It's my nature, nosey. Because I was sure you hadn't done it, Clare, in spite of all your tricks and evasions.'

'Who asked you – '

'Nobody.' I shrugged. She was taking exactly the attitude I had anticipated. 'But all the same I thought I'd like to prove your innocence. Then there was the suggestion that Oliver might've been involved, so it wasn't any longer a simple matter of proving your innocence, because I really had to prove who was the actual culprit. And I have.'

She stared at me balefully, with blank eyes and not a blink. 'Who is this person, you interfering bitch?'

I shook my head. I wasn't going to say that. The fact that she'd made her statement as to my ancestry without any intonation, as a simple statement of fact, seemed to place a more vicious emphasis on it.

'You're not the first one to complain that I interfere.'

She gave a bitter laugh. 'Oh . . . I can believe that. Who said it last, this person you claim admitted to shooting Harris? Shouted it in your face, I wouldn't be surprised.'

'Well, no. No anger was involved. We spoke together quietly, just the other side of your hedge.'

'You're lying, of course.'

'But why d'you say such a thing, Clare? I'd have expected a certain amount of gratitude. I can prove your innocence. You ought to be happy. I didn't say I intended to, and that should make you even happier.'

'Ah!' She nodded. I seemed to have succeeded in easing her anger. Then she appeared to realise something. 'You spoke of this, out there? Recently?'

'I told you – a few minutes ago.'

'With people all round you?'

'I think so. It was dark, you see, and at the end the fireworks had finished.'

'Then I'll know.' She nodded positively to herself. 'It'll be all round the countryside tomorrow. They'll come to me, and I'll hear everything. You'll see. I shall know who's made this ridiculous claim, this admission, as you call it.'

Oliver said, 'I don't see what you think you'd gain from that, Clare.'

'I'll know.' She nodded.

'And be able to deal with this person?' I asked quietly.

'I didn't say that.'

'You don't seem pleased.'

'Pleased?' That seemed to baffle her. She went across the room and closed the french windows. 'It's getting quite cool.'

'Isn't it!' I said. I waited until she'd turned back and was facing me. 'But don't assume anybody will be coming to tell you anything, Clare. I don't think they'll come to you – and if you go down to the village, I feel they'll look away and not speak.'

'What're you talking about?' she demanded, becoming more tense with every second.

'Are you familiar with the phrase: *persona non grata*, Clare?'

'Of course. I did Latin at school. Have you gone insane or something?'

'Oh, I'm sane enough, I assure you. And I can feel what's going to happen. When they all accepted that you'd killed Harris there would've been general approval. He was universally hated. When you were sent to prison, and went there with your head high, grandly to your punishment, you were adored for it. The whole thing had an element of proud sacrifice about it, and was coloured splendidly by the violent scene in the background. Oh, how they cheered you this morning! You were back ... their heroine. And you lapped it up. You were indeed the lady of the manor. But now they'll know it was all false. You played it for all it was worth. Not for you the kicking and screaming when they dragged you away. No. It was head high. The proud killer. You fooled them, Clare. They know the genuine executioner now. In the morning it'll be all round the district. And d'you think they'll whisper a word, outside their tight little circle? Not on your life, they won't.'

'Who is this person? You're lying.' She lifted her shoulders in a gesture of contempt. 'I'll know, anyway, when the police go there with a warrant.'

'There'll be no warrant, Clare. Can we put it that there'll be a conspiracy of silence? Yes, silence when you're near – when authority's near – silence when you wave grandly, no answer when you call out: good morning. Because they'll all know you used the situation to inflate your own personal ego. That it's all been a pantomime, with you as Cinderella. But ... I was forgetting ... you won't have to suffer it for long. You may not even have time to see the village in the morning.'

'What do you mean?'

Now she was pale, her eyes still wide, but with a wildness to them. They settled fixedly on my face, searching for a way out from what would sound like purgatory to her. I didn't answer.

'Not long?' she whispered. 'I still don't know what you mean.'

'You didn't want me to prove your innocence, did you, Clare? You were happy with what you'd got.'

I'd made it a direct question. She responded to it. 'No, damn you, no.'

'Shall I tell you why you didn't? I didn't understand. I do now. It had brought you the status you longed for. You had come home to a great welcome. And all this rested on the one fact: that you'd killed Harris, on behalf of the whole community, and you'd paid your debt to society. You wallowed in it, Clare.'

'Oh, this is absurd. You'd better leave.'

'In a moment, Clare. It's motive, you see, a motive that to anyone else would seem paltry. But not to you. You see, if I proved your innocence a large part of your magic aura would have been snatched away. And I was doing this thing. So I had to be removed before I succeeded. How strange, that you'd be prepared to commit a murder in order to hide the fact that you hadn't committed the first. Strange, that is, to someone who didn't know you.'

I paused, waiting for her to say something. She was staring at me with a set, white face. And I was wondering whether there hadn't been just a hint of jealousy in the stabbing. Oliver was infinitely desirable – to both of us. But she said nothing.

'But Clare, you loved the adoration, as you love your guns. Both affections so very destructive. Shall we go now, Oliver? I'm very tired.'

In fact, I could barely remain on my feet.

'You're insane,' she whispered.

'I shall phone the police – Superintendent Vosper – first thing in the morning, Clare. Were you so foolish as to use one of your own knives?' I caught the flick of her eyes, which was as good as an admission. 'And I suppose, here, they'd come in sets. Now ... if I were you ... I wouldn't try hiding or burying the rest of the set. That would look bad. And if you went out to buy a matching knife ... well, you'd find nobody would sell you one, and it'd look bad if the police arrested you while you were searching the shops. Think about it. Think about it, Clare.'

Oliver was at the french windows and was holding open the right-hand one. I didn't like to turn my back on her. My nerves ached with the strain, expecting the Darne to be hurled at my head. But there was no sound as we walked out, not even a whimper, and we reached the corner of the house before we heard anything. Then it was a crash of glass. She had thrown the Darne at one of her cabinets.

'You were wrong on one point, Phillie,' said Oliver, as we approached the belt of trees.

'What was that?' I didn't really care.

'The knife. Even if it matches a set she's got, it wouldn't be proof. Not something you could use in court.'

'I know. But it doesn't matter. She'll confess to it. Claim it, perhaps. She's so stupid, really. The death of Harris – everybody took that as a justifiable homicide. Clare will think that killing a policewoman, even if in mistake, is the same. But it's not the same, Oliver, is it, even though I was the intended victim?'

'No, love,' he said, 'it's not at all the same.'

The car stood where we'd parked it, now apparently isolated. There was no sign of any other vehicle, but nevertheless I had an impression that we were not alone. The deeper shadows beneath the trees seemed restless, and were moving.

I stopped so abruptly that it almost jerked my hand from beneath Oliver's arm.

'Oliver,' I whispered. 'The keys! They're still on the terrace. I threw them . . .'

'At me,' he confirmed.

I was abruptly very tired indeed. The thought of walking all the way back for them was appalling. The thought of waiting there while Oliver went to get them was even worse. The car was no more than a heavier block of darkness in a surrounding darkness, one that was restless and expectant.

Then the car doors swung open. The interior light indicated that Glenn was at the driver's door, Josie at the passenger's. They held them wide. And was Glenn smiling? In any event, he inclined his head.

As I reached his side, I saw that the key bunch was dangling from the ignition lock. Then I understood. Glenn had overheard my disagreement with Oliver, and he'd seen me throw the keys at him. That Glenn had more recently gone to the terrace to rescue them for me, indicated that he must also have overheard what had been said to Clare.

I slid on to the seat. As Glenn slammed the door with one hand, he put the other to his mouth, inserted two fingers, and whistled shrilly. I'd always wanted to be able to do that, but had never mastered it. I would have to come back and learn the secret, I thought. Or perhaps not.

An engine, far off, had thumped into life, then settled down, and the strewn coloured lights, draped each side of the driveway, glowed feebly, flickered, then settled down to their full glory.

The sides of the drive were lined with people, who'd behaved so

189

superbly that not one sound had come from them. Scattered with different colours, their faces glowed. And they were all smiling.

I pushed the window switch, and they slid down, the better for both of us to see. I started the engine and slid the box into drive. The car eased forward, and then the gentle pattering sound, which I'd taken for a sudden rain shower, became a clapping of palms. No other sound. Smiling faces and gently applauding hands.

I tried to smile, but I was exhausted, physically and emotionally, and all I achieved was tears. I stared ahead, barely able to see, and slid the car slowly into movement. There was a ridiculous urge to wave a hand languidly in acknowledgement, but I resisted it.

Who the hell did I think I was? Clare?